IRÈNE NÉMIROVSKY

The Fires of Autumn

Irène Némirovsky was born in Kiev in 1903 into a wealthy banking family and immigrated to France during the Russian Revolution. After attending the Sorbonne in Paris, she began to write and swiftly achieved success with *David Golder*, which was followed by more than a dozen other books. Throughout her lifetime she published widely in French newspapers and literary journals. She died in Auschwitz in 1942. More than sixty years later, *Suite Française* was published posthumously for the first time in 2006.

VINTAGE
INTERNATIONAL

Also by Irène Némirovsky

Suite Française

Fire in the Blood

David Golder

The Ball

Snow in Autumn

The Courilof Affair

Dimanche and Other Stories

All Our Worldly Goods

Jezebel

The Wine of Solitude

IRÈNE NÉMIROVSKY

The Fires of Autumn

Translated from the French by Sandra Smith

Vintage International
Vintage Books
A Division of Random House LLC
New York

A VINTAGE INTERNATIONAL ORIGINAL, MARCH 2015

The Cataloging-in-Publication Data is on file at the Library of Congress.

Vintage Books Trade Paperback ISBN: 978-1-101-87227-7
eBook ISBN: 978-1-101-87396-0

www.vintagebooks.com

Printed in the United States of America
10 9 8 7 6 5 4 3 2

This book is dedicated to the memory of Denise Epstein, Irène Némirovsky's daughter, who passed away in 2013 at the age of 83. From 2004, when *Suite Française* was first published in France, until her death, Denise travelled the world, working tirelessly to promote her mother's canon and re-establish her as one of the most respected writers in twentieth-century France. It was my privilege to meet her in 2006, when *Suite Française* was first published in English. She told me, 'I could not accept my mother had died until I saw her re-born.' We became great friends and shared many happy memories of travelling and speaking together at events. Denise was an extraordinary woman who is greatly missed.

TRANSLATOR'S INTRODUCTION

Irène Némirovsky was born in Kiev in 1903, the only child of a wealthy Jewish banker and his adulterous wife. At the time, upper-class Russian families spoke French, and since her mother had no interest in raising a child, a French governess was engaged for Irène. The family also spent most holidays on the French Riviera, so Irène considered French her first language. The Némirovskys were forced to flee their home after the Russian Revolution and finally settled in Paris where Irène attended the Sorbonne, studying French and Russian literature.

Irène married Michel Epstein, another Russian Jewish immigrant, in 1926 and had her first daughter, Denise, in 1929, the year that her first published novel, *David Golder*, made the writer an instant commercial success. Their second child, Élisabeth, was born in 1937. Irène continued writing at least one novel and several short stories every year until she was deported to Auschwitz in 1942, where she died soon afterwards.

The Fires of Autumn is the eleventh novel to be translated into English by this prolific author who was almost entirely forgotten before the publication of her unfinished masterpiece, *Suite Française*, written in a small village in Vichy France as the Second World War raged all around.

The Fires of Autumn, written at about the same time, was no doubt inspired by the reminiscences of many French soldiers and their families who had suffered through the First World War and were once again re-living those horrible experiences. As the Editor's Note to the new French edition (2011), which I have used for my translation of the novel, explains:

> *Irène Némirovsky completed* The Fires of Autumn *in the spring of 1942. It was published posthumously in 1957 by Albin Michel.*
>
> *L'Institut mémoires de l'édition contemporaine (IMEC) – a French association that archives literature of the twentieth century – is in possession of two copies of the typescript of this novel, one of which contains handwritten corrections by Irène Némirovsky. The first was used as the basis for the 1957 publication. The current edition is based on the second typescript, the result of the author's revision in which she made cuts, additions and modifications that were sometimes quite significant.*
>
> *Olivier Philipponnat, Irène Némirovsky's biographer, and Teresa M. Lussone, who wrote her philology dissertation on Némirovsky, worked together to produce this new edition, retaining nonetheless three chapters from Part I of the novel – the fifth, sixth and ninth chapters – that the author wanted to remove but which allow the contemporary reader better to understand the ravages of the 1914–18 war.*

Like *Suite Française*, this novel follows the fate of several families, whose paths intertwine. It is a riveting study of French, especially Parisian, life from the eve of the First World War right through to the outbreak and early years of the Second World War, depicting the terrible human cost of war as well as the corruption, greed and political expediency that were factors leading to a breakdown of morality in inter-war France.

The Fires of Autumn provides us with insight into the minds of ordinary people, their lives and loves in the midst of war, and the scars that remain when war ends. Through Némirovsky's beautiful, lyrical writing, this novel works as a prequel to *Suite Française*, offering a panoramic exploration of French life between 1913 and 1942. It is both an important historical document and a sensitive depiction of both the best and worst of human emotions.

I would like to express my gratitude to Alison Samuel for her invaluable help in editing this book.

Sandra Smith
Robinson College, Cambridge

Part One

1912–1918

1

There was a bunch of fresh violets on the table, a yellow pitcher with a spout that opened with a little clicking sound to let the water pour out, a pink glass salt cellar decorated with the inscription: 'Souvenir of the World Fair 1900'. (The letters had faded over twelve years and were hard to make out.) There was an enormous loaf of golden bread, some wine and – the *pièce de résistance*, the main course – a wonderful blanquette of veal, each tender morsel hiding shyly beneath the creamy sauce, served with aromatic baby mushrooms and new potatoes. No first course, nothing to whet the appetite: food was a serious business. In the Brun household, they always started with the main course; they were not averse to roasts – when properly cooked according to simple, strict rules, these were akin to classics of the culinary art – but here, the woman of the house put all her effort and loving care into the skilled creation of dishes simmered slowly for a long time. In the Brun household, it was the elderly Madame Pain, the mother-in-law, who did the cooking.

The Bruns were Parisians of some small private means. Since the death of his wife, Adolphe Brun presided over the table and served the meal. He was still a handsome man; bald and with a large forehead, he had a small upturned nose, full cheeks and a long, red moustache that he twisted and turned in his fingers until its slender tips nearly poked his eyes. Sitting opposite him was his mother-in-law: round, petite, with a rosy complexion crowned with fine, flyaway white hair that looked like sea foam; when she smiled, you could see she still had all her teeth. With a wave of her chubby little hand, she would brush aside everyone's compliments: 'Exquisite . . . You've never made anything better, dear Mother-in-law . . . This is just delicious, Madame Pain!' She would put on a falsely modest little face and, just as a prima donna pretends to offer her partner the flowers presented to her on stage, she would murmur:

'Yes, the butcher did me proud today. It's a very nice cut of veal.'

To his right sat Adolphe Brun's guests – the three Jacquelains – and to his left, his nephew Martial and Brun's young daughter, Thérèse. Since Thérèse had just turned fifteen a few days ago, she had put her curls up in a chignon, but her silky hair was not yet used to the style she tried to hold in place with hairpins, so it was escaping all over the place, which made Thérèse unhappy, in spite of the compliment her shy cousin Martial had whispered to her:

'It's very pretty, Thérèse,' he said, blushing quite a bit. 'Your hair I mean . . . it's like a cloud of gold.'

'The little angel has my hair,' said Madame Pain. She was born in Nice, and even though she left at the age of sixteen to marry a ribbon and veil merchant from Paris, she still had the accent of her native city, as sonorous and sweet as a song. She had very beautiful dark eyes and a lively expression. Her husband had left her destitute; she had lost a daughter who was only twenty – Thérèse's mother – and was supported by her son-in-law; but nothing had affected her cheerful disposition. With dessert, she happily drank a little glass of sweet liqueur as she hummed a song:

Joyful tambourines, lead the dance . . .

The Bruns and their guests sat in a very small dining room flooded with sunlight. The furniture – a Henry II sideboard, cane chairs with fluted legs, a chaise longue upholstered in a dark fabric with flowers – bouquets of roses against a black background – an upright piano – everything huddled together as best it could in this small space. The walls were decorated with drawings bought in the large department stores near the Louvre: young girls playing with kittens, Neapolitan shepherds (with a view of Mount Vesuvius in the background) and a copy of *The Abandoned Woman*, a touching work depicting a woman who is obviously pregnant sitting on a marble bench in autumn, weeping as a Hussar of Napoleon's Army disappears in the distance among the dead leaves.

The Bruns lived in the heart of a working-class area near the Gare de Lyon. They heard the long, wistful whistles of the trains, full of resonance, that passed them by. But at certain times of the day, they could feel the faint, rhythmic, metallic vibrations coming from the large iron bridge the metro passed over as it emerged from deep beneath the city, appearing for a moment under the sky before fleeing underground again with a muffled roar. The windows shook as it passed.

On the balcony, canaries sang in a cage and, in another, turtle-doves cooed softly. The typical sounds of Sunday rose up through the open windows: the clinking of glasses and dishes from every floor, and the happy sound of children from the street below. The brilliant sunlight cast a rosy hue over the grey stonework of the houses. Even the windows of the apartment opposite, dark and grimy all winter long, had recently been washed and sparkled like shimmering water in the bright light. There was a little alcove where the man selling roasted chestnuts had been since October; but he was gone now, and a young girl with red hair selling violets had materialised to take his place. Even this dark little recess was filled with a golden mist: the sun lit up the dust particles, the kind you get in Paris in the spring, that joyful season, dust that seems to be made of face powder and pollen from flowers (until you realise that it smells of dung).

It was a beautiful Sunday. Martial Brun had brought in the dessert, a coffee cake with cream that made Bernard Jacquelain's eyes light up with joy. They ate it in silence; nothing was heard but the clinking of teaspoons against the plates and the crunching of the little coffee beans hidden in the cream, full of heady liqueur. After this brief moment of silence, the conversation started up again, just as peaceful and devoid of passion as a kettle simmering gently on a stove. Martial Brun was a young man of twenty-seven with beautiful doe eyes, a long, pointy nose that was always a bit red at the tip, a long neck he kept tilted to one side in a funny way, as if he were trying to hear some secret; he was studying medicine and talked about the exams he was soon to take.

'Men have to work so hard,' said Blanche Jacquelain with a sigh, looking over at her son Bernard. She loved him so much that she felt everything applied to him; she couldn't read about an epidemic of typhoid that had broken out in Paris without imagining him sick, even dying, and if she heard any military music, she immediately imagined him a soldier. She looked darkly, sadly, at Martial Brun, replacing in her imagination his nondescript features with those of her adored son, and thinking that one day Bernard would graduate from one of the great universities, showered with prizes.

With a certain sense of complacency, Martial described his studies and how he sometimes had to stay up all night. He was overly modest, but a thimbleful of wine made him suddenly eager to talk, to impress others. As he was bragging, he ran his index finger along the back of his collar – it was a bit tight and irritating him – and he puffed his chest out like a rooster, until the doorbell rang and interrupted him. Thérèse started to get up to answer it, but little Bernard got there first and soon came back accompanied by a plumpish, bearded young man, a friend of Martial, a law student named Raymond Détang. Because of his liveliness, his eloquence, his beautiful baritone voice and his effortless success with women, Raymond Détang inspired feelings of envy and gloomy admiration in Martial. He stopped talking the moment he saw him and nervously began brushing up all the breadcrumbs scattered around his plate.

'We were just talking about you young men and your studies,' said Adolphe Brun. 'You see what's in store for you,' he added, turning towards Bernard.

Bernard did not reply because at the age of fifteen, the company of adults still intimidated him. He was still in short trousers. ('But this is the last year . . . Soon he will be too big,' his mother said, sounding regretful but proud.) After this hearty meal, his cheeks were fiery red and his tie kept slipping. He gave it a hard tug and pushed his blond curls off his forehead.

'He must graduate from the Polytechnique, the most prestigious Engineering School, among the top of his class,' his father said in a booming voice. 'I would do anything in the world to give him a good education: the best tutors, anything; but he knows what I expect of him: he must graduate from the Polytechnique among the top of his class. He's a hard worker though. He's first in his class.'

Everyone looked at Bernard; a wave of pride rushed through his heart. It was a feeling of almost unbearable sweetness. He blushed even more and finally spoke in a voice that was breaking, sometimes shrill and almost heart-rending, sometimes soft and deep:

'Oh, that, it's nothing really . . .'

He raised his chin in a gesture of defiance and pulled at the knot in his tie so hard it nearly ripped, as if to say:

'We'll see about that!'

He was excited by the dream of one day seeing himself become an important engineer, a mathematician, an inventor, or perhaps an explorer or a soldier, having encounters with a string of beautiful women along the way, surrounded by devoted friends and disciples. But at the same time, he glanced furtively at the bit of cake sitting on his plate and wondered how he could manage to eat it with all those eyes staring at him; fortunately his father spoke to Martial and diverted everyone's attention, leaving him in obscurity once more. He took advantage of the moment by wolfing down a quarter of his cake in one mouthful.

'What branch of medicine are you planning to specialise in?' Monsieur Jacquelain asked Martial. Monsieur Jacquelain suffered from terrible stomach problems. He had a blond moustache, as pale as hay, and a face like grey sand; he was covered in wrinkles like dunes furrowed by the sea breeze. He looked at Martial with a sad, eager expression, as if the very fact of speaking to a future doctor might be enough to discover some secret cure, but one that wouldn't work on him. He instinctively placed his hand on the spot where the illness made him suffer, just below his sunken chest, and repeated several times:

'It's a shame you haven't got your qualifications yet, my dear boy. A shame. I would have come to you for a consultation. A shame . . .'

Then he sat there, deep in anguished thought.

'In two years,' Martial said shyly.

Urged on by their questions, he admitted he had his eye on an apartment, on the Rue Monge. A doctor he knew wanted to retire so would pass it on to him. As he spoke, he could picture all the pleasant days ahead . . .

'You should get married, Martial,' said the elderly Madame Pain with a mischievous smile.

Martial nervously rolled the soft part of the bread into a ball, pulled at it so it took the shape of a man, stabbed at it with his dessert fork and raised his doe eyes to look at Thérèse.

'I'm thinking about it,' he said, his voice full of emotion. 'Believe me, I'm thinking about it.'

For a fleeting moment, Thérèse thought his remarks were directed at her; she wanted to laugh but at the same time felt embarrassed, as if she'd been left standing naked in public. So it was true then, what her father, her grandmother and her friends at school were saying: ever since she had started putting up her hair, she looked like a woman? But to marry this kind Martial . . . She lowered her eyes and watched him with curiosity. She'd known him since she was a child; she liked him very much; she could live with him as her mother and father had lived until the day the young woman died. 'The poor boy,' she suddenly thought. 'He's an orphan.' She already felt a kind of affection and concern that was almost maternal. 'But he's not handsome,' she continued thinking. 'He looks like the llama at the zoo in the Botanical Gardens: gentle and slightly offended.'

In an effort to stifle a scornful laugh, two dimples appeared on her rather pale cheeks; all the children of Paris had pale faces. She was a slim, graceful girl with a soft, serious face, grey eyes and hair as fine as mist. 'What kind of husband would I like?' she wondered. Her thoughts grew sweet and vague, full of handsome young men who looked like the Hussar from Napoleon's Army on the print opposite her. A handsome, golden Hussar, a soldier covered in gunpowder and blood, dragging his sword behind him through the dead leaves . . . She leapt up to help her grandmother clear the table. She felt a jolt that brought her back from her dreams to reality; it was a unique and rather painful feeling: someone seemed to be forcing her to open her eyes while shining a very bright light in front of her.

'Growing up is so tedious,' she thought. 'If only I could stay the way I am . . .' She sighed rather hypocritically: it was flattering to inspire admiration in a young man, even if it was only the well-mannered Martial. Bernard Jacquelain had gone out on to the balcony and she joined him among the cages of canaries and turtledoves. The steel bridge vibrated: the metro had just passed by. A few moments later, Adolphe Brun came out to the children.

'The Humbert ladies are here,' he said.

They were friends of the Brun family, a widow and her daughter Renée, who was fifteen.

Madame Humbert had lost her brilliant, charming husband early on. It was a sad story, but a good lesson for the youngsters, or so they said. Poor Monsieur Humbert (a talented lawyer), had died at the age of twenty-nine for having too great a fondness for both work and pleasure, which do not go together, as Adolphe Brun remarked. 'He was a Don Juan,' he would say, shaking his head, but with an expression of admiration, mixed with condemnation and a tiny bit of envy. Twirling his moustache and looking pensive, he would continue: 'He had become very conscious of his appearance. He had thirty-six ties' (thirty-six stood for an exaggerated number). 'He had started to indulge in luxuries: a bath every week. He caught the chill that killed him coming out of one of the public baths.'

His widow, left with no money, had been forced to open a milliner's shop to earn a living. In the Avenue des Gobelins stood a boutique painted in sky blue; high up on the roof was a plaque bearing the inscription: '*FASHIONS by GERMAINE*' finished with a gold flourish. Madame Humbert launched her creations on her own head and her daughter's. She was a beautiful brunette; she carried herself with majestic dignity, showing off one of the first new straw hats to come out this spring, trimmed with a burst of artificial poppies. Her daughter wore a modest creation of tulle and ribbons: a stiff bonnet but as light as a lampshade.

They had been waiting for these ladies before going out to finish their Sunday in the fresh air. And so they all headed for the metro at the Gare de Lyon. The children walked in front, Bernard between the two girls. Bernard was painfully aware of his short trousers and looked with anxiety and shame at the golden hair that shone on his sturdy legs, but he consoled himself by thinking: 'This is the last year . . .' Besides, his mother, who spoiled him, had bought him a cane with a gold knob and he played with this nonchalantly. Unfortunately, Adolphe noticed it and muttered: 'He looks like a dandy with that cane in his hand . . . ,' which spoiled all his pleasure. Lively, always on the go, slim with beautiful eyes, to his mother he was the personification of masculine beauty, and with a jealous pang in her heart, she thought: 'He'll have so many conquests by the time he's twenty,' for she intended to keep him at home until then.

The young women wore black cotton stockings with nice tailored suits that modestly covered their knees. Madame Humbert had made a hat for Thérèse just like Renée's, an impressive creation decorated with chiffon and little bows. 'You look like sisters,' but what she really thought was: '*My* daughter, my Renée, is prettier. She's a little doll, a kitten with her blond hair and green eyes. Older men are already starting to notice her,' she continued thinking, for she was an ambitious mother who could foresee the future.

Emerging from the depths of the underground, the little group came out of the metro at the Place de la Concorde and walked down the Champs-Élysées. The women carefully lifted the hem of their skirts a bit as they walked; you could see a respectable ruffle of grey poplin under Madame Jacquelain's dress, a reddish-brown sateen for the elderly Madame Pain, while Madame Humbert, who had an ample bosom and made the most of her 'Italian eyes', was accidentally showing off a dapple grey taffeta ruffle that rustled silkily. The ladies were talking about love. Madame Humbert let it be known that she had driven a man wild with her strict morals; in order to forget her, he had to run away to the colonies, and from there he had written to tell her that he had trained one of the little natives to come into his tent at bedtime and say: 'Germaine loves you and is thinking of you.'

'Men are often more sensitive than we are,' sighed Madame Humbert.

'Oh, do you think so?' exclaimed Blanche Jacquelain. She had been listening with the same haughty, sharp expression as a cat eagerly eyeing a saucepan of hot milk (she stretches out her paw then pulls it back with a brief, offended miaow): 'Do you really think so? It's only we women who know how to sacrifice ourselves without any ulterior motive.'

'What do you mean by ulterior motive?' asked Madame Humbert; she lifted her chin and flared her nostrils as if she were about to whinny like a mare.

'My dear, you know very well what she means,' replied Madame Jacquelain in disgust.

'But that's human nature, my dear . . .'

'Yes, yes,' said the elderly Madame Pain, nodding her head and jiggling her jet-black hat covered in artificial violets, but she wasn't really listening. She was thinking of the bit of veal (left over from the blanquette) that she would serve that evening. Just as it was or with a tomato sauce?

Behind them walked the men, holding forth and gesturing grandly.

The peaceful Sunday crowds walked down the Champs-Élysées. Everyone strolled slowly, no doubt feeling heavier because they were digesting their meals, because of the heat – early for the time of year – or simply because they felt no need to rush. It was an amiable, cheerful, modest group of ordinary middle-class people; the working classes didn't venture there, and the upper classes only sent the very youngest members of their families to the Champs-Élysées, supervised by nannies wearing beautiful ribbons in their hair. Along the avenue, they could see students from the Military Academy of Saint Cyr walking arm in arm with their lovely grandmothers, or pale students in pince-nez, from the prestigious Polytechnique whose anxious families gazed lovingly at them, high school students in double-breasted jackets and school uniform caps, gentlemen with moustaches, young girls in white dresses walking down to the Arc de Triomphe between a double row of chairs where other students from Saint Cyr and the Polytechnique sat, with other gentlemen and ladies and children identical to the first group, wearing the same clothes, the same expression, the same smile, a look that was cordial, curious and benevolent, to such an extent that each passer-by seemed to see his own brother by his side. All these faces looked alike: pale-skinned, dull-eyed, and nose in the air.

They walked even further, right down to the Arc de Triomphe, then to the Avenue du Bois de Boulogne, to the Boni de Castellane Villa whose lilac silk curtains fluttered out on to the balconies in the light breeze. And then, at last, the horse-drawn carriages arrived in a glorious cloud of dust, returning from the races.

The families sat on their little metal chairs. They studied the foreign princes, the millionaires, the famous courtesans. Madame Humbert feverishly sketched their hats into a notebook she took out of her handbag. The children watched in admiration. The adults felt contented, satisfied, without envy but full of pride: 'For the pittance we paid for our chairs and the price of the metro, we can see all of this,' the Parisians thought, 'and we can enjoy it. Not only are we spectators at a performance, we are also actors (though with the most minor of roles), with our daughters so beautifully decked out in their brand-new hats, and our chatter and legendary gaiety. We could have been born somewhere else, after all,' thought the Parisians, 'in a place where even seeing the Champs-Élysées on a postcard would have made everyone's heart beat faster!'

And they settled back comfortably in their chairs.

'Did you see that pink parasol trimmed with lace roses?' they said, slightly critically, as if they owned the place. 'It's too much; I don't like that sort of thing.'

They recognised the celebrities that passed by:

'Look, there's the actress Monna Delza. Who's she with?'

The fathers told their children stories from the past:

'Five years ago I saw Lina Cavalieri having lunch with Caruso over there,' they said, pointing towards the windows of a restaurant. 'Everyone was gathered round them and looked at them as if they were curious animals, but that didn't dull their appetite.'

'Who's Lina Cavalieri, Papa?'

'An actress.'

Towards evening, the children were starting to drag their feet. The powdery sugar from the waffles fluttered through the air. A fine dust rose slowly towards the sky, a golden dust that crunched between the teeth; it veiled half of the Obélisque in mist at the Place de la Concorde, shrouded the pink flowers on the chestnut trees; the wind carried it towards the Seine and it gradually fell to the ground while the last of the horse-drawn carriages and the Parisians headed for home.

The Bruns, Jacquelains, Humberts and Raymond Détang sat down on the terrace of a café for a drink:

'Two grenadines and eight glasses of wine.'

They drank in silence, somewhat tired, rather light-headed, pleased with their day. Raymond Détang fiddled with his little beard and began showing off for the benefit of the woman sitting next to him. It was a hot evening. The first street lamps were being lit and the sky was turning a pale mauve, almost sugary, you could say, like the colour of violet sweets. It looked good enough to eat. 'Ah, this is so nice . . .' the women sighed, and 'It's almost too nice to go back home, isn't it, Eugène?' But Eugène or Émile (her husband) shook his head, looked at his watch and simply said: 'Time for supper.' It was nearly seven o'clock and all the little Parisian families would soon light their lamps and sit down to dinner. The delicious smell of stew and fresh bread would do battle for a few moments with the scent of the perfumed dust that the expensive ladies had left in their wake; it would compete with it and, in the end, win the battle.

The Bruns and their friends parted at the Étoile metro station. They settled the bill – 'And I still owe you some money for the waiter's tip . . . Yes, I insist; the man who pays his debts is richer for it . . .' Then everyone went back home.

2

In 1914, Martial Brun ordered a bronze plaque for the door of his future home on the Rue Monge; it was engraved with these words:

DOCTOR MARTIAL BRUN
EAR, NOSE AND THROAT

The apartment would not be available until the end of October; it was now the 14th July. Martial went to see his friend, the doctor, who was still living there. After saying goodbye to him, he stopped on the staircase, took the plaque out of his pocket and polished it until it gleamed. Then he tiptoed back up the stairs, held it against the wooden door for a moment, tilted his long neck even further to the side and thought: 'That's really nice', and began to daydream. There was a polished oak bench on the landing; the windows were made of coloured glass and their reflection covered the stairwell in translucent light, as in a church. Martial imagined a procession of patients arriving to consult Doctor Brun. 'That excellent Doctor Brun . . .' he whispered softly, 'Martial Brun, that famous doctor . . . Do you know Doctor Brun? He cured my wife. He removed my daughter's adenoids.' He could almost smell that odour of antiseptic and clean linoleum wafting out of his consulting room. No more studying! He had earned his diplomas! That blessed moment when a Frenchman could say: 'I've sown well. Now it is time to reap.' And in his mind, he mapped out the future. He assigned a date to each event in the years to come: 'I'll move in here in October. I'll get married. I'll have a son. The second year, I'll be able to have a holiday at the seaside . . .' His life was planned in advance, sketched out right down to every success, right up until he was old, until he died. For naturally, there was death. It had its place in his domestic calculation. But death was no longer a wild animal lurking in the corner, lying in wait, ready to pounce. It was 1914, for heaven's sake! The century of science, of progress. Even death seemed diminished in the light of such knowledge. It would wait in the wings for an appropriate moment, the moment when Doctor Brun would have fulfilled his destiny, lived a long, contented life, had children and bought a little house in the country, the moment when the white-haired Doctor Brun would fall peacefully asleep. Accompanying him on his path, Doctor Brun imagined Thérèse. He had always . . . he stopped at the word 'loved' as it seemed to him, heaven knows why, bordering on the improper. He had always hoped to make her his wife and the mother of his children. She was eighteen and he was thirty. Their ages were appropriate. She wasn't rich but she had a small dowry of safe investments: Russian bonds. And so, everything was in place: the house, the money, the wife. His wife . . . But he hadn't yet put the question. He had been content to make allusions, to sigh, pay compliments, to squeeze her hand furtively, but that was surely enough. 'Women are so shrewd . . .'

Once again, Martial gave himself a stern talking to:

'I will not let another day go by without asking her if she will marry me. It would be simpler to talk to Uncle Adolphe, but I must take a modern approach. It must be her decision.'

He was supposed to see her that very evening, for they were going out together. It was the 14th July and they were going to watch the dancing at the Place de la République. Adolphe Brun was very strict about everything Thérèse saw or read: she was not allowed any popular novels; he went through her reading with a fine-tooth comb and only allowed her to see matinees of classical French films; but to him, the streets of Paris held no danger. Its sights, its atmosphere, the gaiety, the hustle and bustle – he allowed Thérèse to enjoy these things as an old Indian brave would allow his children to play on the prairies. To outsiders, this was a wild place full of perils – but to him, it was the most peaceful countryside.

Standing in front of the carousel with its wooden horses while the orchestra played, or perhaps in the dark street they would take to walk home – the youngsters in front, the parents behind – he would say to her . . . What would he say to her? 'Thérèse, I have loved you for a very long time . . .' or 'Thérèse, you alone can make me the happiest, or the most wretched of men.' Perhaps she would say: 'I love you too, Martial, I do.'

Martial could feel his heart pounding at this idea; he took a little mirror out of his pocket and anxiously looked at himself, hanging his head down even more than ever and almost sweeping his long eyelashes against the mirror, for he was short-sighted. He had taken off his pince-nez so he could see himself: 'She has to be able to see my eyes,' he thought, 'my eyes are really my best feature . . .' For a moment he studied his terrified eyes, his pointy red nose and the black beard that hid his cheeks. Then he sighed sadly, put the mirror back in his pocket and walked slowly down the stairs.

'She's a serious young woman. Respectable women do not care about good looks. We'll make a family together . . . We have to have the same likes and dislikes . . .'

Then he weakened:

'I'll love her so much,' he thought.

He had dinner with the Bruns. Nothing had changed at their

house. Nothing would ever change. Her father sat in his shirt-sleeves reading the newspaper in his usual place, at the head of the table, the same table, the same armchair, the same newspaper, the same Uncle Adolphe that Martial was used to seeing, with his bald head, his wide blue eyes, his long red moustache. Grandmother was in the kitchen; Thérèse was setting the table. In the future, he would come to this dining room with his wife and children. He felt very happy. He took Thérèse's hand; she pulled it away gently but she smiled at him, and that knowing smile, somewhat mocking but friendly, filled his soul with hope. Of course she had guessed everything.

After dinner, Thérèse went to put on her hat.

'Are you coming with us, Mama?' asked Adolphe, winking mischievously at his nephew to encourage him to hear what he said next: 'Aren't you afraid you'll get too tired?'

'Me? Get tired?' the elderly lady protested with indignation. 'Speak for yourself with your varicose veins! I have strong legs, I do, thank the Lord! And besides, someone has to keep an eye on Thérèse.'

'Well what about me? And Martial? Don't we count?'

'You . . . when you see those Chinese lanterns, you stand there like a child with your mouth hanging open. And Martial is too young to look after a young woman.'

'Oh, I'm too young,' protested Martial, delighted. To hide his lack of composure, he picked up the newspaper that his uncle had just put down. 'Anything new in the paper?'

'The Caillaux trial is starting on Monday.'

Martial leafed absent-mindedly through the *Petit Parisien*, and read out loud: 'Monsieur Maurice Barrès was elected President of the League of Patriots'; 'In Sarajevo, after the assassination, attacks on the Serbs . . .'

He folded up the paper, carefully smoothing it out. He shuddered slightly, his shoulders twitching as if he felt a chill run through him. He even thought: 'What could be wrong with me? I'm shivering. I must have stopped wearing my flannel underwear too early this year.' He made it a rule to keep wearing it until the 15th August, because you can never be certain at the beginning of summer. Certain . . . this little word suddenly resonated in his mind. What had made him shiver was not the early signs of a cold, but something within, something that had nothing to do with anything physical . . . Anxiety. No, that was too strong a word. Sadness . . . Yes, that was it; suddenly he felt sad. He had been beaming all day long and now suddenly . . . Mere mortals knew nothing of what was thundering through every Embassy in Europe, and yet he sensed a kind of agitation in these high places, something feverish, the shock of opposing electric currents that struck him every now and then, just as you sometimes see sheep safely sheltered in their folds anxiously raise their heads when they sense a storm raging in the distance. The assassination of that Austrian prince . . . The crowds the day before yesterday, demonstrating in front of the Statue de Strasbourg at the Place de la Concorde . . . Words, rumours, talk, words . . . one word . . . But a word that doesn't belong to our century, thank goodness.

'It smells of gunpowder,' he said out loud, showing the newspaper to Uncle Adolphe and trying to sound as if he were joking. 'It smells of war . . .'

'Well, if there is a war, we'll fight,' said Adolphe, twirling his moustache and puffing out his chest. 'We'll eat rats, like during the siege.' Then he turned towards the women and asked impatiently: 'Well, are you coming? We're going to miss the fireworks.'

'Tonight, I'll ask her, I'll definitely ask her,' Martial said to himself, and, oddly enough, this time he knew he actually would do it, he wouldn't shy away. The feeling of sadness remained in his heart, but not only sadness, a sort of extreme awareness of his entire being, as if he were alone in a room and could hear footsteps outside.

Thérèse found him standing in the small entrance hall. He was staring at the door, his neck straining forward, his nose red and his forehead covered in sweat. She started laughing:

'You frightened me. What are you doing standing here? Come along, let's go, Papa is going downstairs. Close the door. Don't step on my skirt. You're so clumsy! You'll tear the hem.'

All four of them went out on to the street; it was already alive with the sound of celebrations. Violinists were tuning their instruments at the intersections. In front of the small cafés, the squares were marked off for the dancing, a rectangle of pavement lit by paper lanterns and the moon. They could see the swaying shadows of the trees on the ground. The night had something gentle about it, something soothing and sensual that intoxicated the young men and women. Young girls wearing boaters and white blouses raced by, raising their skirts up to their calves. Soldiers danced with chambermaids. On the Avenue de la République, there was a fair, stalls, the smell of hot oil, gingerbread, gunpowder, circus animals, noise, shouting, gunshots and fireworks.

Martial took Thérèse's arm.

'Here, right now, immediately,' he thought.

He shouted into her ear and later on, she would recall his hoarse, anguished voice, merging with the roaring of the captive lions, the sound of the *Marseillaise* and the hum of the carousels.

'Thérèse, I love you. Will you marry me?'

She couldn't hear what he was saying. She gestured to him to say no more, then smiled and pointed to all the people around them. He looked at her with terror in his eyes, gasping with anguish. She felt sorry for him and gently squeezed his hand.

'Is that a yes?' he cried. 'Oh, Thérèse . . .'

He could think of nothing else to say. He put his hand under her elbow and supported her with respect and infinite care, as if he were carrying a priceless vase through a great crowd. She was touched by his gesture. 'He wants me to understand that he will always protect me, always love me.' He wasn't handsome, he wasn't eloquent, but he was a decent man and she felt affection for him. She had always known that she would end up marrying him. Yes, even when she was still a very young girl, when he let her ride piggyback . . . Once, when she was nine, he had carried her all the way to the top of the Colonne de Juillet at the Place de la Bastille. She had felt safe in his arms, and occasionally opened one eye to look down at the square, very far below . . . Yes, that day she had thought: 'When I grow up, I will marry Martial.'

They had left the broad avenue now. They walked down the calmer, darker streets. They crossed the Seine. The adults walked behind them.

'He's asked her,' they said. 'He's talking intently, gesturing with his arms. She's listening without saying anything. That's it, he's done it. It was meant to be. He's a decent young man.'

'Will you dance at their wedding, Mama?' Adolphe asked his mother-in-law, straightening a leg to make her a small bow.

Madame Pain dried her eyes. She was remembering her own daughter. But it was just a sad, fleeting thought. She was too old to think about the dead for long. In old age, the dead are so close that you forget about them. You can only imagine things that are far away. She imagined Thérèse's wedding, the honeymoon, the wonderful meal . . . the child that would be born.

She nodded her head and, her voice quivering with emotion, her eyes still full of tears, she automatically began to hum:

Joyful tambourines, lead the dance! . . .

They had arrived at the Pont de la Tournelle. They watched the fireworks above the Seine, saw Notre Dame, the water and the skies all illuminated. Then the water was black, the sky had turned red, threatening, on fire.

Martial stood beside his fiancée. They were engaged. 'I'm starting a new chapter,' he thought, flustered. 'I'm beginning a new life. What was I before? A man on his own. Unhappy. From now on, whatever happens, we'll be together. Nothing will come between us.' He had succeeded; all was well.

3

A boy of seventeen wearing trousers that were too short and too tight, for he had grown so quickly, no hat, his hair thrown back off his face, gritted his teeth and clenched his fists to hold back the sobs rising in his throat: Bernard Jacquelain walked down the street behind a regiment on the march. It was the 31st July 1914, in Paris.

Every now and again, Barnard glanced around, curious, attentive and terrified, like a little boy who has been taken to the theatre for the first time. It was an amazing spectacle, on the eve of war, for only men who had gone soft in the head, old fools like Adolphe Brun, or the . . . (he quickly spat out a swear word that had all the pleasure of novelty, for he had only recently learned it at school), those . . . like Martial Brun claimed there wouldn't be a war, that at the last moment the governments would pull back, refusing to be responsible for a European massacre . . . They really didn't understand there was something sublime about all this, thought Bernard. To think that a single word, one act could cause war to break out, and war was heroic, similar to all the upheaval wreaked by Napoleon – imagine knowing this and pulling back! You had to have ice in your veins. For a moment, he imagined he was the Tsar, the President of the Republic, a great military leader.

'Forward!' he murmured, stretching out his arm, his eyes full of tears. 'For the honour of our flag!'

'Yes, there will be a war,' he told himself again. 'And I, I, Bernard Jacquelain, will have lived through heroic times like Austerlitz and Waterloo. I will tell my children: "Ah! If only you could have seen Paris in 1914!" I'll tell them all about the shouting, the flowers, the cheering, the tears!'

In reality, it was not like that at all. The streets were quiet, the iron shutters on the shops lowered. You could see carriages loaded up with baggage going by. But Bernard knew there had been patriotic demonstrations that very morning in various parts of the capital and, as for the rest, he embellished, his thoughts wandered into invisible apartments, he explored the depths of the hearts and souls of the Parisian population:

'There's a woman who is looking at the soldiers and crying. Poor thing . . . She's thinking about her husband, her son. And that other woman who watches them march by, such sadness in her eyes. She looks like Mama . . . What will Mama say when she finds out that I want to join up, "enlist before being conscripted" as they call it? For I've made up my mind, I'm not waiting until it's my turn! Besides, everyone agrees it will all be over in three months. Then what will I do? Stay at school, slog away like a fool, get punished with extra homework like a little kid when there is this, this glory, this bloodshed, this war? No, no, no! No, thank you! I want to go, and right away, go far away, and do everything! God, what beautiful weather it is, how hot the sun is! How striking that soldier's uniform with its red trousers! And the horses! Can anything ever be more beautiful than a fine-looking, lively animal that prances, nuzzles his reins and has lather in his nostrils? I want to be a cavalryman, a dragoon, because of their helmets. Oh, the young ladies are blowing kisses to the soldiers! How proud those men must be. Women love soldiers. I want to be loved, but not by just one woman, by many women; I want them to fight each other for my favours, while I simply stand among them, watching, in my handsome uniform . . . When they see the way I look at them, they'll know I am their lord and master. But all of that is really childish. I'm no longer interested in women. No! Not even that little chambermaid who gives me the eye when we pass on the stairs. I want to live for the smell of gunpowder, war and glory! There's an old man who must have fought in '70; how moved he must be! Don't worry, Monsieur, I'm here, me, little Bernard Jacquelain, and I'll bet you anything that I will bring back Victory under our flag! Oh, I want to sing, to shout, to leap! They can say whatever they want but I'm joining up, I'm joining up, I've made up my mind. I'll be eighteen next week. How old do you have to be to join up? It will be a nightmare if I can't make it happen. Oh, that music! They're playing over there. The trumpets are blaring, and the drums . . . My God, it's beautiful! To advance to the sound of that music and then, charge! Swords drawn! Bayonets fixed!'

His emotion and exhaustion – he had walked through half of Paris – left him out of breath. He had to stop for a moment to lean against a wall. The battle music sent shivers down his spine, filled his eyes with tears. He suddenly felt as though he were being flayed alive, every muscle, every nerve was exposed as the sounds of the trumpets swept over him; and every single note was being played on his body, on his own flesh. Every beat of the drum battered his bones. 'And that's how it feels,' he thought. 'At least, that's how it will feel when I'm a soldier. I'll be part of the regiment like . . . like a drop of blood is part of the red river that flows through my heart.'

He pulled himself up to his full height with pride: he stood to attention, listening to the fanfare that faded away in the distance. The air still quivered like the string on a violin. To Bernard's ears, everything was singing: the river, the ancient cobblestones, the mass of people. The crowd was tightly packed now; everyone rushed towards the newspaper stands. The men talked endlessly, gesturing broadly, waving their walking sticks about. You could hear them saying: 'The Tsar . . . the Kaiser . . .' Their faces were pale, drawn, serious. Bernard looked at them scornfully:

'Old men! They're all talk. *I'm* going to act; *I'm* going to join up,' he thought.

His elbows tight against his sides, chin raised, jogging along and imagining himself charging behind the raised flag, Bernard crossed the street, went into a bakery, bought two pastries, ate them standing up with a fierce look on his face, then took the metro home; he wanted to announce his decision to his family that very evening. 'Mama will cry, but Papa will back me up. He's patriotic. Mama is too, but women are weak. The most important thing is to talk like a man. This is what I'll say: "Papa, I love and respect you. I have always obeyed you. But now, someone stronger than you is in command: our country, Papa, it is the call of France!"'

He was charging up the stairs when the concierge stopped him: his parents were at their neighbours, the Bruns, and were waiting for him.

'So much the better,' Bernard thought, quivering with pleasure. 'I'll tell them in front of the Bruns . . . That will impress them all . . .'

He felt particularly pleased to be impressing Thérèse. She had hardly paid any attention to him for some time now; she was engaged . . . 'Engaged,' he murmured, shrugging his shoulders. 'Everyone thinks it's natural for a girl of my age to get married, to lead the life of a wife . . . But if I were to say I want to get engaged, they'd cry their eyes out. But actually, he's going to leave, her fiancé! Their marriage will be postponed indefinitely. Anyway, what do I care! Really . . . really . . . Women . . . !'

Still running, he got to the Bruns' house; the key was under the mat. He went inside. He saw his parents and Martial in the dining room. His mother looked at him and whispered: 'What's wrong?' she asked, sounding frightened. 'You're covered in sweat.'

'Nothing,' he replied, but thought proudly:

'There must be something remarkable in my eyes. I am a man, a warrior.'

He said a quick, patronising hello to this group of women and old men (Martial's thirty years seemed close to decrepitude to him).

He looked at him curiously. Martial was seated at the table; the tablecloth had been pushed back and he was sorting out letters from a small old suitcase open in front of him. Ever since finishing the lycée, Martial no longer lived with the Bruns, but he left a trunk and some other things of his at their house because he didn't have room for them in his small student lodgings. With extreme care, he separated the papers, tearing up some of them and putting the others in different coloured folders:

'These are photographs of the family, Uncle Adolphe. And these are the ones I took of Thérèse at Tréport when she was four years old. My diplomas. The bill from the engraver of the brass plaque you know about . . .'

He fell silent and sighed, deep in thought:

'Doctor Brun. Ear, Nose and Throat.'

'I'm putting the money in an envelope, Uncle Adolphe; please take it to him for me and apologise that I'm late in paying it: I really haven't had a minute to myself. And this is something of my mother's, a watch with her initials on it that I would like Thérèse to have.'

'You can give it to me after our wedding, darling,' Thérèse said softly.

It was the first time she had mentioned their forthcoming marriage in public. She blushed and handed back the watch he held out to her; it was gold, old-fashioned with a long chain.

'I suppose you'll get married when the war is over,' said Bernard, his voice as husky as a young cockerel, with a hint of unconscious cruelty.

'We're not waiting until then,' said Martial. 'I'm not leaving right away, at least not going over there immediately . . .'

He gestured to indicate some unknown far-off place.

'My teacher, Professor Faure, has arranged to keep me with him. They're setting up new hospital trains in the provinces. As soon as they're ready – it will take three or four weeks – they'll leave for . . . over there . . . ,' he said again, 'and me with them. But that will give us time to celebrate our wedding.'

'Three or four weeks!' cried Bernard. 'But it will be over by then!'

Martial shook his head:

'No, it will be a long war, a very long war.'

The elderly Madame Pain had said nothing up until then. She had just sat with her hands folded on her lap, lost in thought.

'If I were you, my children,' she said, 'I'd wait . . . That's no kind of marriage; the husband off in some hell, his wife in Paris! After the wedding, just a week together . . .'

'A week? Even a day together would be wonderful, Madame Pain!'

'Well, you see? One day and then you'll be separated. Perhaps for six months, who knows? You've said yourself that it will be a long war! No, no, my dears, let things work themselves out: when everyone's had enough of fighting, life will get back to normal. For now, it's as if everyone's gone mad, but that can't last.'

'I'll do whatever Thérèse wants,' Martial said quickly. 'If she doesn't want to be married to a soldier . . . The wife of a soldier . . . I know that I'm offering her a difficult future, one that is very different from what I had dreamt of for her . . .'

'But Martial,' said Thérèse, 'we're already committed to each other.'

'It's not the same thing,' Madame Pain grumbled, 'not the same thing at all. You're a child, you don't know what you're talking about.'

But Thérèse just shook her head and said nothing, tight-lipped, with a look of determination that Madame Pain knew very well.

'She'll do just what she wants,' she said softly. 'And besides, it's not as if Martial will be in any great danger: he's a doctor . . .'

'That's true,' said Bernard, scornfully. 'And besides – mark my words – by the time he and his well-equipped, fancy train get to Berlin, we'll already be there.'

He turned bright red and pushed his unruly hair off his forehead with his ink-stained hand.

'Papa, Mama, don't try to stop me. I've made my decision and there's no turning back. I'm not waiting to be conscripted. I'm joining up.'

'Imbecile! Not another word!' his father shouted angrily.

'Papa, Mama, I'm telling you: I've made my decision and there's no turning back.'

'But you're only seventeen,' groaned Blanche.

'I'll be eighteen in three days.'

'But you're only a child!'

'That's what the enemy will think,' replied Bernard, and he thought: 'That was a good thing to say!'

Then Adolphe Brun intervened. He banged his fist on the table with one hand while furiously twirling his left moustache with the other.

'You all make me laugh, the lot of you! You know nothing about politics. You'd think you were a bunch of village idiots! I'm an old Parisian; I can't be fooled. Your war will fizzle out! I'm telling you, I am. Much Ado About Nothing. All that pointless sabre rattling, and in the end, the diplomats will come to an agreement and everyone will go back home. And why? Because that's the way it's always been! Yes, I know, there was the Hundred

Years War and Napoleon, but all that is history! These days, everything gets worked out in the end. Songs will be written about it, a satirical revue at the end of the year and that will be that! You know that they can't pull the wool over my eyes,' he said again, trying to put a crafty expression on his honest face he believed was befitting a true Parisian born and bred. He winked at everyone several times:

'Exactly one year from now, we'll talk about your war again,' he concluded, 'and we'll have a good laugh.'

Everyone was silent.

'And we'll have a good laugh,' he said again.

At that very moment, they heard the sound of trains passing by. Sharp, shrill whistles rang out as the carriages seemed to surge out of the station, rumbling, thundering, with the hurried, raucous roar of a herd of furious charging beasts. Everyone listened; they had never heard so many trains going so fast.

'Those are the military convoys, of course, aren't they?'

'Already?'

'Yes, absolutely! They must have started moving the troops yesterday.'

'We've heard them roaring by for the past three nights,' said Thérèse.

Blanche Jacquelain burst into tears while Adolphe Brun turned very pale and simply kept saying:

'I'm telling you we'll soon be having a good laugh about it, believe you me.'

4

Bernard managed to witness one more event with the innocent eyes of a non-combatant: the wedding of Martial and Thérèse.

The marriage was held at the beginning of 1915. 'The groom is returning from the front,' Adolphe Brun had told his friends when he invited them to the wedding reception. 'He'll be in Paris for twenty-four hours; he'll tell us what's happening.'

For at the time, soldiers were greeted like ambassadors of a foreign country who carried fearful secrets, secrets that were only kept from their nearest and dearest by the demands of discipline. Every single one of them, from the most humble foot soldier to a battalion's medical doctor, like Martial, 'knew things', or so the civilians thought. They had knowledge of what the great military leaders were plotting, the date of the next offensive and the mysterious plans of the enemy.

'Well, when is it going to happen? When?' Madame Humbert eagerly asked Doctor Brun as soon as she saw him. What she meant was 'The Victory. When will we claim Victory?' And when Martial did not reply, she cheerfully wagged her finger at him. 'He's so secretive; he doesn't want to tell us a thing,' she said, simpering, then becoming serious again:

'Well, can you explain what they're doing, why we aren't advancing?'

Martial had not remained behind in his fine hospital train for long, a train that could hold up to eight beds per carriage and one hundred and twenty-eight wounded men in total, or so the newspapers proudly reported. Those trains were used for show, to comfort the civilian population and for the edification of the neutral nations. The wounded soldiers were transported in freight trains and cattle wagons, bleeding, in terrible pain, dying all along the small regional branch lines. After the first days, the really awful days, Martial had been allowed to transfer to a first-aid post on the front line. 'He's a hero, no one can doubt that,' thought Bernard as he studied him with jealous admiration, for he was still in the depot: he was just a child; he wore the uniform of the army, of course, but the military medals, the honourable injuries were for the others, he told himself, looking at Raymond Détang's arm in its sling. Détang, on convalescent leave, had come to the wedding and was now having dinner at the Bruns' house, in their little dining room crammed full of furniture. It was raining; the wood-burning stove gave off a gentle, somewhat stifling heat. They had toasted the newlyweds, the Allies and Victory. Bernard had still not lost his enthusiasm for drinking as much as he wanted, without risking being told off by his father and mother. He was sitting between the two soldiers. Martial, thin, sunburnt, with sunken cheeks and a pinched nose, pulled at his black beard. Raymond Détang was plump and had a healthy, glowing complexion; he had shaved off his beard and was getting many flattering compliments from the ladies. Because of his appearance, the way he spoke, his gentlemanly demeanour which he used to flatter and reassure civilians ('Don't you worry, now; they're done for, listen to what I'm saying, it's just a matter of months'), because of his war stories and his healthy chubbiness, Raymond Détang fitted the ideal of a soldier as imagined by civilians in their hearts far better than the silent Martial.

'That's it, all right,' said Adolphe Brun as he listened and drank his champagne, deep in thought. 'That's it, all right. They always keep a good sense of humour. I heard about one soldier who was hit by a shell and had both his legs blown off. "That's a bit of luck," he said. "Now I won't have to wash my feet any more!" Then he died. Now that's a real French soldier . . .'

'Monsieur Détang, is it true they've managed to make the trenches more or less comfortable?' asked Madame Jacquelain.

Meanwhile, Bernard, who had achieved an extraordinary state of lucidity thanks to the champagne, but the kind of lucidity that emerged in bursts and was then suddenly hidden by a heavy curtain or a wall of dense fog, this young Bernard found a strange resemblance between these two men (Martial and Détang), as if they were related. He took a long time trying to understand the nature of this similarity. 'They look feverish,' he thought in the end as he looked into their deep-set eyes. Yes . . . even Raymond Détang's eyes shone with a worrying glimmer. Both these men sat stiff and straight, rather too straight, as if they were standing to attention, as if, in spite of their muscles, their nerves were on edge, lying in wait, on the alert. 'They aren't really like us,' thought Bernard as he recalled the soldiers he'd seen when they'd returned from the front. They were different, unusual. The battlefield had dragged men down, crushed them, and war did not willingly return the ones who had not yet been devoured. People talked about the regular leaves they would soon be granted, but for the moment, people turned around in the street whenever one of these fabulous heroes walked by, looking at them with curiosity, respect, love. They had cheated death, these '*poilus*', the 'hairy men' as people called the ordinary soldiers hesitantly, apologising for using such a vulgar expression (the women preferred to call them '*pioupious*', 'the young Tommies'). 'And in a few days,' thought Bernard, 'I'll be just like them. There will be an immeasurable distance between me and my parents, my friends. Martial . . . Détang . . . To think that Détang always seemed a downright idiot to me, and Martial a ridiculous smug fool. But they've done so many things; they've seen so much. They've killed other men. Détang says he uses his bayonet, that he skewers them like chickens. As for Martial, naturally, that isn't his job, he dresses the soldiers' wounds while they're under attack, with shells falling all around him . . . And to think that he could have stayed behind the lines but didn't so he could serve his country better, that he put off his wedding, even though he really wanted it . . .' Not knowing how he could show what he felt, Bernard shyly touched Thérèse's arm.

'Will you think of me once in a while, when I'm gone?' he asked.

And immediately he berated himself: it was a silly thing to say, whiny, unworthy of a warrior. But he suddenly felt his heart fill with tenderness. Everything around him, these familiar faces, the little dining room that was so warm and peaceful, the table on which he and Thérèse had played card games and backgammon, everything, the little pitcher with the clicking spout he had found so funny when he was little, right down to the pink glass salt cellar sitting in front of him, everything seemed pleasant, friendly and full of precious, deep significance. 'This might really be the last time that I'm warm, that I feel good, that I want for nothing,' he thought. 'I might be killed as soon as I get over there. Brrr . . . it feels really strange to think about that . . .'

A cold little chill ran across his shoulders, so sharply and suddenly that he turned his head, as if someone had breathed on his back:

'If I am killed, at least I will have experienced this, which is better than anything in the world: Papa, Mama, our family and friends. I will never have travelled or been in love . . . *"I am prepared to die, O Goddess, but not before having known love . . ."*.* Martial . . . One night with the woman you love, your wife . . . Thérèse . . . No, I mustn't let myself think such thoughts. I must respect Thérèse. It isn't possible that I could be killed as soon as I get over there, is it? But then again, if that does happen, what glory! Everyone will love me, feel sorry for me. I will remain alive in people's memory, I will remain alive as a hero. Yes, as I fall to my death on that far-off battlefield, facing the enemy, I will feel that great surge of love upon me. It will console me, rock me gently to sleep. What is that thing we call Glory? It is to be loved by as many people as possible . . . Not just my parents and my friends, but even by strangers. And I, too, I will be happy to have died for them. For there's no doubt about it, if there were no daring fellows like me to defend you, you'd be shaking in your boots, ladies,' he concluded, imagining he was speaking to all the women whom he found lovable, sweet and kind.

'They'll think about me. They'll worry about me . . . They'll send me packages, letters, nice things to eat. And if I come back . . . with a medal for valour . . . we'll celebrate it here. Everyone will drink a toast to me. Then *I'll* be able to say, just like Détang: "I held the enemy back with my sharp bayonet. Strike! I pinned him to a wall like a butterfly." Yes, but what if it's the enemy who . . . Humph! I'm not going to think about that. One thing at a time. For now, I'm happy,' he told himself, and had some more to drink. He settled back in his chair like an old veteran, legs apart and hands in his pockets. It wasn't very polite, but too bad! It was the audacity of the hero: they

* The final lines of 'Sophocles' Song at Salamis' by Victor Hugo, from *La Légende des Siècles*, 1877.

just had to put up with it. Détang offered him a cigar; he lit it while looking furtively at his mother. Would she finally understand that he was now a man, that you don't forbid a man from having a cigar, especially the night before he's heading for battle? But no! She would not let it go: she clasped her hands together and spoke to him as if he were a child she'd caught playing with matches:

'Oh, Bernard!'

'What do you mean, oh, Bernard!' he thought. 'These women are unbelievable, honestly!'

'Won't that be bad for you, my dear?'

'Of course not, Mama, not at all,' he replied with affectionate indulgence. He even added: 'I'm used to it, you know,' even though it was the first cigar he'd ever had in his life. He took a long puff of it with a serious expression on his face.

Thérèse had no white dress, no bouquet of lilies, no crown of orange blossom. She was a war bride so wore a modest grey suit and a black hat.

'Twenty-four hours,' thought Martial, 'twenty-four hours and six have already gone by. One day and one night! That's all? My God, is that all? And what if I don't come back? To think that we might have been born fifty years ago . . . or twenty-five years from now, when there would be no war . . . Ah, we haven't been lucky! Détang has assured me that I could have been sent to the rear if I'd used my connections. But that would not have been honest. There are so few men in the first-aid post at the front that students and veterans from the Territorial Army are given the most terrifying responsibilities. It's true that I could also be useful elsewhere and . . . No! No! That's cheating! You don't compromise, you don't make a deal when it comes to your duty. You don't go into things half-heartedly. You sacrifice everything, your life, your work, everything you love.'

He slowly rubbed his closed eyes, picturing once more the

cellar, half under water, where he tended the wounded. That was home to him. For a long time he would know no other. He smiled as he recalled the 14th July, the day when he stood on the staircase at the Rue Monge and planned his future. It was sad and funny to think about that . . . 'Ah,' he sighed, 'this filthy war.'

Adolphe Brun looked at him, outraged. Yes, he had forgotten the rules of the game. Here, among civilians, it was not acceptable to speak ill of the war. It had to be described as wonderful, savage, but inspiring. My God, those things were true, of course. But as a doctor, he mostly saw the other face of war, a face with a deadly grimace. How did young Bernard Jacquelain see it? Eighteen years old with a broad chest, strong muscles, sharp reflexes, piercing eyes . . . Perfect prey for the war! He felt sorry for him, but his pity was the cold, clear-eyed pity of a doctor. During an operation, the arms and legs are sacrificed to save the rest of the body; men are snatched up and thrown into the fire, him along with many others, so that the country may survive . . . He accepted this. It made him sad, but he accepted it. 'You can't cheat,' he said to himself once more.

All the while, he was growing more and more desperately impatient; he looked at the time and wondered when he could politely leave with his wife. A small gold clock sat opposite him on the mantelpiece; it ticked away very quickly, with the sound of a rodent gnawing away at a piece of furniture. Nearly three o'clock . . . At three o'clock he would leave the Bruns; he would walk down the staircase, Thérèse on his arm; they would head for a little hotel he knew in Versailles where they would spend their wedding night. And the next day, while she was still asleep (his wife . . . her hair falling over her neck, her shoulders, just as it did when she was a child, her fine, sweet-smelling hair . . . that cloud of spun gold . . .) while she was still asleep, he would very quietly leave, without saying goodbye, without even kissing her, because his heart would break if he had to give her one last kiss and see her eyes fill with tears.

Finally the meal was over. Madame Brun carried the empty cake dish into the kitchen, the one that had held her masterpiece, her triumph, a specialty of Savoie filled with cherry cream. Not a crumb was left. She had been so overcome with emotion by making this dessert that she had hardly noticed anything else, the wedding, or that Thérèse had left . . . But nothing would change, because tomorrow, with Martial back at the front, Thérèse would return to the room she had before she was married and her life would carry on as if nothing had happened. The elderly Madame Brun was delighted at this thought with the sweet childlike cynicism of the elderly.

In the dining room, the men had fallen silent, one after the other. Even Adolphe Brun had not been able to take part in the women's chatter for long; Madame Humbert's loud, strident voice could be heard above everyone else's, like the big drum in an orchestra, and during certain patriotic tirades, she sounded like a shrill, heartbreaking fife, while Renée's voice was a flute alongside hers and Madame Jacquelain sighed like a mandolin. Thérèse was visibly trying to be cheerful, talking and laughing; it was the moment when she began to learn how to behave like a soldier's wife, no crying, no lamenting in public, rarely talking about herself and never about the one who was 'over there', the woman who continues waiting for him when everyone else has stopped waiting, the one who remembers when everyone else has forgotten, the one who hopes against all hope.

The women were talking about the war.

They descended from such lofty conversation to discuss the theatre; the Parisian theatres had reopened in December. Madame Jacquelain exclaimed that it was sacrilege: 'How can people go out in the evening when our dear little soldiers are so miserable? I wouldn't dare do that, not me . . .'

Madame Humbert did not agree:

'But come now, my dear, it all depends on the performance. At the Comédie Française they've been showing *Horace*. Marthe Chenal sang the *Marseillaise* at the Opera House. Well, what do you want? We need things like that to keep our spirits up. Civilians need that.'

'We're young,' said Renée, 'we need to take our minds off things.'

She looked at Détang and smiled brightly, provocatively. She and her mother had always dreamed of finding her a rich husband. But the war was wreaking terrible havoc with the men. 'Soon, it won't be a question of choice. It will be like it is at the butcher's: since August, you had to take whatever you could get,' Madame Humbert had said with a disillusioned sigh, as she sewed her hats beneath the lamplight every evening. 'Soon a lad like Détang, with no fortune and no prospects, a nobody, will seem like a good bargain, just as long as the war agrees to send him home with at least one arm or leg.'

'He's not stupid,' Renée would say to her mother, 'he's only as enthusiastic as necessary. It's very odd: he never gets carried away. He gets everyone else to speak. He does talk a lot but he never actually says anything. He's got a true Southern personality. He told me that if he makes it through this war he wants to go into politics, and it's not a bad idea for him. He could be successful.'

'Yes,' her mother replied, 'but you must be very careful and not give in to him at all. He's the kind of man who only gets married as a last resort. I know the type: your father was just the same.'

Now she turned to Madame Jacquelain. 'Don't forget about business here in Paris. Businesses have to thrive. Women are starting to think about their clothing again, thank goodness. I've designed a gorgeous new style of hat. It's inspired by the times: it's a policeman's hat. Very elegant looking and all the rage. It has an embroidered insignia, a piece of braid and a gold tassel, or even feathers and a rosette; no one will wear anything else this winter.'

Amid the hum of the conversations, the little clock on the mantelpiece, with its silvery tones, very quickly, shyly, struck three times. It was time for everyone to go. Martial stood up, trembling. Since he was leaving the next day, he wouldn't be seeing his family and friends again. The kisses and handshakes began; Madame Jacquelain quietly begged Martial: 'If my son is sent to the front lines, you'll look after him, won't you?' (She imagined the front was a kind of lycée where the older boys could defend and protect the younger ones against the unfair attacks of the Germans.) Monsieur Jacquelain spoke in his deep, hoarse voice: 'You'll think of me . . .', for during dinner, he had made sure to get some medical advice from Martial and made him promise to prepare a diet for his stomach troubles 'as soon as he had a free moment'.

Martial nodded and nervously pulled at his beard, where a few grey hairs were already beginning to show. Thérèse had stood up with him.

'I don't often have any free time over there,' he pointed out gently.

But Monsieur Jacquelain refused to believe it:

'There are surely quiet moments; you can't be operating all the time. It would be impossible for anyone to do that. In the newspapers, they report there are very few sick people and that the wounded heal very quickly, thanks to their good morale. Is that true?'

'Umm . . . morale . . . of course . . .'

But Adolphe Brun had pulled his nephew towards him and was hugging him; then he let him go and looked at him, his wide, bright eyes full of tears. He wanted to say something, make a joke . . . tell some funny story that Martial could tell the other soldiers that would make them say:

'Those old blokes from Paris, I mean . . . they're really something. They still know how to laugh.'

But he couldn't think of anything. He just slapped the doctor on the shoulder, on his thin, yielding shoulder beneath the thick material of his uniform:

'Off you go, my boy . . . ,' he muttered, 'you're a good, brave lad.'

5

The first-aid post was set up in the cellar; the house, solidly built and very old, had good foundations. It was a comfortable house in French Flanders, three kilometres from the German trenches. It had once looked squat, resilient, reassuring, its solid pillars framing the low door with its large rusty nails. A part of the house remained standing, the part where the silhouette of a tall, slim, mysterious woman wearing a turban had been sculpted above the casement window. The village had passed from one side to the other during the fighting that autumn in 1914. For the moment, the French occupied it. In this never-ending war that had started a few months before, people battled fiercely over a fountain, a forest, a cemetery, a bit of crumbling wall. The sudden advances of the enemy were no longer to be feared, but the bombardments grew more terrifying with every passing day; rubble piled up over the ruins. On sunny days, what had once been a pretty little French village (every gate was decorated with roses in bloom) now resembled a demolition site. Sunny days were rare. In the rain, obscured by the fog, it looked like a cemetery for houses, a heartbreaking sight. But the first-aid post stood firm.

'Even if the house crumbles, the cellar won't be affected,' Martial had said. 'So of course it will hold up.'

He was very proud of his cellar; it gave him pleasure to look at the thick walls, the vaulted stone ceiling above his head and the small alcoves that were dug out of the rock; one of them was his operating room; the other was where he slept; the third was a luxurious bedroom reserved for high-ranking officers who had been wounded. In his cellar, Martial could give free rein to his desire to be a home-owner, a feeling that circumstances had never before allowed him: orphaned when he was eight years old, he had moved from a school dormitory to a barrack room by way of furnished student accommodation. Everywhere, even in his dingy lodgings on the Rue Saint-Jacques as a first-year medical student, he had tried to 'make it into a home for himself', as he used to say with emotion. He had patched up the curtains that hung in ribbons, washed the skirting boards, polished the rickety night tables and arranged his books and family photos on the bookcase. He had spent so many hours imagining his future apartment on the Rue Monge: the living room with a yellow sofa, a leafy plant on the piano . . . his bedroom (the large bed and wardrobe with a mirror on the door), his consulting room. All of that had been taken away from him and replaced by a cellar in a strange house up north. Unfortunately, water was coming through the floor in certain places: the canal was nearby and, damaged in several places by the bombs, threatened to cave in at any moment and flood everything. The climate wasn't exactly ideal; the entire region was soaked with rain and covered in mud. Everyone slept in a thick, whitish sludge that continuously shifted and sloshed about; they ate the rainwater that fell into their soup – more rainwater than soup – they fought, fell, died in mud.

A well-situated, enormous staircase led up from the cellar; the men lay on its rough, uneven, wide steps. Their wounds had just been dressed; they were waiting to be evacuated to ambulances. Some of them slept on their haversacks, others on the bare stone; a smell of idoform, blood and damp seeped from the walls. Sickly, sweet clouds of chloroform hung in the air. From the tiny room where he worked, the doctor could see the wounded men newly arrived from the most recent battles. First their shapeless shoes weighed down with clods of yellowish mud that they banged, in vain, against the floor to loosen the clinging earth, the entrails of the gutted land they carried with them; then their drenched, torn, stained greatcoats, stiff with encrusted mud, then the hollow faces almost hidden by their full beards. Some of them had boots, helmets and faces so covered in mud that they looked like shapeless masses of silt on the move; others had every single strand of hair in their moustache caked in mud. It was a war zone where you could no longer tell which bodies were yours and which were the enemy's – the mud covered them with the same shroud.

The stretchers came down; trembling, panting, bleeding bodies were placed on the wooden trestles used as operating tables; if there was no more room on the trestles, they were laid on the ground. One corner of the cellar had been closed off with an improvised partition – a piece of canvas thrown over two metal rakes they had found in the garden and stuck into the ground: this was the morgue.

At the beginning, what wore the doctor out most was the incessant movement around him, all the strange faces that went by, reappeared, disappeared, a crowd, a crush of French soldiers and German prisoners, blonds, dark-haired men, the haggard features of the dying, the pale, astonished faces of children wounded for the first time who make an effort to show off, to put on a brave face, to smile, farmers who say 'Out you come, out you come!' and groan and seem to want to rip the pain from their bodies as if they were pulling out a plough that had got stuck in the mud – the weak men who cried like women, the silent ones, the courageous, the cowards and the ones who didn't hold back: 'Just my luck!' they would say, 'I'm done for' when their injury was 'really nasty', and even those who – just like in the newspapers intended to feed the patriotism of the masses – murmured as they turned pale from the pain: 'Oh, it's really nothing! I'm sure they can patch me up.'

He had seen so many of them! Even his brief moments of sleep were peopled with enormous crowds. He would fall asleep and dream that he was being crushed on all sides by strangers who prevented him from moving, who grabbed his hands, breathed on his face with the smell of tobacco and rough wine, stretching out their bloody stumps to him, calling him with tears in their eyes. He would gently push them away, but they would clutch at his clothes, trying to pull him towards them. They grabbed him from behind and made him stumble and fall. Then they would stamp on him with their heavy shoes, as if he were caught in a charge. They would cry out, and the heart-rending, shrill sound of their voices would wake the doctor up. Then he would find himself surrounded by groaning wounded men once more and he would get back to work.

It was raining. The rain fell into the trenches, on to the fields pitted with craters, over the grey corpses, the pale blue horizon, the ruins. It transformed the earth into a foul-smelling marshland. It caused the few drains that were still intact finally to crack so that water flooded into the cellar. It gushed through the tiny window, splashed over the stretcher where they had just placed a man whose two legs had been blown to bits. The lights went out. At the very same moment, the staircase leading up to the house was flooded. Shouting and swearing, the soldiers who weren't badly wounded rushed outside. It was night. Bombs were falling. Every now and then a rocket coming from the enemy lines would hover for a moment in the sky like a star, then fall and light up a bit of crumbling wall and the yellow eyes of a cat wandering among the stones. They had to evacuate the cellar. Before making the decision, the doctor stood motionless for a moment, his head leaning to one side and with a thoughtful expression on his face, as if he were deciding whether to operate: circumstances had forced the 'Ear, Nose and Throat' specialist to metamorphose into a surgeon who dealt with urgent casualties. For a moment, he had the idea that they might be able to draw off the water using small bottles and canvas buckets, but the water kept on rising.

So he started evacuating the men; the able-bodied men supported the weaker; the stretcher bearers carried the stretchers. The man whose legs had been blown to bits was the first to be carried out of the cellar. They climbed the staircase knee-deep in water. They went through the house. There was one room that had remained intact, a beautiful bedroom containing a large mahogany bed with swan-neck carvings; the fine sheets had been torn from the bed and dragged on to the floor.

Outside, Martial managed to organise his group and the procession headed towards the nearest ambulance. The road was dangerous because of the gunfire and shells. Day was just breaking when they arrived; they could see a strip of fiery light above the devastated field: it was a November dawn; a bitter reddish morning sky filled with crows in flight.

Martial kept staring at the stretcher as he walked; this was the most seriously wounded man and Martial had wanted to save him; he still hoped he could. The injured man was a farmer, tall, stocky, solid and strong. He wasn't speaking any more; he looked at Martial with a fierce expression so full of hope that it pained him, then he clenched his teeth and closed his eyes. He was still conscious. He didn't even cry out when the water splashed over him. He let himself be carried out without so much as a moan. Now he was moving forward, rocking on a stretcher carried by two men. Martial had had time to give him a caffeine injection on the doorstep, just before they left.

When he reached the ambulance, he called for his men; the stretcher passed close to him and he leaned over and drew back the blanket that covered the wounded man's face:

'Good God! But that's not him!'

It was someone else, a sly little fellow with sallow skin who started groaning in an unbearably loud, shrill voice as soon as anyone came near him. He had a broken femur.

'But, good Lord, where's the other man?' Martial shouted.

The two stretcher bearers looked at each other horror-struck: they had got the wrong patient. The man whose legs had been blown to bits whom the doctor had given an injection and placed on the stretcher must have been left back at the first-aid post; he was surely dying in the abandoned house.

Martial was seething with fury. This was another new characteristic he had acquired, a result of army life, the kind of anger that so easily takes hold of your soul. So courteous, so shy in ordinary life, since he became a soldier, he gave way to bursts of rage which, once they had passed, left him feeling shame, remorse and a sense of pride, all at the same time. Even the gentlest of men is sometimes pleased to frighten his equals, and the two stretcher bearers trembled as they listened to him, watching him shake his fists, his frail fists at the end of those long, thin arms:

'You morons! Idiots . . . You stupid sons of b . . . !'

He shouted all the swear words he knew in their faces and invented a few of his own:

'Now we're going to have to go and find him,' he said at last.

'Go and find him? Damn it,' the soldiers protested, 'but it's daylight!'

Martial refused to listen: he insisted on having his wounded man. He remembered the look in his eyes, the look of a man who was placing his life in Martial's hands, his own precious life. He was such a brave man! A man who had not moaned, or screamed or shown off, a man who had suffered with dignity, in silence . . . A real man! And he was the one who had been abandoned.

He started out with the two stretcher bearers. A shell exploded; Martial rolled to the ground. When he got up, he was safe, but the soldiers had disappeared; the stretcher was left on the road and since there was no sign of the two men, Martial assumed they had made a run for it. Without thinking, he shook the dirt from his greatcoat and continued on his way, sometimes crawling on the ground, sometimes walking, his head and shoulders bent, as if fighting a violent storm. It was raining, of course. Through the din of the shells and whistling bullets, you could hear a nearby river roaring: swollen by the constant rain, it had overflowed and was flooding somewhere in the mist.

Finally, Martial saw the first few houses at the edge of the village, at least what was left of them. Amid the fog, a fountain seemed to float in a watery mist. A farm had collapsed, leaving only an open gate still standing, a kind of Arc de Triomphe leading to the ruins. Martial got his bearings. Here was the house; there was the silhouette of the mysterious woman carved into the stone; greyish water lapped all around her.

'At least I'm lucky that those two stupid asses had time to get him out of the cellar,' he thought. 'The poor man. If he has to die, it's better if he's out of the water. But he won't die. He seemed determined, strong.'

He went into the house. Almost immediately, he crashed into the mutilated man lying on the stretcher, his head thrown back, his cheeks drained of blood. But he was alive. He was looking at him. He was looking at him! Martial grabbed his hand:

'What's all this, my poor boy, have they just gone and ditched you here? But I'm here now, you haven't been forgotten. Don't worry, I'll get you well again, come on . . .' he muttered, and the wounded man smiled; at least, a slight movement of his lips made Martial understand that the man whose legs had been blown to bits was trying to smile.

'The stretcher bearers will come and find us,' the doctor thought. 'My two lads must have got back by now and they'll send someone.'

If the roads weren't blocked, the stretcher bearers would come in daylight to take the wounded men to the ambulances. Otherwise, they had to wait until dark, but night fell early at this time of year. In this rain, soon there would be only darkness, the sound of lapping water in the night, a blind and deaf battle – but relative safety, in spite of everything.

'We'll get back, my boy, won't we? We'll both make it back.'

He talked to him almost tenderly; he felt almost fatherly towards this soldier, a kind of active, strong, masculine pity that no one had ever inspired in him until now. He changed the dressing on the wounds, gave him something to drink and waited.

But no one came.

'If you weren't so big, we would manage on our own, wouldn't we? But I can't carry you on my back . . . you can see that very well . . . the elephant and the flea,' he joked. 'What did you do before the war? Farmer? Wine grower? You look like a wine grower. We'd be happier back at your place sipping a nice white wine, wouldn't we?'

He talked to him without expecting or wishing for any reply, he spoke for himself as much as for the wounded man, to forget, to make the time pass more quickly.

The bombardment was incessant. Every now and again, a veritable earthquake shook the ruins. For a long time now, not a single pane of glass had remained in the windows; the wind and rain flowed freely into the room. Soon, when night fell, he would go out and find help; he knew that these ruins, which appeared deserted, gave signs of life at dusk. Soldiers returning from the front lines, the wounded, stretcher bearers, they all emerged from behind the bricks and mortar.

He and the man were in the bedroom, near the bed with the swan-neck carvings; the walls were covered in yellow wallpaper dotted with little flowers; on the mantelpiece stood a lamp with a leafy pattern on its shade, some framed photos above and, in one corner, a mahogany pedestal table with a bronze leg. In spite of everything, it was comforting to be surrounded by four walls with a roof over their heads. It was necessary to forget certain things, of course – the shattered windows, the ceiling that was crumbling in places, the plaster and rubble on the rug, the flooded cellar, the deep, muffled sound of explosions. But by making just a little mental effort, as he stared at the large bed – he lifted the sheets off the floor, smoothed them out, tucked them under the thick, soft mattress – he felt almost happy.

'When the war is over, when I'm old, after I've retired, Thérèse and I . . .'

He never finished his thought; it was cut through as if stabbed by a blinding light: a 105mm Howitzer shell had exploded in the bedroom, killing Martial. One entire section of the floor smashed open, crashed down, crushed deep into the earth, carrying the dead body with it. But the wounded man on his stretcher was not hit. He was found a while later by a division that had just been relieved and had left the front lines to get some rest. He was taken to an ambulance where the remains of both his legs were amputated. He survived, and is still alive today.

6

Bernard was wounded. He was walking down a road, fleeing towards the rear, along the banks of the Aisne; the road was littered with dead bodies. Everything and everyone – columns of men, horses, trucks, cannon, long lines of refugees dragging carts full of furniture behind them, with women between the shafts, even a clump of bare trees, dead for four years, decapitated by shells or poisoned by gas that the autumn wind or a hail of bullets had violently bowed over in the direction of the retreat – everything and everyone seemed to be fleeing.

The First and Seventh German Divisions had attacked the Sixth Division of the French Army from north of the Aisne to the Montagne de Reims. The enemy managed to cross the Aisne, and get as far as the Vesle River. On the evening of the 28th May, everyone was saying that the defences of the Vesle had been breached, that the English were pulling back, that Soissons had fallen. Bernard knew none of this. He had been wounded at the beginning of the attack. Now, he and a group of men, all injured in the recent battle, were looking for the first-aid post. But it no longer existed, destroyed by artillery or overrun by the advancing waves of the enemy. Bernard was told they had to keep going. When he tried to climb into a truck, he was pushed out; there were too many wounded. He kept on going, his eyes blinded by a kind of bloody mist; one shoulder was torn open and fragments of shell were lodged in his cheek.

Along both sides of the road, or rather the track that remained of the wrecked road, stretched a ravaged plain, hollowed out, dug up, turned upside down, a chaotic mass of loose stones, yellowish slimy mud, shell-craters, crosses (even those were broken and had tumbled on top of each other, riddled with bullet holes, torn out by artillery fire); there were empty tin cans, helmets, boots, clothing in tatters, bits of wood and metal debris. Every now and again, you could see a section of wall that was still standing, or three stone blocks, or a slight mound on the ground, a pile of rubble – and that was all that remained of a house, a village, a church. In other places, overturned tanks, partly sunk in mud, entirely covered in dust, seemed to be reaching steel shards towards the sky. It was the bedlam of the crucial days of war, a moving wave of vehicles from three armies. Munitions caissons, small flatbed trucks for repairing the railway lines, supply wagons, ambulances, lorries loaded with petrol, troops being shifted to the rear into new positions, everything sped past Bernard like a river of grey metal. Mines had blown up the road; bridges made of wooden beams had been thrown over the shell-craters.

Every so often, the entire procession stopped under fierce artillery fire because an overturned vehicle was blocking the road, causing a deadly bottleneck. Herds of animals would come out of nowhere, followed by fleeing villagers; confused, terrified, bellowing cows charged into the trucks or ran off into the fields.

It was burning hot, a stifling spring day. Men walked through the dust, breathing it in, spitting it out again; dust mingled with their blood and sweat.

'My God,' thought Barnard, as he marched on as if in a dream, sometimes climbing back up on to the road, sometimes falling down on to the devastated stretch of land. 'My God, please let me live through this, please let it end! Please let me rest . . .'

He was twenty-two years old. He was eighteen when war was declared, nineteen in the Argonne, twenty at a hospital in Marseille, not even twenty-one on the hills of Mort-Homme during the Battle of Verdun. He had aged without having had the time to grow up; he was like a piece of fruit picked too early: bite into it and all you will taste is its hard, bitter flesh. Four years! He was so tired.

'I want to rest,' he murmured with painful determination, talking to himself through the dust, 'I want to rest, not just today but forever, forever. I don't want to die, just close my eyes and not give a damn about anything. Whether we attack or run away, win or lose, I don't give a damn any more, I don't want to know any more. I just want to sleep.'

But sometimes, when he felt a little stronger, he would think:

'No! I won't rest forever. If only I can get out of here alive, I'll enjoy everything I never had. I'll have money, women, I'll enjoy life, I will . . .'

He had never before felt that way. During the early years of the war, he had been serious, stern, with bursts of juvenile cheerfulness, but completely determined to become hardened and to win, thanks to a heroic act of will. Perhaps he had overestimated his strength? Physically, he was strong, resistant to pain and exhaustion; he had become a man with broad shoulders who stood tall and was energetic and alert. Mentally, though, he had been wounded in a way that nothing in future could ever heal, a wound that would grow deeper every day of his life: it was a kind of weariness, a chink in his armour, a lack of faith, pure exhaustion and a fierce hunger for life. 'And I'll live for me, and me alone,' he thought. 'I've given them four years,' and what he meant by these words was a sense of an entire hostile world set against him – leaders, enemies, friends, civilians, strangers, even his own family. Especially civilians! Those . . . It was the time when the home front thought they had sacrificed enough, shed too many tears over blood that had been spilled and could never be recovered, blood they could no longer stop from flowing. Profiteers, politicians, every kind of mercenary, workers spoiled by high wages, who all thought only of themselves and left the front lines twitching, bleeding and dying. 'And why?' thought Bernard. 'It's pointless: no one will win. Everyone is exhausted. Each country will end up back on its own borders, but drained, spent, dying. And in the meantime, the civilians are still alive. While we're rotting away in the trenches,' he continued thinking, 'those nights in the trenches, long nights on sentry duty, or that instant just before the battle: ominous moments you could never forget.'

He thought all of this as he walked along the road, among the other soldiers moving fast like him, suffering like him. No one could help him. No one could make his cross any lighter to bear.

'It's so heavy,' sighed Bernard in a kind of delirium, tottering beneath the weight of the military kit he was still carrying over his bloody shoulder. Those poor guys! How could they possibly help me? Some of them are worse off than me. Me, me . . . But I'm nothing. Whether I live or die means nothing. All the civilians with their lies: "Heroes, Honour . . . giving your life for your country . . ." To tell the truth, they don't even really need me. Modern warfare requires machines. An entire battalion of heroes would be better off replaced by a perfect armoured tank that, without patriotism, without faith or courage, would annihilate as many of the enemy as possible. And the civilians can sense that. They keep on saying that they love us, admire us, but it's just what they're expected to say; all of them are thinking that we're nothing and they know that even an inanimate machine is more valuable than we are. That's what is so serious. We used to be real men . . . But since we can't turn ourselves into machines, since we're no longer really men, we feel degraded, as if we were beasts. What is it they say? "Don't try to understand. Don't think." Become mindless! We have to be like that dead horse,' he said, staring at it.

They were scattered everywhere along the road, cadavers with long teeth, wounded horses, worn-out horses, some disembowelled by an exploding shell, all that remained of an English regiment in retreat. Such a confusion of races, of blood, of languages surrounded Bernard! He saw Scotsmen, Hindus, Africans, German prisoners. All these different faces had the same expression: a kind of exhausted grimace that gave their young faces the look of death. Of hell . . . And a few kilometres from there, in Paris . . . 'No! Paris has been bombed. They are suffering there too . . . But further away, in the cities . . . in Cannes . . . Or the cool, beautiful houses in Geneva . . . in Madrid . . . in the United States, where the young men are well out of it, young men who can swim in the sea or drink chilled punch . . . Oh, just to eat some ice cream . . . The sun on an open wound is torture! And the sun on a helmet . . . My brain is being boiled. What did Papa say during my last leave? "They won't be very demanding, the ones who make it back. It will take very little to make them happy!" He was so wrong! But everything they say is stupid,' he thought bitterly. 'Stupid, stupid, stupid . . .'

He stumbled, felt as if he were losing his footing: blood was seeping through the dressing that a nurse had hastily applied during the battle; warm blood ran down his arm, and he no longer knew whether the sickly stench of butchery came from the dead horses or from his own body. He fell down. 'No one will carry me, will they?' he said to himself. 'Well, then keep on walking or die, boy.' With superhuman effort, he stood up, kept going. A small group of wounded men were behind him, each man gritting his teeth, each one dragging his weary legs. Then came a stretcher with a wounded man on it, followed by another carrying a corpse. Then some African soldiers rolling their wide, terrified eyes to the heavens. Then grey soldiers in long greatcoats. Then a Hindu riding a small black horse. Then more trucks, tanks, cannon. And Bernard, who kept on walking . . .

7

The war dragged on; a long-range cannon fired on Paris; the Allies were preparing themselves for 'three, ten, twenty years of war, if necessary', but everyone, even the Germans, knew that peace would come eventually. No one could imagine how it would come, whether it would arrive with the sly, soft footsteps of the diplomats or the arrogant strides of the conquering warriors. What would it be called? A truce with no winner, a victory, a defeat? But there were subtle signs of its approach. 'There's no reason why it should end,' people said out of habit. 'It will only be over when we're all dead.' But every now and then, a timid little voice would suggest: 'Still, it can't go on forever. Force of circumstances will put a stop to it. It will end because everything ends.' The young retorted harshly: 'It will end because everyone's had enough.' There was an outcry: 'Coward! Defeatist! You're not a true patriot.' But these were merely empty words: the truth was they had had enough. They were dazed by the thundering weapons, they'd had their fill of blood and glory.

Madame Pain came back from the greengrocer's, emptied her bag full of vegetables on to the kitchen table and announced:

'It won't go on for much longer now. All we have to do is wait!'

'Well she can tell herself to be patient,' thought Madame

Jacquelain, her heart breaking with anguish. 'She doesn't have anyone over there.'

It was over: the holy alliance of the early days, the time when each person suffered on behalf of everyone, when glory and mourning were shared equally among all the French. Four years later, everyone had his own personal destiny, and it had nothing to do with the fate of France. Martial was dead. They all talked about him; his picture had place of honour in the dining room: a framed photograph decorated with a red, white and blue rosette and black mourning crepe. He was in his uniform; he looked taller, more imposing than he had in reality; he had straightened his neck for the camera lens rather than shrinking it as he normally did when he tugged at his beard or rubbed his tired eyes . . . He looked straight ahead of him with an expression that was strange, wise, attentive, kind, yet with a barely perceptible hint of coldness, a kind of detachment, as if, from that moment on, in the village behind the lines where he had been photographed a week before he died, he was saying goodbye to everyone, forever. Thérèse placed fresh flowers in front of his picture every day.

Madame Jacquelain was pale, emaciated, her face distorted by nervous tics. She couldn't sleep any more, barely ate. Lying in her bedroom, she thought about Bernard sleeping in the mud of the Somme or in the sand of Flanders; when she was eating, she imagined him going hungry; when she rested, that he was tired. When she read the list of the dead, she told herself: 'Tomorrow it could be him.' When the son of one of her friends was killed, she cried because she could see her own son's face beneath the features of the young victim. But whenever she heard that a soldier had been saved, found shelter, was safe, she bitterly reproached God that her own son was still in danger – and for how much longer?

Bernard was fighting in the Aisne region.

Raymond Détang had married Mademoiselle Humbert, and had managed to organise things so that he remained in Paris.

The Bruns had nothing to live on apart from Thérèse's money, 'but I'm not worried about the Russian stocks,' Monsieur Brun said, ever the optimist. 'The Russians will pay up in the end. They are true friends and even though I miss the Tsar, who was a good man, in spite of everything, I'm not angry that the people are now a Republic: their system of government was behind the times. So I'm not worried at all: they will pay their debts. But in the meantime, in the meantime, it's difficult . . .'

And it was difficult; they lived as they had before, but they looked like people who had set out on a journey one beautiful fine day in a gentle breeze, with parasols and straw hats and who suddenly see the weather change, a storm brewing and the rain drenching the ruffles on their muslin skirts.

Everything seemed strange, distorted, out of joint. This war no longer resembled the one that began in 1914: with its tanks, planes and armoured vehicles, with its soldiers in gas masks, this was nothing more than war on an industrial scale, an enormous company that traded in serial massacres, death on a production line. This Paris where all the languages in the world could be heard, these cafés where the French no longer felt at home, this echo that reached the scandalised but curious Frenchmen, the echo of ever increasing numbers: 'He made a million on war supplies, a million . . . Two, ten, twenty million . . . There are people making millions while our sons . . . They aren't decent Frenchmen . . . They aren't patriots, but . . . money . . .' What they didn't say was: 'Pleasure . . .' They would not have dared. And besides, that word would have sounded almost offensive to the lower middle classes. They didn't take to pleasure easily, they didn't enjoy themselves in 'good' society, among 'the right kind' of people. No! No one would have dared speak of pleasure and yet, whispered rumours spread from one person to another that in Paris itself, even while it was being bombed, in certain areas, in clubs open only to members, soldiers on leave, women, foreigners danced the tango and other dances as well, frenzied, obscene dances that had daring names; every night, drunken Americans smashed the windows at Café Weber; pilots, the war's 'flying aces', behind the wheels of cars, speeding along at a hundred miles an hour, swerved on to the pavement and killed women. These rumours were strange, almost incomprehensible, sinister in a way, or so thought Adolphe Brun. There was something about all this that frightened him: he no longer recognised the French. Its people spoke a new language that was no longer the light-hearted slang of 1900; it was teeming with Anglo-Saxon expressions. There were new customs and, most importantly, certain words no longer elicited the same reaction from him as in the past. The most sacred words – 'Frugality . . . Marital fidelity . . . Virginity . . .' – had gradually become old-fashioned, almost laughable. There was a painful contrast between what you read in the newspapers and what you heard in the street, on the metro, in the shops, it was like a nightmare where you see a great crowd of men in top hats who are otherwise stark naked; you wonder: 'Can they see what they look like? Who do they think they are fooling?'

On the other hand, however, the persistent bombardments did not concern Monsieur Brun. He would stand at the window in his nightshirt when the sirens began to wail. He felt a sort of pride during the air raids. This was history, something that had happened before, experienced by an entire race of people through him, a noble kind of danger.

Thérèse was a nurse, along with Renée Détang. The two women worked in the same hospital. Renée often went out in the company of young American soldiers and laughed scornfully when Thérèse refused to go along.

'You're so middle class, such a homebody, my poor girl! And yet, you're free. As for me . . .'

She took a small mirror from her handbag and looked at her exquisite cat-like face with its tiny nose and wide green eyes; small curls of a harsh, metallic gold colour escaped from her nurse's cap:

'Well I think that life is short and you have to make the most of it. I'm not doing anything wrong.'

'You're not?'

Whenever Thérèse made fun of someone, her eyes sparkled and her round face with its turned-up nose took on a bold, frank expression.

'I'm just having a good time,' said Renée.

'That's what I thought. You're appalling.'

'Do you think a life like yours is fun? The hospital, then back home to clean the floors with steel wool? Polishing the saucepans? For what? You're not married any more. Making yourself a pretty collar on Sundays to put on your uniform? Why? You don't have a lover. Aren't you ever tempted at all, Thérèse?'

'No,' Thérèse said quietly. 'No, never.'

And yet, temptation wafted all around a woman in the words she heard spoken, in the very air she breathed. A tall, handsome lad in uniform smiles at you in the street and you think: 'Tomorrow he'll be gone. No one will know. Why not?' Jewellery, perfume, clothes from a boutique on the Rue de la Paix when your hair reeks of idoform and blood, when you are wearing a starched uniform and a nurse's cap that covers your forehead, when you have hardly any money. When you have become a soldier's pen friend, when you have chosen a farmer who writes to you at Christmas: 'Thank you so much, my dear benefactress, for the new sweater and the pipes. I told my wife how spoiled I am . . .' and then you watch your friend going out with Americans . . . Temptation, and the most dangerous thing of all . . . missing being loved when your husband is dead . . . But that was nobody's business.

'I don't know what you mean. I'm always busy and I'm never bored. Cleaning the floors? Well, I like doing that! I like a wardrobe that's been polished and shines, the smell of stew that's been slowly cooking, a new hat made out of two flowers and a ribbon.'

'You'll never find another husband if you stay hidden within your four walls.'

'I'm not looking for a husband. But tell me, what about yours? Doesn't he see anything?'

'Nothing. And besides, he's not the jealous type.'

'That's odd. I . . .'

'You'd be jealous, Thérèse? Well, really! Holding on to a man against his will isn't worth the trouble.'

'Yes, but as far as I'm concerned, I enjoy taking the trouble.'

'Like with the stew and the hat?'

'Exactly. I like putting effort into things. It gives me pleasure. When I fall in love . . .'

'So you will fall in love then?'

'Why not? I'm twenty-two years old and was only married for two months. I sincerely mourned my husband. I cared for him a great deal but I was never in love with him. Love . . . But what you call love makes me feel ashamed and rather frightened.'

'There is no other kind of love in 1918,' said Renée, getting up.

They said goodbye. They had been standing under a courtyard entrance waiting for the rain to stop. They went their separate ways. It was a stifling hot day. The brief shower had barely dampened the dust. Now it began rising again, casting a haze through the air, and the last rays of a bright red sun sparkled through the fine mist. An enormous American officer passed by, crushing a plump little woman against him – she only came up to his waist – and behind him came another officer who blew a kiss to Thérèse when he saw her. When she looked away, he pulled a handful of various crumpled bills from his pocket: thousand franc notes, hundred franc notes, worthless money at the current exchange rate. All around the Champ-de-Mars, near the Eiffel Tower, people selling oriental carpets, peanuts and obscene postcards lay in wait, ready to pounce on potential customers. A group of young girls, high school students, walked past Thérèse.

'What a great time we had at that club yesterday,' they chirped. 'It was wild!'

Young women wearing mourning veils and pink stockings were on the prowl. It was wartime. They had been bombed all week long. They'd be bombed again perhaps. The Germans continued to advance. It was war. This scourge on the immense body of the world had unleashed great waves of blood. Now everyone could tell that such a wound would not heal easily, and the scar would be ugly to behold.

8

My little boy will be so happy, thought Madame Jacquelain as she came out of the circus where she had just reserved a box for the performance the next day. It was an extravagance . . . everything was so expensive. Too bad! Bernard was on leave, recovering from being wounded in the Battle of the Aisne; Bernard deserved to be spoiled on his last night in Paris.

He'll be so happy! He liked the circus and the theatre so much. He used to dream about going to those wonderful matinees of French classics a whole week before he went. His very pale little face would concentrate intently as he looked at the stage: 'Mama, it's so beautiful!' – 'What could he do when it's three against one?' – 'I hope he dies!' – 'Those were real men, Mama!' He always had such noble feelings. And as for the circus! The horses! He loved everything that pranced, pawed the ground, all the sounds and the bright lights. I think his injury has tired him out, she continued thinking. He's not . . . He's really changed. I can't put my finger on it but the things he says, his mannerisms . . . He no longer has that spontaneity that was so sweet . . . But of course, I'm forgetting that he's actually a young man now. Even though he was twenty-two, she thought of him with gentle indulgence, just as she had in the past: 'He's eight years old. We've cut off his curls but he's still a baby' or 'He's fifteen and even though he pretends to be a man, he's still a child at heart.' Oh, just let this war end, end, end! Just let her little boy, her child come back alive with only a tiny little wound, just enough for her to shed tears of pride, to have an excuse to pamper him. Yes, just let her little boy be given back to her and let them live the life they used to have. Bernard with his books, reading beside the lamp in the dining room, while she knitted him socks. It would be hard work to make up for all that lost time. She was ambitious for him. He'd be the first to be accepted at one of the top universities, and afterwards, oh, afterwards! He'd earn a good living. He'd get married. He'd have children. It would be heaven . . .

'And that's not all,' she thought, stopping on the pavement. 'Now let me see, there are two more seats in the box. I'll invite Thérèse and her grandmother. What should I wear? I have to make my soldier boy proud. My mauve taffeta dress with Aunt Emma's cameo.'

Happily thinking of everything she had to do, she ran after a bus that had already pulled away.

'I must stop by at the Bruns to invite the ladies,' she thought.

Thérèse accepted with pleasure, happy at the thought of seeing the young soldier again. They agreed to meet at the circus, by the entrance, a subtle suggestion by Madame Jacquelain who thought: 'The men should pay for the programmes and the usher when we arrive. It's expensive but more gallant.'

Thérèse and her grandmother waited amid the crowd, trying to find the handsome young man in uniform whom she had last seen when he was on leave in 1915, because ever since then, she had been so busy at the hospital that she had not had time to meet up with him when he had been in Paris. She smiled and looked straight in front of her, then suddenly let out a cry of surprise: that tall, skinny young man with a small, dark moustache in a neat, trim line above his thin lips, that young man with the deep-set eyes and a scar on his cheek who was walking towards them between the Jacquelains, could this be Bernard, the little boy she used to play with?

'Oh, Grandmother, look at him . . .'

But Madame Pain was very agitated by all the movement around her and was trying to protect her black silk dress – it was the one she had made for Thérèse's first Communion (Thérèse had altered it, shortened it, made it look more like the fashion of the day) – and so Madame Pain saw nothing.

They sat down in their box. Thérèse was between her grandmother and Madame Jacquelain, whose face looked pale and preoccupied. Thérèse thought that the fact that Bernard was leaving the next day was already spoiling her happiness. How hard it was to be a mother! How many tears, how many sleepless nights, how much anguish she must have felt these past four years! She squeezed Madame Jacquelain's hand affectionately.

'I'm terribly upset, Thérèse,' she whispered. 'My husband and Bernard had a fight.'

'A fight? About what?'

'Well, when I came home with the tickets for the box, really pleased to surprise my boy, he kissed me and said: "You're really sweet, Mama, but I already have plans for tonight, I'm supposed to meet my friends." – "Tonight? Your last night, Bernard? How could you do that? The little time you have here belongs to me, your mother! You owe it to me; I've suffered too much," and I started to cry. He was touched and was about to give in. Unfortunately, his father intervened. He's not always diplomatic; he upset him, and then . . .'

She fell silent, her heart heavy, hiding the most important, the most painful part of the argument: Bernard needed money; he had gone out the night before to play poker; he had lost five thousand francs. It was an amount of money they would have considered spending on an operation or for his education, for something serious, legitimate, reasonable, but for gambling! 'You, Bernard, a gambler!' even though she tried to tell her husband that it was just a passing phase, that he'd met up with the wrong kind of people, 'Papa' wouldn't listen to a word. 'At his age, at twenty-two . . . still a kid . . . to lose five thousand francs playing poker! . . . And what sort of a game is that anyway? Just a kind of baccarat. It wasn't until I was forty years old and balding that I first bet on anything, five francs on *petits chevaux* in Dieppe. And today, that's the type of place you intend to go instead of coming to a respectable performance with your family and friends?' And Bernard . . . My God, Bernard . . . what have they done to my good little boy? Bernard sighed with a kind of ironic bitterness: 'I'm happy to die for you both but don't give me a hard time!' She had had the presence of mind to remind her husband that getting all worked up was bad for his stomach. But what an argument, such a scene! 'You have no respect for your father, my boy. You are undermining the principles of this family.' Bernard listened to him with a cold, impassive look on his face, as if he pitied us. My God! To fight when he's leaving the next day, going back to that hell knowing he may never come home again! She watched the horsewoman grabbing at paper hoops and tears formed a kind of prism of the brilliant lights around her so that everything seemed to dance, shimmer and leap inside the ring.

'Dear Madame Jacquelain, try not to get upset,' Thérèse said softly. 'What do you expect? They've seen so many horrible things; they need to be entertained to help them forget what they've seen.'

'Exactly,' said Madame Jacquelain, wiping the tears from her eyes, 'and what could be more entertaining than the circus to take your mind off things?'

'Yes, of course, but for a young man of his age, it's perhaps a little . . . childish.'

'But what do you think they do when they get together, then?'

asked Madame Jacquelain, scandalised and extremely curious. 'Do they get drunk? Invite women around? But why? I mean, why has he changed so much?'

She turned towards Bernard:

'You're having a good time, my darling, aren't you? A really good time?' she asked anxiously, her voice quivering with hope.

'Of course I am, Mama.'

'It's funny,' he thought, 'that they can't understand. My heart has been bombarded by violent emotions for the past four years and now needs to beat more strongly than in the past, to beat at a pace that is no longer childish. Poker . . .' But no, he wasn't a gambler. He just liked spending money. Spending money! What a sacrilege that was in the eyes of these middle-class people! He'd acquired a taste for it, though, a taste he had not had before his previous leaves. He'd acquired several new tastes and not all of them were low. Books for example . . . Dostoyevsky, André Gide, the poetry of Rimbaud and Apollinaire. Something within him was becoming sophisticated, demanding, vaguely sensual. Money lost at poker . . . He hadn't cost his parents much during the past four years. His father would just have to spend less on his tonics, that's all.

His father sucked the tip of his moustache, looking irritated and his mother was crying. But what could they be thinking, for heaven's sake? That he would come back the same as when he left? That after four years of war he would be just as naïve, just as childish as in the past? Four years . . . His tongue burned, tasted mouldy, as if he'd been drinking 100 proof alcohol. Everything seemed dull, bland. And besides, nothing was of any importance. That was what caused the abyss between him and these people. They were so terribly serious, poor souls . . . As for him . . . Oh, he wasn't going to get upset about it. Everything would work out, nothing was of any importance. You live today, you die tomorrow. When you think about it that way, five thousand francs lost at poker and the righteous anger of his father were a joke! He half closed his eyes, stifled a yawn. Not a decent woman in sight . . . Women . . . The things he'd seen and done . . . Behind the lines, in the hospitals, you could take your pick. Everyone said they'd become easy since the war started. But he thought they had always been like that. It was in their nature: man was made to kill and woman to . . . A simple and brutal way of looking at life. Too brutal? Too simple? Rash and lacking in nuance? Perhaps. It wasn't his fault. And besides, who gave a damn . . . He glanced over at Thérèse. Now there was one he could get . . . But he didn't have time to begin the assault. He was leaving the next day. He looked at the ring where little horses with long tails were trotting about. His mother turned towards him, smiling with delight:

'Do you remember how much you used to like them, Bernard? When you had Thursdays off, remember?'

He coldly thought back to the memories she conjured up before him. The delights of family life! The humble pleasures of the Parisian middle classes! Free waffles and orangeade in the large department stores on rainy days and, when the weather was good, a wrought iron chair beside the Champs-Élysées watching the fortunate people of this world drive past in their fancy cars. A sudden feeling of envy pierced him to the core: 'I won't always be sitting on a wrought iron chair, will I? Ah, how I long to be rich!' Over there, in the place he'd just come from, it wasn't the same. Everyone was equal in war. But on the home front . . . They were revving up to have a good time! And to think that people were talking about regeneration, a revival of morality after the suffering of the war! Could they really not see that everyone had loose morals, that all they wanted to do was eat as much as possible, get drunk, go wild. Whether they were winners or losers made no difference. With pride or in despair, the beast would be released, the beast you had carried within yourself and kept under control for four long years.

After the show, Madame Jacquelain asked her husband to buy everyone some hot chocolate. She was determined that the evening be a total success. Surely her little boy would have nothing to complain about: his parents had gone all out for him. He could even have a drop of Benedictine.

They had lost Armentières and Soissons; the Fifth Division of the British Army had been pushed back. Bombs were falling on Paris. But in this café, set up in a cellar beneath the Champs-Élysées, there was such a crowd that people had to wait to get a table. The Bruns and Jacquelains too smiled and waited with the unshakable patience of Parisians who do not like paying for their pleasures but who will gladly suffer to ensure they enjoy themselves, queuing in the rain at the ticket window of a theatre, trudging the corridors of the metro, travelling in a packed third-class train compartment to spend two hours at the seaside. And besides, it was good sport. They had to keep an eye out for a table where someone had paid the bill, thread their way through the groups who weren't as on the ball and triumphantly claim their place. At last they were seated; the ladies ordered hot chocolate and Bernard a black coffee, much to the disappointment of Madame Jacquelain.

'Go ahead, Bernard,' she whispered, 'do order a Benedictine . . .' then, speaking even more quietly: 'Papa won't say anything.'

'But Mama, I can't stand Benedictine; it makes me feel sick,' Bernard protested with a tense smile.

His mother looked sad but said nothing more.

At the next table, a soldier was in the company of some very beautiful young women wearing make-up.

'But that's Monsieur Détang!' exclaimed the elderly Madame Pain.

He heard her and turned around. Heavier, his complexion rosier than ever, he had an unusual upper lip that made him look like a wolf, thought Thérèse. People said he was a good lad, that he would 'make his way in politics'. 'He's on first-name terms with some Ministers,' Madame Humbert told them. 'He's very well respected, a young man with a future, and kindness itself.' Madame Humbert had insinuated to Madame Jacquelain that with his connections, his influence, he could get Bernard away from the front line, but Madame Jacquelain's old French blood had revolted:

'We'll have nothing to do with that sort of thing,' she had replied haughtily. 'My son isn't a shirker.'

The use of that word had somewhat spoiled the relationship between the two women, but Raymond Détang smiled most cordially at everyone, greeting them as warmly as possible; he had the eager attentiveness of Southerners who hide their coldness like the ice cream at the centre of that dessert known as 'Peach Melba': a layer of smooth, warm chocolate covers a kind of hard stone of ice that hurts your teeth.

'Thérèse! You've finally taken a break from that damn hospital? I hardly ever get to see my wife . . . wait a minute, is that you, our little Bernard? How's things?'

'Not bad, Raymond. How about you?' Bernard asked casually. He was shocked to be addressed so familiarly and replied in kind.

But Raymond didn't seem offended that this kid who had addressed him as 'Monsieur Raymond' four years ago was now putting himself on an equal footing. He replied with good humour. And besides, he was used to being familiar with all sorts of people, shaking hands all round, and delivering speeches with ease. He immediately launched into a knowledgeable, lively treatise, in a very loud voice, on the most recent developments in the war. Strangers listened to him with respect. Someone whispered:

'That man is very clever . . . He seems to know what he's talking about.'

'So what are you doing in Paris?' asked Bernard.

Détang lowered his voice:

'I'm on an assignment,' he said, sounding mysterious. 'I'm going on a long trip to the United States soon. I can't say any more than that, but I hope to contribute, in some small way, in forging a solid link between our two countries. The war is actually about to end. Everyone can sense it. So now, we have to start planning for peacetime and the most important economic and political issues have to be resolved.'

'Lucky devil,' grunted the young man. 'You're going to get a free trip with flowers, fanfares and parades while the day after tomorrow, I go back to work "somewhere in France".'

Raymond looked at him sceptically and frowned. At the corners of his lively eyes appeared an intricate network of fine, yellowish lines.

'You poor boy, come on now . . .'

They were surrounded by the noise of the crowd; Bernard looked around him with an expression of scorn and curiosity.

'Paris is strange now,' said Raymond Détang, and he seemed to be offering the spectacle to Bernard and the women with the same gesture as a director pointing out a group of characters on stage. 'You have no idea what's being bought and sold here, what schemes people are cooking up. Sometimes, it makes you want to take your head in your hands and ask yourself "Is this why we've gone to war? The Marne, Verdun, our dead young men, all that to end up like this? A jumble of mercenaries, profiteers, schemers, American munitions sellers and Bolshevik spies?" Compared to all that, this is lively, amusing. Vile but lively, you can't say it isn't. And there are such opportunities!' he added, leaning in to whisper in Bernard's ear.

'Like women?'

'Oh, women . . . there are far too many women. No, business opportunities. Ah, if only I had some investment capital . . .'

He was lost in a dream for a moment and his hands – he had very beautiful hands, well cared for, expressive, with quivering fingers that curled up slightly at the tips, spiritual, worrying hands that clashed with the easy-going directness he affected – his hands trembled and stretched out as if reaching for some prey.

'You'll find some money, I'm sure of it,' whispered Bernard.

The two of them spoke very quietly amid the noise while Thérèse remained pensive and the others watched the crowd in open-mouthed astonishment.

'But I'm not interested in money,' said Raymond, recovering his mocking manner of good little boy. 'I am a true son of France, I am, sensitive, generous, a dreamer, always ready to sacrifice my own most legitimate interests to some greater ideal. So in America, where it's raining gold at present, not a single cent will end up in my pocket. My mind is completely focused on enormously important deals that affect all of humanity . . . I literally have no time to think about myself, and that's a shame, a real shame, because, as I've already said, there are opportunities and no one should sneer at making money. It's a powerful lever, a tool that can do a great deal of harm but also a great deal of good,' he declared in a beautiful, throaty voice that could easily be heard above the noise of the conversations and the clatter of dishes and glasses. 'When are you going back, Bernard?' he suddenly asked.

'Tomorrow.'

'Tell me, you speak English, don't you? Aren't you a real fount of knowledge? When you were a child, you won all the school prizes. I remember that, just as I remember everything. I have a remarkable memory.'

'Yes, I do speak English.'

'Yes, but careful now, is it a good, modern English, good commercial English, no what-do-you-call-its, nothing as old-fashioned as Shakespeare? If so, could you come to the United States with me, as my secretary?'

'You're mad! I just told you that I'm leaving tomorrow.'

'My dear boy, everything can be arranged. You must start from the principle that nothing in this world is impossible. Mind you,

I'm not promising you anything, but I have contacts and a certain amount of influence . . .'

He gave a self-satisfied little laugh.

'A certain amount of influence,' he said again. 'You could say that you are extraordinarily lucky. I am actually looking for a clever lad who could help me over there, for I am a true son of France, and I have never been able to get a single word of those damned foreign languages to stick in my thick skull. It's annoying and I'd like to work with someone honest, kind, someone like you, really, and I'd like to help you too. Your mother's heart is being squeezed dry knowing you're in danger. To enlist voluntarily at the age of eighteen, wounded twice, fighting throughout the entire campaign, you deserve a bit of a break, and so does she . . .'

'It's quite funny,' thought Bernard, 'to think that all I have to do is agree, say yes . . . I know what he really wants. He must be looking for some little trustworthy fool to help him with his shady munitions deals or to win a contract to manufacture shoes for the army. Ah, those bastards . . . The United States, the good life, money, women, while we . . .'

At the same time, he felt as if someone had slapped him across the face. No, worse than that! As if a lump of wet mud had hit him in the face.

'Thank you, but that isn't possible,' he said curtly.

The big man seemed truly surprised:

'Really, that doesn't appeal to you? Well, I understand and admire you, to tell the truth! I wasn't offering to get you out of your responsibilities, you know that very well, but to continue serving your country. The country doesn't only need our blood, it also needs our intelligence, all our superior qualities. But no matter, I do admire you, my boy, it's noble, gallant, so very French! It warms my patriotic heart to see a soldier like you. You're a little hero.'

He turned towards Madame Jacquelain:

'Madame, you should be very proud of your son.'

'I should, shouldn't I?' said Madame Jacquelain, her eyes welling up with tears, while Bernard, furious, protested:

'No! That's enough! You're making a bloody fool of me!'

'Me?' exclaimed Détang, and tears dimmed his booming voice. 'You're not being fair to me, my boy. Do you really think it doesn't lift our hearts to watch the youth of France accomplishing such marvellous things? You are only doing your duty, of course. And we are doing ours. For me, it's by crossing the dangerous ocean to bring America the respect of her sister Republic. For you, it's rushing back to the trenches. The beauty of what is happening now in France is even more pronounced against the background of the corruption and dishonesty that I spoke of a little while ago. You are right, my boy, totally and utterly right! Be a soldier, a simple soldier, see only the task ahead. Leave to us what will perhaps be the even more arduous task of preparing the future peace, and allow me to drink to your good health,' he concluded with a sweet, paternal smile.

He ordered some champagne and they all drank it, after much protest. Madame Jacquelain was sobbing into her glass, out of love, pride and anguish.

9

'How this child has changed,' said Madame Jacquelain, sighing.

They had gone back home through the dark streets. There had not been any air raids for a week, but everything stood ready in case they had to hide in the basement – a shawl for Monsieur Jacquelain, his belladonna drops, a few small pieces of jewellery, some family mementos, all packed into a little case on the mantelpiece where everyone could see it.

In the next room, Bernard spent his last but one night under his family's roof. These final hours of his leave were so painful to his mother that she sometimes thought: 'I'd really prefer it if he never came home. It would be better for me if he weren't brought to me only to be taken away again so soon.' And this time, in addition to her usual suffering there was something else: another source of gnawing, surprising pain. Her boy had indeed become a stranger. She didn't know who he was any more. She began to wonder if really and truly the end of the war (even if her son came through it alive), if the end of the war would really put a stop to all her worries.

'He used to be such an easy child,' sighed Madame Jacquelain.

She combed her thinning grey hair before going to bed. She settled their old cat Moumoute for the night in the basket they carefully carried down to the basement when the air raid sirens sounded. She washed and lay down next to her husband. He was still awake. She could hear him sighing in the darkness, the muted, painful groans he made when his stomach cramps gave him trouble. She got up to make him some herbal tea with his drops. He drank it slowly; his long, yellowish moustache hung down into the cup; he sucked one end of it, looking pensive.

'It's the hot chocolate that's made you feel ill,' said Madame Jacquelain.

He gestured that it wasn't, thought for a moment, then suddenly cried out:

'It is really unbelievable that this child is extorting five thousand francs from me for a gambling debt, that he tells me in the most insolent manner that he's made up his mind and won't be continuing his studies after the war, that he speaks to me without any affection, with no respect . . .'

'Papa!'

'With no respect, I'm telling you! The moment I open my mouth to express my opinion on the course of events – opinions that, my God, are just as valid as his and that I find, moreover, in a slightly different form in my newspaper, written by the best journalists – this . . . this little brat contradicts me and only just stops himself from ordering me to keep quiet! It really is unbelievable to have to put up with that from my own son and to have to stop myself from slapping him . . .'

'Papa, I'm begging you, you're getting yourself all upset!'

'. . . Slapping him; just because he's twenty-two and is fighting in the war. In everything he says, in everything he does, he implies: "What? If it weren't for me . . . ? You'd be in a terrible state if it weren't for me!" Yes, of course he's doing a fantastic job, it's war, I forgive him everything, but if he comes back with that sense of insubordination, of self-pride, what will become of us?'

'It will pass.'

'No, no, it won't pass.'

He gloomily shook his head. He seemed to be contemplating some terrifying vision, as if he were watching monstrous, shadowy shapes from the future rising before him; he could only make out a few sketchy features; he described them in his naïve way; the rest remained hidden from him, or only appeared for a split second. He was feeling his way, trying to understand, shrinking back:

'He's holding a grudge against us, that's what it is, he's holding a grudge against us. He told me that . . .'

'What? What did he tell you?'

'Oh, silly things, jokes, but things that revealed a terrifying state of mind. He dared to say that the soldiers didn't give a damn about Alsace-Lorraine or getting our land back!'

Madame Jacquelain let out a wounded cry:

'Papa! He didn't really say that!'

'Yes, he did. And that we, the civilians, had gradually got used to the idea of war, that we pretended to be suffering but that we weren't really, that only they, they knew what true suffering was, and that now, all they ever thought about was one thing – to end the war and to have themselves a good time to make up for what they had lost.'

He fell silent, picturing Bernard's hardened face as he said over and over again:

'They don't give a damn about anything, nothing at all. Having a good time. That's all they care about. He told me that because I was talking to him about his studies and he absolutely refuses to continue with them.'

'But why, why? I don't understand.'

'Because he's become lazy, I dare say! He told me that we were all just dupes, that very soon all you would need is a bit of luck and some influence in order to earn millions, and that a life like ours already disgusted him. It's the mentality of war transposed into peacetime. It's terrifying. I told him: "My boy, audacity,

System D and thinking on your feet, being hard-hearted, all that is fine in wartime because patriotism makes it acceptable, but in peacetime, it will create a generation of crooks." "No! A generation of shrewd people," he replied. I do believe, Mama, that he's just showing off, exaggerating, but, in spite of everything, something is going on inside him that terrifies me. And it's got to the point where . . . if I talked to him about certain things, like honour, integrity, the inviolable duty to work hard, I think he'd laugh in my face. Our son has been corrupted.'

'But who has done this to him? Perhaps he has friends who are a bad influence?' asked Madame Jacquelain who still thought that a soldier's life, in 1918, was simply the continuation of a student's life.

'Perhaps . . .'

'But Papa, be fair, he has extraordinary patriotism and decent feelings. Think about what Raymond Détang offered him: to get away from the war, out of harm's way, to escape from the stress of war to go on a wonderful trip to the United States, and he refused. It broke my heart to see him refuse such an unheard of thing, but at the same time, I was proud of him. No! He's a good boy, a good Frenchman!'

'The war still has a hold on them,' murmured the elderly Monsieur Jacquelain. He fell silent, confusedly picturing in his mind the war as an enormous steel frame that cut straight through and supported these weary men, forcing them into a proud, rigid stance. But when the war was over, they would collapse.

'No, they'll forget,' said Madame Jacquelain. Being a woman, she assumed that the two sexes had the same short memory.

'War is never forgotten,' said Monsieur Jacquelain. 'I've never been to war, but still I will never forget it.'

They sat in silence, trying to unravel the enigma of their son together, thinking about it, looking at it from every angle, understanding nothing. A form of revolt? No. Revolt is tinged by fanaticism, and there wasn't a hint of fanaticism in Bernard, just a kind of bitter, soul-destroying cynicism.

'But how does he expect to earn his living if he doesn't go back to his studies? You can't have a career without qualifications . . . Have you asked him about that, Papa?'

'Yes. He sniggered. "Do you really not see what's going on around you?" he asked me.'

Madame Jacquelain began to cry:

'And here I thought I would make him so happy by taking him to the circus . . . So, you mean, he's no longer my child, no longer my little boy?'

'Well, that's another matter. You're being silly . . .'

'No, no, it is the same thing,' his stubborn mother said again. 'It's all the same thing. My child, my good little boy, so generous, so open, so affectionate, he's gone. That's all there is to it, he's gone.'

They finally stopped talking and soon Monsieur Jacquelain's snoring could be heard, mingling with the purring of the old cat in her basket. But Madame Jacquelain could not manage to fall asleep. She finally got out of bed; wearing her grey flannel bathrobe, with her thinning locks of hair falling down over her sunken cheeks, she silently crossed her bedroom and went into her son's room. He was asleep, his face was pale and smooth. My God, would he come back? My God, if he did come back, would he be happy? What still lay in store for him? He was only twenty-two. To think that it wasn't enough that she had to worry about the present, but, in spite of herself, the future frightened her as well. What if Bernard began leading a life of debauchery? Blessed Virgin Mary! This horrifying, awful, incomprehensible war. She vaguely sensed that the 'fire', as men called it, did not only burn the hearts and bodies of poor children, it also lit up strange, shadowy, confused ideas that once lay dormant, buried deep within them.

'No, he's a good lad. He has a good heart,' she said once more.

She wanted to kiss him but didn't dare. In the end, she simply pressed her lips softly against Bernard's hand, just as she used to when he was asleep in his cradle. She went back to bed, thinking:

'It will pass. 'We'll create such a good little life for him. He'll want to go back to school again and he'll love being at home. He'll work hard. He'll make up for lost time. He'll get his degrees. He'll be a good boy . . .'

10

A station, somewhere in France, one night in June. Bernard was going back to the front. Soldiers were swarming on to the platforms. Some were sleeping in the waiting rooms. Some walked by speaking loudly, laughing, and against the backdrop of the starry sky or the shadowy light of the station café, their silhouettes stood out: strong, thickset, heroic, already popularised a thousand and one times in films and photographs, the image of a soldier in the Great War, with his heavy shoes, his haversack on his back, a pipe in the corner of his mouth, his hard face, his laugh, his piercing eyes. It wasn't a crowd, it was an army. The war held them together; war crucified man but held him upright as well. Did any of the leaders, more aware than the others, ever imagine the moment when peace would come, when the army would become a mass of people once more? That was the moment they should have been anticipating, preparing for in the midst of war, but it was difficult. Peace was being improvised just as war had been. That had been a success. So everything would be a success. The pride of the soldiers in themselves was immense. Bernard shared this sense of pride, just as he shared all the feelings of the other soldiers when he was with them. His own, unique soul, complex and contradictory, had been replaced by a collective soul, one that was simple and strong. Like the others, he believed himself to be invincible; he thought he was amazing, and, like the others, he knew that he would hold his own until the very last day of the war, he wouldn't give an inch, but afterwards . . . oh, afterwards!

He stretched out his legs, sighed, threw his head back and looked up at the distant sky, daydreaming vaguely of various things. What a long way he had come in the past four years! First, the enthusiasm, the joy of self-sacrifice, the desire to die for your country, for future generations, for future peace . . . Prepared to die, as long as death was heroic and had purpose, but soon the idea of death terrified him – oh, how he had hated death, how he had feared it, just as he had doubted God and blasphemed as he looked at the little blackish heaps lying between two trenches, dead bodies as numerous and insignificant as dead flies in the first cold snap of winter . . . And yet, even that moment held a rather tragic beauty. But that time too passed. He got used to the idea of death. He no longer feared it, he thought of such things coldly and with terrifying realism. He was nothing. He no longer believed in God, the immortal soul, the goodness of mankind. He needed to get as much pleasure as he could out of his short time on this earth, that was all there was to it . . . 'If someone like Raymond Détang comes looking for me again after I've done my duty . . .' He thought about one of his friends who had enlisted at the age of eighteen like him, an amiable boy who had been killed two months before, a good, pious lad who used to say: 'You never stop doing your duty.' What a joke . . . He wouldn't harm anyone, he thought, but they'd better stay the hell off my back. All around him, men walked with heavy steps, chatting cheerfully. They reeked of tobacco, cheap wine, filth and sweat.

What would he find when he got back to his sector, Bernard

wondered. They were expecting serious offensives. But the civilians thought and talked about that more than the soldiers. 'Supremely confident,' said the newspapers. 'No, we're simply numb with exhaustion,' murmured Bernard. But still, perhaps the worst was over? Perhaps he would live to see them marching into the towns, the parade through the Arc de Triomphe? 'Just think, the ones marching in that parade will be the shirkers like Détang, while I, I'll be food for the rats. Hell, I don't give a damn!' he said once more, and as he waited for his train, he made himself as comfortable as possible on the sacks of oats that had just been unloaded, then fell peacefully asleep.

Trains went through the station at regular intervals, and when they did, the air filled with smoke and the sharp, shrill sound of the whistles. Bernard dreamed that he had been wounded, that two men carried him on a narrow stretcher along a bumpy path, that he was being pushed and jostled; then he noticed that they weren't ordinary stretcher bearers marching alongside him but two angels with long floating hair and snow-white wings. In his dream, he could hear himself groaning and shouting: 'You're hurting me, let go of me! I don't want to go with you!' The angels smiled and shook their heads without replying, walking even faster. It was a winter dawn; the sky shone with the dazzling purity. The long hair of one of the angels brushed against his face. Bernard, in a trance, thought: 'It's over. Finally. We're here.' But the angel said:

'You have not gone yet. You are only just about to leave, my poor soul. We're leaving. We're leaving.'

He woke up. One of his friends was punching him and saying over and over:

'We're leaving! Hey you daft thing, you ain't staying here are ya?'

Yawning, sighing, amid the rattling of tin, the clanking of

metal, the appalling din of army boots clattering against the ground, the troop swarmed out of the station's café, the waiting room and the refreshment stands on to the platform, and then stormed the train.

Meanwhile, that same night, Thérèse was on duty in the hospital; she was watching over a young soldier who had recently had an operation and was resting. Very pale and very quiet under his sheets, he was coming back from a faraway place. Thérèse gently wiped the large drops of icy sweat that flowed down his face like tears. Every now and again, she stood up and did her rounds, walking in between the beds, among the sleeping or groaning men. Then she would go back and sit down next to the young boy. He had caused her a lot of anguish. My God! So many had died! But a few had been spared, all the same, saved by her. The wives, mothers and fiancées of these soldiers were never happy with the care they received, they always seemed to think they could have done better, done more. And they were jealous as well. They resented the nurses for having taken their places at the bedside. 'But at least we will send a few back to them,' thought Thérèse, 'and such hopeless cases!'

For some time now, whenever she saw these wives, these mistresses coming to the hospital and throwing themselves at the recovering soldiers, clutching them tightly, carrying them like prey, or so it seemed, far from the hospital, far from death, she felt abandoned, unjustly and cruelly abandoned. The short-lived affairs, the flings, the brief storybook romances between nurses and convalescents filled her with horror. But her heart needed love. She was a loyal, affectionate woman. She saw desolation and horror all around her. Everyone was saying that Europe, civilisation, the entire world was collapsing, that the century was destined to end in catastrophe, that everything would perish, drowned in blood. But she still hoped for a husband, a home, children, and she instinctively felt that the destruction of everything was a mirage, a lie, while she, she lived the truth.

It was a time when certain men let themselves sink into despair, when certain women sank into debauchery, but Thérèse and many others cared for the wounded and dreamed with confidence of the future.

Part Two

1920–1936

1

At the beginning of November, the first formal meeting of the forty-one states that made up the League of Nations took place in Geneva. In France, the financial and political set that Raymond Détang had worked his way into since his return from America considered this event from a perspective that was not quite the same as that of the ordinary man in the street – that is to say, they did not really wonder whether war was going to become impossible in future (the war was over, forgotten, dead and buried), but what the repercussions would be on the careers of those in line for ministerial posts and how to make the most of it, both financially and in terms of personal satisfaction. Like any new, unexplored opportunity, this one frightened many people; even in the Détangs' circle, they couldn't agree on how this League of Nations should be treated: with irony or fervour? As a universal panacea or a temporary fix? This troubled Renée Détang. She had decided to celebrate the opening of the sessions but she wondered how best to strike 'the right chord': a dinner where people could express serious opinions – which might become the basis for establishing the political circle she wished to preside over – or a reception where, in between cocktails, people would exchange witty pleasantries, gently mocking this recent event (and then she would say, with that graceful little pout that so became her: 'Oh, hush, now. I'm telling you that this is a great hope for the world!'). In addition, a reception would allow a good mix of people; given the Détangs' social status, they weren't yet in a position to choose their contacts. 'Anyone and everyone to pad out the room', as Madame Humbert always said. A lot of noise, a lot of champagne, a great crowd of people, a certain amount of inevitable waste, but perhaps, amid the swarm – like a prospector who discovers a few specks of gold buried in the sand – they too would find one or two or ten desirable recruits, influential people in Parliament or the Stock Market.

'Raymond is on a first-name basis with everyone who really counts,' Renée confided in her mother, 'but that's just the kind of familiarity you find in schools and prisons, part friendship, part complicity; it has to be transformed into *contacts*. And that is a completely different thing.'

At the beginning, the Détangs carefully prepared what they called their 'war strategy'; they intended to climb the Parisian social ladder cautiously, one step at a time, taking one bastion after another, but at the end of a few months, they realised this technique was useless, embarrassing and outdated: anyone can get into high society by just walking straight in, or more precisely, there was no such thing as high society. There was an enormous fairground where anyone who wanted to could get in; it wasn't even necessary to hide your background like in the good old days: they were living in a cynical world that glorified the sludge from which a man had risen. It was the era of the nouveau riche, a time when if people asked someone how he had earned 'all that money', he would smile and reply: 'In the war, of course . . . like everyone else.' Raymond Détang, however, was not cynical. In politics, cynicism is a clumsy tactic; voters wish to be treated as noble creatures. Raymond Détang was one of those men who could most skilfully manipulate key phrases: 'Civilisation based on law and logic . . . France, the path of enlightenment for all mankind . . . World peace . . . Science and Progress . . .' He was not even cynical about himself, except for very rare moments when he felt depressed. He honestly considered himself an eminent statesman who exists solely for the good of the people. At the time, he was not yet a Member of Parliament; he was organising his electoral campaign with infinite care: it had to be a work of art. He was earning money. Money, at this point in time, had not yet become the wild, wayward beast it turned into between 1930 and 1939 when it could only be captured through dangerous close combat; now, it was a small, tame animal that was easy to catch. Détang played the Stock Market. And since his connections to certain political figures were well known, groups of foreigners entrusted him with what he called 'setting up contacts' – preliminary conversations that would facilitate economic or other kinds of deals.

He had created close ties to several important businessmen in the United States who had become valuable, influential friends. He had acted as intermediary in orders placed by the French Republic in America for the reconstruction of ravaged territories. However, as he put it, he had become too important for such work. There was an entire category of transactions that would be impossible for him to carry out once he was elected, 'at least they would be impossible if carried out under your own name', as Renée put it. The married couple got along well together; they supported one another. Every now and again, Raymond felt he was still in love with his wife. Renée was one of those Parisian women who seemed not to be made of flesh and bone but rather of a sort of malleable plastic that could be transformed to fit the changing fashion. When Raymond had first met her, she had a funny little face with a fringe that fell over her eyes; she had been petite, curvaceous and as soft as a cat. Now she was the very model of the woman of the post-war years. She had lost weight; she had long, strong muscles; she looked taller. Her skin, covered in glossy golden make-up, looked darker and her blond hair was cut like a boy's. All these features were fresh and new at the time.

And this was how she appeared to Bernard Jacquelain: wearing a short, straight sleeveless dress that showed off her bare arms and beautiful legs, though her mouth was already marked with fine, bitter wrinkles. He had not seen her since the beginning of the war. After being demobilised, he had returned to live at his mother's house in Paris. The elderly Monsieur Jacquelain had let himself get carried away by the mad, reckless spending of the time; other men bought cars, travelled, paid for mistresses: but Monsieur Jacquelain, after tense, secretive calculations, decided to have an operation. He had dreamt about it for ten years, only putting it off because of the cost. But the entire world was giving in to pleasure; even Madame Jacquelain had paid fifty-nine francs for a felt hat; small businessmen had houses in the country where they spent what they called their 'veekends'. Why not me? thought Monsieur Jacquelain as he looked resentfully at a new pair of shoes that Bernard (without telling him) had ordered from a shoemaker. This was unprecedented in a family in which the women bought their clothes at Galeries Lafayette and the men at Belle Jardinière. Yes, why not me too? We save, we do without, we put money aside for our children who will only squander our money once we're gone. I won't refuse myself anything either, not me, he thought. And so he reserved a room in a private hospital in Neuilly without telling anyone. Sixty francs for the room. Ten thousand francs for the operation. They cut open his stomach and he died.

Bernard made applications to obtain a pension for his mother as the widow of a retired civil servant. All the applications ended up with Raymond Détang. Everyone in Paris who wanted something hovered around him: people looking for jobs, recommendations, favours, military honours, permission to open tobacco shops, or simply asking to have a speeding ticket withdrawn. Raymond

Détang replied to everyone, without exception, with unfailing cordiality: 'You did the right thing by coming here. I'll think about what the best thing is to do to sort this little matter out for you. Personally, I can't do anything, but I have a friend . . .'

'He knows absolutely everyone,' people said when they left, 'he's amazing.'

His status as someone who had influence, connections, powerful friends was far more useful to him than a reputation for integrity, intelligence or even for having a great deal of money. It became quite common, in certain circles, to say of Raymond Détang:

'Go to him first with your request before talking to anyone else about it. He has all the Ministers in his pocket . . .'

Or even:

'Ask Détang for his tips on the Stock Market. He knows all the wheeler dealers.'

He was not yet a politician, or a financier, but he functioned as a kind of conduit between politics and finance. He was the person who knew everything before anyone else, the one who was 'in the know', the man about whom everyone said:

'What exactly does he do? I couldn't tell you, but he's someone important.'

To the people he received in this way, to talk about business, people he felt might turn out to be useful to him, he never failed to say:

'Look, let's talk about this again. Where? Why not come to my house? Say on the 20th? My wife is entertaining some friends. There'll be dancing. Good heavens, you've just made me think: I must remind someone about it . . .'

And he would nonchalantly name some famous person.

Bernard Jacquelain was not invited as one of the people who 'might turn out to be useful' some day, but as part of a smaller, though no less important group: the 'gigolos'.

'Find me as many gigolos as possible,' Renée had told her

husband. 'There are never enough of them,' she added, sounding annoyed.

When she entertained, the 'gigolos' padded out the room, so to speak. They needed to be everywhere. In order for the reception to seem dazzling and luxurious, there had to be a crowd of young men with slicked-back hair and tireless legs standing in all the doorways, at the buffet table, in the smoking room. Every woman normally had three or four of them following her around; some women went as far as to have six, but they were the foreigners: where gigolos were concerned, as in all other things, it wasn't done to go too far. These gigolos were nice young men who carried out their professional duties conscientiously. If Renée saw any of them standing still, she would tell them off:

'Well, what do you think you're doing?' she would mutter angrily, 'go and dance with the Baroness.'

In such social circles, gigolos weren't paid but they were well fed. Stuffed with foie gras and caviar on toast, living in dusty furnished accommodation where they only spent a few hours each day in a deep sleep – between eight o'clock in the morning and noon – life for them was sweet.

When Bernard walked over to her to say hello, Renée didn't recognise him. He was young, good looking; she gave him a vague, friendly nod, indicating behind her to the back of the reception room where he should join the other actors with walk-on parts crammed between the crimson curtains, waiting for the first bars of jazz to start playing. Everything was exactly as it should be, and just as it was everywhere else at this time: an orchestra of black musicians wearing red jackets, smoke so thick you could cut it with a knife, a crush of people, endless chattering, ice cream melting in little Venetian glass bowls, cigarettes with gold tips, swizzle sticks for the champagne, flowers, lipsticks carelessly tossed into the ornamental vases, couples stretched out on low loveseats in the dark corners of the room, a bar set up in the long entrance hall, old women with dyed hair on the dance floor, necklaces bouncing and clicking against their dried-up, sunken chests.

Renée was always dancing, sometimes without even knowing the name of the man who held her in his arms. When Bernard asked her to dance and asked how Madame Humbert was, she looked at him, confused:

'My mother is fine, but how the devil do you know her?'

'Well, very nice; that's a fine thing to say! You really don't know who I am?'

'Do you actually believe that I know most of the people here?'

'Well, then, it seems we're at a masked ball. I'll give you some clues. Let's see, my lovely masked lady, do you remember a very modest little shop, painted sky blue, with a sign that said "*FASHIONS by GERMAINE*" in gold letters and, in the back room, a round table covered by a Turkish cloth; three children played at having a doll's tea party around that table, you, a little girl who was the same age as you named Thérèse Brun, and a little boy . . .'

'Bernard Jacquelain!' she cut in. 'Now I remember. That Bernard had lovely eyes.'

'I think he still does,' said Bernard, sounding smug, sensing that was the right tone to take in these surroundings.

She smiled at him and they twirled around for a moment in silence. He looked at the scene over her head. He breathed in the scent of her hair. What a learning experience for a young man! Four years of carnage and, finally, as if he were emerging from a dark, blood-filled tunnel, this reception room full of lights and women, all there for the taking, this light-hearted atmosphere, heady and intoxicating. Oh, good heavens, he had truly understood during his last leave before the Armistice that people who took anything seriously were nothing but . . . dupes. Nothing anyone did, or said, or thought meant a thing. It was all a sort of futile babbling, the kind that madmen and babies talk. Everything around him merged into a golden cloud; all he heard was a mixture of laughter, black jazz singers and fragments of conversation:

'Well, he should go and see Thingy, Whatshisname, you know who I mean? The Minister's Secretary. He'll see to it that he gets the Croix de Guerre.'

'It's difficult because of the scandal. He was found to be a deserter, after all.'

'Oh, but that was all so long ago, my dear . . .'

'She's been with him for six months; didn't you know? He started out as her mother's lover . . .'

'What's making you smile?' asked Renée.

'Nothing. How different things are.'

'Yes, I know. Everyone who fought in the war is flabbergasted, at first. What do you expect? It's only natural. We have the right to laugh a little after the things we've seen. I mean it; don't look at me so derisively. I was a nurse, you know. It wasn't always very amusing . . .'

'Bah! Women splash about in blood as if it were the most natural thing in the world.'

'Do be quiet! You're so bitter.'

'Who, me? From now on, my motto is "Don't worry about anything in life". Since I did come back from *over there*, everything will work out. I will commit the worst foolishness, the greatest follies with an easy conscience, certain that nothing will affect anything and that everything will continue to go on as in the past, for better or for worse. I no longer believe in catastrophes, since the last one failed miserably. I no longer believe in misfortune, or in death. All of humanity now has the state of mind of a child who is not afraid of the bogeyman any more.'

'But you have to believe in love,' she said, fluttering her eyelashes.

'That would be very nice.'

He gently pulled her closer to him. They broke away from the crowd. She led him through a few rooms, some in half-darkness where they could hear whispers rising from the plush divans, others dazzlingly bright where well-fed, fat men discussed politics. They heard snippets as they passed:

'Germany will be banned from any involvement in the League of Nations. Viviani said so. That will teach them.'

'The people want . . .'

'The people do not want . . .'

'Leave the wine merchant alone.'

Renée touched up her lipstick in front of a large, three-panelled mirror.

'What have you been doing since you were demobilised?' she asked him. 'You don't have a lot of money, do you?'

'No, not a penny. I'm looking for a way to earn a living.'

'It's not difficult these days. You can do interior decorating for foreigners, sell old masters on the black market; you don't even have to know much about anything. Then there's the Stock Market, of course. Prices are skyrocketing. My husband could help you out, you know. I'll talk to him about you and . . .'

He had moved closer to her and was watching her in the mirror. She turned her head slightly towards him and their lips met. After a moment, she slipped out of his arms, rather breathless, and finished her sentence:

'. . . and he'll find a way for you to earn a living. Doing the least possible and earning the most possible. Ideal, don't you agree?'

2

When Bernard became Renée's lover – the day after their first encounter – he felt a strange sensation: the pleasure of his conquest was somewhat tainted by a feeling of resentment, not only because she had given herself to him so quickly, but because she had not even deigned to hide the fact that she would have slept with any other man like him, as long as he was young and attractive . . .

'Really,' he thought to himself as he made love to her, 'these women are such sluts.' She opened her eyes; he had fallen back beside her, his face expressionless, his eyes staring blankly into space.

'What are you thinking about?' she asked.

'About you, my love,' he replied.

She looked at her watch:

'It was good, wasn't it? Pass me my stockings; I have to get out of here now.'

They parted on the damp street. Behind them was the hotel where they had just spent the past two hours; in front of them, the Parisian pavement shimmered like a black mirror beneath the rain and lights. In the darkness, the arc lamps formed a bright mesh of sparkling facets, like halos, plays of light that made Bernard feel dizzy, dazed as he already was by the warm, stifling, perfumed darkness of the hotel room.

'A good body . . . Nice curves,' he thought as he left Renée. 'She knows how to use it too . . . It would be very stupid to get attached to a little beast like her.'

He had enjoyed their lovemaking, but a nagging feeling of dissatisfaction lingered within him, a feeling that came less from his body than his soul.

He went home. It was the time of day when the schoolboys were coming out of the 'Institution Etienne-Marcel' where Bernard had been a student before moving up to the lycée. Chubby-cheeked young boys ran after the bus. He watched these adolescents who walked along swinging their briefcases by their sides. It wasn't so long ago that he himself . . .

'I was a good little boy,' he thought, 'I swallowed everything I was told. Now . . . The war took me when I was too young. It's a funny thing, war. The men who are in at the start and those who come out at the end are different people. First they send in the mature men, people who know what they want, whose characters won't change; they get killed, and then they take the youngsters; and afterwards, everyone is surprised when they come back changed. Whatever happens, I know that I, personally, will no longer put myself out for anything, or anyone. This Renée . . . I could have truly loved her. But none of these women gives a damn about love. What they need is . . .'

He didn't finish his thought. He was standing at the courtyard entrance in front of his home. He looked at it – a building where rent was inexpensive, the place where he was born, where his mother still lived. My God, how shabby and ugly everything was! In his mind, he could picture the sitting room with the heavy green curtains decorated with silver palm leaves, the folding bed set up for him in the dining room, the narrow, dingy kitchen . . . How different it all was from Détang's private house, full of noise, joy and light; how strikingly different!

'He's clever, he is, I'll give him that! I'm just a sucker. Naturally,

I'll go to his house, get recommendations from him, take advantage of my relationship with his wife,' he thought. But at the same time, something deep inside him protested, felt indignant, something, someone, who was like him, like the real Bernard, and yet was no longer him, just a shadow of what he had once been, a troublesome memory.

He climbed up the staircase where the stench of herring reigned supreme. Through the closed doors, you could hear children crying, dishes rattling. A little old man with a very pale, wrinkled face was walking up ahead of him, carrying a loaf of bread under his arm, a long, golden baguette. He thought about his father and remembered how he used to go downstairs every evening at the same time to buy bread and the newspaper (*L'Intransigeant*), then he would come back upstairs, eat dinner and scold his son: 'We haven't been put here on earth to have fun . . . It's when you're still young that you should put some money aside for your old age,' and Bernard was horrified by that way of life.

'Everyone tells you: "You are all heroes. You are better than us." And then, when you come back: "Sorry, my boy, but while you were out risking your neck, I've been feathering my nest. You should go back and finish your beloved education. Get your head down in those books. Take the life your father and mother led before you were born as your ideal."' How different this place was from the Détangs' home. 'And yet, it was me, me, who went to war for four years, while he . . . He tried it for a bit, didn't like it and found a way out. No you don't, my friend: we're going to share!' thought Bernard. 'And we've started by sharing your wife, and that's the truth,' he muttered, and that idea made him feel better.

At home, in the dining room, his mother was knitting by the light of a lamp; Thérèse was keeping her company. She had come up to say goodnight to her neighbours, as she sometimes did ever since Monsieur Jacquelain had died. Thérèse heard the key turn in the lock:

'Here's your son.'

She looked up. Bernard came into the room.

'Why are you wearing your new overcoat?' his mother asked.

Sometimes Thérèse barely recognised Bernard. He had friends, ways of enjoying himself she knew nothing about and found difficult to imagine. He didn't seem very happy . . . He didn't answer Madame Jacquelain's question, nor did he obey her when she continued:

'Please switch off the lights in the entrance hall, my darling. You're never careful. Everything is so expensive.'

She was nervous when she spoke to him, now that he was a man, as if she always feared he would snub her.

He sat down between the two women. The wood-burning stove was lit. The dining room was very small, with imitation brown wood panelling and artificial flowers in blue vases. On the mantelpiece, between the vases, was a photograph of Bernard in uniform, his arm in a sling.

'Where have you been, my darling? I didn't wait for you to have dinner. There was a nice piece of veal with vegetables for you. How will you use the leftovers tomorrow, Thérèse?'

'Grandmother will make an onion sauce to go with it . . .' she replied.

Their familiar voices soothed him but didn't calm him down. He still felt annoyed, as if a swarm of wasps were plaguing him.

'I saw one of your old friends today, Thérèse,' he said quietly, with a slight snigger.

She guessed he meant Renée Détang.

'I never see her any more. She has so much to do . . .'

'She does indeed,' he murmured.

'She's very pretty,' said Thérèse with a little sigh.

'I wonder if this one would sell herself so easily,' Bernard suddenly thought. He adjusted the flame on the wood-burning stove without saying anything, then looked up; Thérèse realised he was watching her. Silently, and for quite a long time, he studied her face as she sewed, enjoying making her blush; she felt the kind of embarrassment and confusion, mixed with pride, that the most respectable women feel when they realise that a young man finds them attractive.

'But why?' she wondered. 'He's never looked at me like that before.'

Then:

'No, I'm mad. He's known me for such a long time . . . We're childhood friends . . . There's never been anything between us . . .'

And finally:

'He has beautiful eyes . . . They aren't as blue as they used to be, more grey, like the grey of a raging storm . . . What difference does it make to me? I'm not going to fall in love with this boy . . . He's the same age as me . . . Are he and Renée Détang . . . ?'

Suddenly, she felt jealous of Renée, so violently jealous that she was ashamed and frightened; she forced herself to remember Martial, as if his memory could exorcise that particular demon. She scolded herself harshly: 'Well now, are you going to become just like all the other mad women who chase after young men? You must be worthy of Martial.' But Martial was dead and this man was very much alive, and sitting quite close to her.

She stood up and folded away her embroidery.

'I have to go home,' she said curtly, 'Papa will be worried.'

'I have to go out as well,' said Bernard, 'I'm expected somewhere. I'll walk down with you.'

They left the room without paying any attention to Madame Jacquelain who cried out in a pleading voice:

'Don't come home too late . . . Bernard, I'll wait up for you! Bernard, you've come home at three o'clock in the morning three nights in a row. Whatever will the concierge say?'

'I couldn't care less. Let her say what she wants,' murmured

Bernard. He could feel Thérèse trembling against him. He had taken her arm and felt a rush of pleasure. Here was one woman who wouldn't give herself like some whore . . . Here was a woman who could make him feel proud to be a man again, a conqueror, while when he was with Renée, he was demoted to an inferior rank: he became someone who was taken and tossed aside when he was no longer found attractive.

He pulled her closer to him; she tried to pull away; he held her more tightly.

'Why are you trembling?'

'I'm cold.'

'Cold? It's as mild as can be,' he said, mockingly.

A warm breeze from the west flowed through Paris. They took shelter beneath the great outer doors leading to the courtyard as rain began to fall. Thérèse didn't really know what she was doing; she followed Bernard, as docile and enthralled as in a dream. She vaguely understood what was about to happen: compliments, words of love . . . My God, he wanted her to become his mistress . . . he would pursue her, write to her, wait for her in the street. But she would resist and know how to defend her honour until the day he asked her to marry him. Yes, in a flash, standing in the shelter of that dark door, listening to the sound of the rain in the street, she imagined a long and happy life . . .

They noticed that opposite them, on the other side of the street, a cinema was open. A little tinkling bell summoned the passers-by.

'Come on, we'll go inside for an hour and wait for the rain to stop,' said Bernard.

'I thought you were expected somewhere,' she protested feebly.

'I'm not. I just said that so I could spend some time with you.'

He led her across the street; they went into the darkened theatre. It was the time of silent films. Great wavering shadows flickered across the screen above their heads; a piano hidden in the shadows played Toselli's *Serenade*. They were alone at the back of a box. They could hear the sound of rustling programmes, sweets being sucked or crunched, the occasional sigh, sometimes a kiss. There were very few people in the cinema. Bernard had sat down behind Thérèse; he leaned forward, held her face in both his hands, pulled her slightly back towards him and kissed her.

What? So soon? Without deigning to say a word to her, certain she would consent, the way you kiss some little maid in the hallway? She felt a great surge of modesty, of wounded pride; it was so violent that it swept away any desire or tenderness she might have felt towards him.

'Have you gone mad?' she stammered with difficulty from between her crushed lips.

But he held her firmly by the shoulders and she couldn't pull free.

'What are you going to say next, "What do you take me for?" or "Let go of me or I'll scream!" My God, Thérèse,' he said, mockingly, 'you are so . . .'

He was trying to find the right word:

'. . . so "pre-war", my poor girl! You mean you can't take a joke?'

She shook her head, dismayed by his words. They humiliated her, made her feel cheap. She had come so close to loving him. She realised now that she had loved him for a very long time . . . But not 'just for fun', not for just a moment's pleasure. She couldn't. She was not made like that. It was horrible that he had managed to make her almost ashamed of such normal feelings.

Meanwhile, the pianist, hidden in the shadows, was managing to dig up from his memory fragments of Beethoven, Mendelssohn and Brahms, creating an artificial medley of background music. It was hot in the cinema; they could hear the rain pattering outside whenever the music stopped.

Bernard lit a cigarette.

'I thought you'd say no,' he said. 'I'll even admit that there's something charming about that. But think about it, my girl. There's not a man today who would offer you anything else. "You want to have some fun? Fine. – You don't? Goodbye." There are too many women and they're all too easy to make it worthwhile . . . pretending you feel something you don't. If you're not interested, we'll just be good friends. But if your heart is telling you . . .'

He suddenly stopped:

'Are you crying?' he said more gently. 'But Thérèse, you aren't going to seriously hold this against me, are you?'

'No, but what you're saying is just . . .'

'The truth.'

'It's degrading to women,' she whispered.

'Is that what you think! They like nothing more. I don't mean a silly little goose from the countryside.'

'I know very well who you're talking about,' she cut in. She was trembling all over with jealousy that she simply couldn't hide. 'If those women like being treated that way, go back to them, but as for me . . .'

'How funny you are, Thérèse . . . since I'm telling you that I won't press you. Women are easy to come by. A good friend, well, that's much rarer.'

'I don't think I'd make a very good friend either . . .' she said, smiling through her tears.

They waited in silence for the film to end. He helped her on with her coat. They left and found themselves outside again, in the rain. There wasn't a taxi in sight.

'I can't wait to own a Rolls Royce,' sighed Bernard. 'Thérèse, there is only one thing I want now: to be rich, as wealthy as possible and as quickly as possible! Do you ever see the Détangs? Now there's a couple that knows how to get the best out of the pretty world we live in. Don't you think so?'

'I don't think that Raymond Détang is an honest man.'

'Bernard stopped in his tracks and started to laugh.

'You are delightful. The words you use . . . Honest! Of course he's a crook. The honest people are you, Papa Brun, poor Martial, and me . . . the poor wretches! The unlucky ones. It hasn't always been that way, perhaps it won't always be like that, but for now, it's the sad truth.'

'You lost four years of your life to the war, I know, but if you would just concentrate on working, you could have a good career, an honest and serious career, and then you wouldn't have any reason to envy the Détangs.'

'But what I envy, my innocent girl, is not what they have but the way they got it: through bluff, through calm, barefaced audacity, a complete absence of scruples and their belief that the world is made up of suckers, that all you have to do is stretch out your hand and reel them in. How can you think anyone would want to work hard when you see something like that? *I'm* going to enrol in the Raymond Détang school . . .'

'You've already enrolled in his wife's school!' she cried, her voice trembling.

'Well now,' he thought, 'she'll also come round, if I can be bothered. They're all the same, of course, but she'll be jealous and a nuisance.'

3

'I would be more than happy to be of service to you, my boy,' Raymond Détang said to Bernard Jacquelain.

This was how he always greeted everyone. They all came begging to him. His role was simply to put them at ease, to show them they were entering a world where nothing was secretive, nothing was difficult. 'Anything for anyone. Come in and help yourself. I am here to serve the people.'

'You did the right thing by coming to me,' Détang continued. 'You're lost, all at sea. You gave four years of your life to France, the best years of your youth. You come to me because I represent our country. (I can tell you in confidence: my election is a sure thing.) You come to me and say: "You're in my debt. You have told me so time and time again. How can you help me?" And I reply: "My time and any kind of influence I might have are yours." (You understand perfectly well that I don't mean you, Bernard Jacquelain, but that you are only a symbol: I mean all soldiers, your brothers.) Take the fate of your country in your hands. Our poor country, she reacts less robustly in peacetime than in war, have you noticed? And you as well, Bernard, you seem less determined, less confident of your own strength than you were in '18. If you had accepted the offer I made you then, if you had gone with me to America, you would have arrived on the scene at a time when they needed real men; you would immediately have entered their world – important industrialists, captains of industry – *the* world, in fact, the only real one, where our future is currently being shaped; you would have had a foot on the first rung of the ladder: afterwards, it would have been up to you to make it to the top with brains and hard work. But that moment has passed. It is unfair, it is cruel, but that is how it is. People . . .'

He stopped speaking and gestured towards the crowded restaurant where they were having lunch.

'People . . . Look around you. Two million men have been killed, and that's just in France. And now everyone is swarming back, we're suffocating again. There are a hundred people for every job. And everyone is intelligent. Everyone can, wants to and must succeed. It's terrifying. And everyone is in a hurry, of course. There's no question of waiting, of becoming wealthy by saving over a long period of time or working terribly hard: everyone wants to be rich and right away. That's what you want as well, isn't it? Well, everyone wants what you want. Just look around you.'

'What we need is another war,' muttered Bernard.

'Please,' said Détang, placing his hand affectionately on Bernard's arm, 'please don't be bitter. Do as I do. I have always managed to retain my faith in man's basic goodness, or rather in his infinite perfectibility, even during the most difficult times. I am convinced that the day will come (and, listen, here is an idea I developed in Toulouse last month), the day will come when this world will be like a banquet where everyone will have a place and there will be enough to eat and drink for all. That is our ideal, and that is what we are working towards. But in the meantime, what a dreadful free-for-all! It's because the world is still poor. We aren't producing enough. That's something the Americans have understood. What a people they are!'

He firmly squeezed a quarter of a lemon over the golden sole he had been served; once he had extracted all the juice, he threw it down.

'So, what can I offer you? Some of my good friends are important bankers. You could have a job at eight hundred francs a month to start with. You're making a face? Good Lord! It's always the same. There are too many people, my friend, too many men, and every influential person is surrounded, like a Roman senator, by a host of protégés looking for patronage, and you have to throw a bone to every one of them. So the carcass has been gnawed bare. You see?'

He gave him a friendly smile.

'Say you want to be the secretary of a politician? You have to know the underbelly of the profession. And it's a filthy one, by the way. So, we're driven back to the old, traditional careers: doctor, engineer, lawyer. You were a hard worker, a slogger in the old days. Go back to your studies. I'm sure that idea doesn't frighten you. Only, it's hard to stand on the sidelines, taking shelter, when it's raining gold, isn't it? Because you're right to say that the downpour will end, that there is a time for everything and to be twenty-two years old just after the Armistice and not take advantage would be truly unfortunate.'

'I'm sure,' said Bernard, 'that if you really wanted to help me . . .'

He hesitated.

'If I am taking the liberty of imposing upon you ("well, well, I'm addressing him more respectfully again," he thought: "the war is over, I'm demobilised, I'm wearing a jacket and an unstarched collar, and I'm experiencing that sense of distance and deference befitting a rich, influential man again"), if I have taken the liberty of requesting a meeting with you, it is because I believed that you had taken an interest in me; Madame Détang, to whom I spoke about this, very kindly reassured me that I was not mistaken, that you had spoken sympathetically of me to her.'

'My wife thinks you're very nice. And as for me, well, I've known you since you were a child. I must tell you that in the situation I find myself, and given the incredible hodge-podge that society in Paris has become, we tend to stick close to the people we know.'

Their conversation was interrupted by waiters coming and going, telephones ringing and all the passers-by who stopped to say hello to him; he was acquainted with everyone on earth. He kissed the women's hands then affectionately patted the gloved fingers he had just brought to his lips as if, of all of them, she were the dearest, most intimate friend. And yet, he did not even know most of their names. In spite of all these interruptions, he never once lost his train of thought or his flow of words. He was in his element in a crowd; he could only breathe easily in the midst of a heavy throng, just as a pike is only happy in the waters of a shallow lake.

'I had considered taking you on to work for me, not on the political side of things. I already have someone for that. No. Here's the thing. I am simultaneously pursuing two goals. I must tell you that during my first trip to America, a trip that has since been followed by many others, as well as meetings with everyone who is anyone over there, I found myself in a position where I could have struck brilliant business deals. I have ties with an American industrial magnate, a man like Ford, who more or less proposed that I be his representative in France, to sell certain products he manufactures; they make everything to do with motors, cars, planes, etc. By accepting this offer, I would have rendered an invaluable service to France. But you can see how things don't always work out as planned: don't think the American is asking for my help because of my pretty face! – no, but because as a politician, I have influence in high places here. I might even be called at any time to serve in the government. But if I wish to remain the man I am and stay clear of scandal, then I must protect myself at all costs, and avoid letting it be known, officially at least, that I have financial dealings with a foreign country. I have enemies. Who doesn't? I hope I will have many more. A man's importance can be measured by the number of enemies he has. And so, my enemies would shout it from the rooftops that I'd been bought, that I was in the pay of American finance. The fact that as a businessman, my value as a politician would be increased (for a quick grasp of reality, a sharp, clear vision, all these things come naturally to a good businessman), the fact that I might actually be benefitting my country by sharing the lead that American industry has over us – all that means nothing to them. They would only see me as a moneyman, loyal only to international finance, me, a man with an ideal, a man who only desires the influence, the greatness and the prosperity of France! So I thought I must find someone who could be my front man, for a basic salary to be agreed and a good percentage in commission. For instance, say I have to import ammunition belts or a specific type of plough or automobile parts to France . . . I'm giving random examples here. I know who to approach for such things, how to deal with them, what bribes have to be made, but I don't make a move, I'm never seen. My name is never mentioned. I sign nothing. I remain hidden in the background. And you mustn't think that such transactions would damage the industry of my own country because French products could be sold in the United States in the same way. Can you imagine the enormous potential sphere of influence that is open to us? Can you see the valuable exchanges, the multiple business links that we could forge between the two countries? Shall I tell you what I really think? You know that I am a fervent supporter of the League of Nations. Just between us, I contributed more than a little to planting the seed of this admirable idea, this great hope, in the minds of various countries. But, it is not that alone, you see, that will allow peace to reign among men. Peace itself is in the hands of commerce and industry. I dream of a statue that will rise one day in a square in Paris to symbolise what I mean: Commerce and Industry, allegorical figures dressed in Grecian robes, standing tall, their hands entwined, and a dove, with an olive branch in its beak, flying up from their joined hands and settling on a globe of the world. Is that not beautiful? That truly is beautiful! At your age, you have to be passionate. Listen, think about what I've said. I can't offer you a great deal now, not yet . . .'

4

'Bernard has a really good position,' Madame Jacquelain said to Thérèse. 'He makes up to five thousand francs a month. He's working for an entire group of American financiers. I'm just a woman, you know, I don't understand anything about such things, but I think he has a good future. His father was wrong to worry about him. *I* knew very well that my little boy was someone. "Mama, I'm doing my apprenticeship," he told me, "I'm learning how to handle important business deals. I'm only an underling now, but little by little . . ." Little by little, he'll stand on his own two feet, Thérèse. You'll see, he'll get his own car. Even now . . .'

She stifled a little laugh:

'If you could see his clothes . . . He ordered pyjamas from Sulka with his initials embroidered on them. He wears a tuxedo to go out to dinner in town. His father would have been scandalised. Don't you think he's becoming very handsome?'

She didn't wait for Thérèse to reply. They were at the Bruns' apartment, one Sunday, in the warm little dining room, a few days after the funeral of Adolphe Brun, who had died of an embolism. He had just finished reading the paper; he was about to drink his cup of steaming hot black coffee, brought to him by Thérèse, the coffee he didn't allow the women to buy for he claimed that their sense of smell was not as sensitive as a man's and that they were incapable of judging the bouquet of a wine, the smell of fruit, the aroma of Mocha. For example, when Monsieur Brun chose a melon, he would carefully hold it in both hands and smell it, with an expression on his face that was almost loving. Monsieur Brun was a sybarite. He breathed in the aroma of the coffee and smiled. He was rather pale: he hadn't felt well for a few days now. He turned his kindly face towards Thérèse, suddenly gasped for air, once, then again, convulsively, like a fish out of water, waved his hand about weakly to protest, as if he were saying: 'But, sir, I don't owe you anything.' He let out a sigh and the end of his long moustache fell down on to his chest. He was dead.

Thérèse was sorting out her father's clothes, kneeling in front of a large trunk with metal bands round it. In the lower compartments were souvenirs of her mother, who had died so young: old-fashioned blouses, silk brocade dresses, some simple but pretty undergarments. All of it had been saved for her, 'when Thérèse grows up, she'll wear some of it,' her grandmother used to say, but she had never dared. She locked the trunk; it would be taken up to the loft where Martial's suitcase was already stored, with the books he had won as prizes, his medical textbooks, the photographs of his mother and father. 'Three lives,' thought Thérèse, 'three poor lives that have left no trace on earth apart from yellowing books and old clothes. My God, I am so alone,' she continued thinking, and she looked over at Madame Jacquelain in despair. 'She's a widow, but she has a son, she's happy . . . Bernard . . . he came to the funeral, but ever since . . . He's part of such a dazzling milieu, so different from in the past. He has mistresses. Renée Détang, without a doubt, and others . . . Well, what difference is that to me?'

A little while later, Madame Pain opened the door to Bernard, and in the dimly lit hallway, the old woman didn't recognise him at first.

'Can I help you, Monsieur?'

Then she brought her hand to her head:

'How silly of me . . . It's our little Bernard. Come in, my child,' she said to him, as she used to in the past when he would come up to see them after dinner, with his school books and notebooks under his arm.

'Hello, Madame Pain,' he would say. 'Can I do my homework here?'

'Thérèse,' she would call out, 'it's little Bernard Jacquelain.'

Then she would open the dining room door, show him in and close it gently behind him, leaving the two youngsters alone between the black cretonne sofa decorated with bouquets of roses and the photograph of Martial on the wall. These darlings . . . She shook her head with a particularly mischievous expression on her face, then quickly and emphatically rolled up her sleeves and went back into the kitchen from where she could hear the children talking quietly. Thérèse was in love with that little boy. Whenever he came near her, she had a certain look in her eyes . . . Madame Pain smiled and sighed: 'My poor Thérèse . . . She has a lovely life; yes . . . But that's not enough when you're young . . . You need tears, passion, love, romantic adventures . . . Later on, you resign yourself to your quiet little life. Then all you ask of God is one thing: to carry on! To carry on peeling the vegetables for the soup, day after day, going down to the dairy to buy milk, reading the serial in the *Petit Parisien*, eating mints to have sweet-smelling breath . . . Nothing more, my God, and for as long as possible. Then comes the time when God sends you an angel from heaven who takes you and leads you, whether you wish it or not, to the ultimate adventure, full of darkness and mystery . . . Terribly inconvenient,' she thought. 'All right now, let's see, do I have enough capers? I wonder if Thérèse will ask the boy to stay for dinner. She's in for trouble,' she continued thinking. 'She's in for a great deal of trouble.' It was just that men had always been difficult to hold on to. To get a man, well, that was easy, all you had to do was have everything in the right place . . . You could always get a man, but to keep him! . . . 'He's not going to make her do something foolish, is he?'

She was no more prudish than the next woman, but when it came to that . . . 'She's no longer a young girl, she's a woman. And, dearie me, you miss it once you've had it. But she must not do that. She's setting herself up for every possible kind of unhappiness. If you are sensitive, you suffer passionately, violently, and if you're not, if you take a second lover, then a third, you end up like Madame Humbert. Now there's a woman who has had a few lovers. An old woman who wears too much make-up, and with cold eyes. But we've never had any bad women in our family,' Madame Pain said to herself, thinking aloud: 'No need to worry about her dying from a chest infection: there's never been any tuberculosis in our family . . .' No, no need to worry. But Thérèse would suffer. Young Bernard had launched himself into society . . . She thought about her dead husband: 'Singers and champagne at twenty francs a bottle, I know what that's like . . .'

She was a decent woman with a vivid imagination that conjured up an amazing abundance of detail of the orgies in which the deceased Monsieur Pain, of the company *Pain and Sons, Ribbons and Veil Merchants*, had squandered all his money; she could see in her mind's eye the image of young women with perfumed bodices standing around a baccarat table, sitting in a private box in the stalls of some little theatre. 'Men have always loved money and life's pleasures. As for women, it's feelings that keep us faithful. We save because we think about our children; we deprive ourselves in order to make sure our little ones can have pleasures that their mothers will never live to see. But men . . . they ruin, they destroy things. So many generations of women who patiently, day after day, sweep up ashes from the carpets, mend torn pockets and holes in socks, keep everything in good order, light the fire when it's about to go out . . .' Thérèse would behave just like all the others; she would gather together precious crumbs of love; she would try to rekindle the sad, flickering light of love. She would save all the money that her man would happily spend the minute he earned it. It was the natural order of things; it was the fate of all women.

Madame Pain hummed to herself as she tidied up the kitchen, then fell silent, saddened: she remembered poor Adolphe who, only a week ago tomorrow . . . But what was the point of crying? There was nothing she could do. 'When it's my turn to go, I really want to leave this world knowing that Thérèse is happy . . . with a handsome husband. He has beautiful eyes, this Bernard . . . when he was twelve years old, he already had eyes to be damned for . . . She couldn't hear them in the dining room any more. 'What are they doing? Rosalie, you're being silly,' she told herself, speaking to the little mirror that hung opposite the stove; it reflected the face of an old woman, a very red face with dishevelled hair (she was always red in the face these days): 'they aren't really children any more . . . Now if my granddaughter is clever, she'll ask him to stay for supper; she's in love with him. I have a very nice piece of hake . . . I'll make them a mousseline sauce to go with it. But I am definitely out of capers. I'll go out and buy some.'

She slipped out of the apartment. She was old and heavy but she had a light step; Thérèse didn't hear her leave or come back. Thérèse was alone when her grandmother returned with the capers.

'But where's Bernard?' the elderly woman asked, sounding disappointed.

Thérèse was sitting at the table decorating her little black hat with some crepe. Her head and shoulders were very still and very straight: as a child, she often held herself in this way, rigid and silent, when she needed to cry but was holding back her tears; her hands seemed to move independently, with a life of their own; they were agile and graceful, fluttering swiftly between the needles and the spools of thread; her hands unrolled the long crepe ribbon; they pushed the pins in deeper. Madame Pain saw that Thérèse's lips were completely white; they formed a pale white line across her face.

'You should have made him stay for supper,' said Madame Pain, trying to sound indifferent.

Thérèse replied in the same way:

'I thought about it, but he had plans . . .'

'Really! There's always time to have supper. Such a lovely bit of hake!'

'He looked for you to say goodbye, Grandma.'

'I went out to get some capers.'

'He was very sorry. He's leaving tomorrow,' she added. 'He's going to America. His mother still doesn't know.'

'What is he going to do in America?' asked Madame Pain.

She sat down and fanned herself with the *Petit Parisien* newspaper she had folded in half; she suddenly felt tired and out of breath: she had gone up and down the stairs for nothing. She had wanted to make such a nice supper for these children . . . Thérèse had let the man she was in love with go . . . The women of today only got what they deserved. They were too proud: 'At Thérèse's age, I would have thrown my arms around his neck, yes, I would,' thought Madame Pain; 'I would have made him wait a good long time for the rest, of course . . . But a nice kiss . . . He would have stayed. What am I going to do now with all these capers?'

'Is he going away for a long time?' she asked.

'Two or three months.'

'Well, then, he'll be back, my dear,' she said, looking fondly at Thérèse's trembling hands. Thérèse did not cry; her voice was calm but she could not stop her fingers from shaking against her will; she picked up the scissors and cut diagonally across a piece of crepe; she put down the sewing.

'I'm not doing anything right; I can't see properly any more.'

She stood up to light the lamp.

'He won't come back often,' she said after a moment of silence. 'He leads a different life over there. What can you do?' She made a vague gesture meant to indicate both America and the strange, exciting world where money was so easy to make, where everything was pleasurable, where women gave themselves to men they did not love.

She sat back down in silence and continued working on the little black hat; it was an old one; they had dyed the felt, for they had to be thrifty, had to count their pennies. Her widow's pension and the Russian stocks were barely enough to keep her going when life was so expensive. Bernard no longer wanted anything to do with this 'middle-class contentment'. Bernard was going to make his fortune in America. Détang had introduced him to politicians and financiers. 'If you only knew what kind of crooked deals they make . . .' said Bernard. He admitted it; he knew it was wrong; he was taking advantage of it; he was swimming in dangerous waters, just like the others. But he, *he* had been to war, yet he thought, and said, that he would have done better to speculate on American stocks. He had no respect for anything, not for women, not for love, not for the ideas for which they had fought.

She pushed the needle in, then pushed it in deeper, pulled it out, pushed it in again, concentrated on her sewing without raising her eyes.

5

When Bernard returned from the United States, he received nearly two hundred thousand francs in commission for having negotiated the purchase of heavy oil to be sent to the French protectorates of Cilicia and Syria. It was not only an excellent deal, but, from a patriotic point of view, it was impossible not to congratulate himself at the thought of the French armies in the Lebanon so well supplied.

'I could have you decorated,' Raymond Détang had said, 'but you're so young . . . Just be satisfied with having helped your country and having pocketed a nice little sum . . .'

Raymond Détang had earned five million francs out of the transaction.

It was an impressive feat; Bernard savoured an intoxicating feeling of pleasure. His childhood had been spent as a lower middle-class boy, holding him back in every possible way; his entire family stood between him and the rest of the world, forming insurmountable barriers; four years in hell and, finally, the golden years of 1920–1921, as spicy and full-bodied as ripe grapes. 'Come and take whatever you want,' said all the men and women. 'Don't even think about whether it's good or bad. We are living in fortunate times, and there are no scruples. Take advantage of it.'

Two hundred thousand francs . . . He bought a car; he rented a bachelor flat. He knew very well that at the rate he was spending money, two hundred thousand francs would only last three to six months . . . But after that, he would surely have earned some more.

'Actually, life has become much simpler,' he said to Thérèse, whom he saw from time to time, when he went to visit his mother. He came over on New Year's Day and, two months later, when he caught a bad cold, he spent a week at home so he could be looked after. It was rather nice to be in his folding bed again with his old, dog-eared copy of *The Three Musketeers*. Yes, life was much simpler. Before, he used to worry endlessly about everything: duty, honour, scruples, responsibilities, love affairs. Now, there was only one problem: how could he earn as much money as possible, and as quickly as possible? And since everyone else in the world was intent only on that one thing, too, he managed to obtain rather pleasing results. During the war it was the same, except then, people thought only about weapons, not much else entered their minds. Now, it was all about money . . . People made money out of everything, out of nothing. Recommendations, preferential treatment, favours, lunches with people from the Stock Market, finding an apartment to rent, a request sent out, a chateau, a painting, a car to sell . . .

'It's very strange,' Madame Jacquelain confided to Thérèse. 'It's impossible to tell when he's being serious.'

'One day,' said Bernard, 'I'll invite you over to my place . . . with Mama, of course, who can be your chaperone. You'll see how nice a beautiful house can be, with good furniture and a servant.'

'And yet, this is where you come when you're ill . . .'

'Naturally; when I have the flu and a head like this, I'm not myself. I get sentimental. Will you come and see me, Thérèse? I have African masks. I have a bathroom with green floor tiles.

I have a Chinese servant and a Siamese cat. Lots of toys, you see?'

She looked at him and thought: 'I love him. I love him even as he is: happy, unfaithful, offhand, loved by other women, blessed with good luck. I would love him even if he were poor and unhappy. He is a good man, intelligent, but I don't respect him the way I respected Martial. He has no conscience. He would make me suffer . . . if he wanted to. But I can't help it. I love him.'

She didn't dare believe he was really inviting her to spend an evening at his place, and yet he was offering just that. He wanted to please Madame Jacquelain and Thérèse's presence would lighten the burden; he was happy to have them admire his beautiful apartment. In truth, Thérèse had a place in his thoughts, a very humble place, but she was dependable. 'Thérèse is a good looking young woman, but she won't hear of it . . . Too bad! Even so, she's worth more than Renée. Oh, that Renée: to despise a woman, to see her exactly as she is, a heartless slut, and to still be drawn to her to the point of suffering, of feeling desperate, of being jealous . . . And her husband . . . All his financial deals . . . Ugh! Some day I'll walk away from all that,' thought Bernard as he went home one day at dawn. 'It's filthy, and ugly . . . Some day, I'll marry Thérèse. But,' he continued thinking with a sudden surge of sincerity, 'once you've had a taste of all that: women like Renée, money like the two hundred thousand francs that falls into your hands just for having signed a bit of paper and taken a pleasure trip to New York or Washington – it's impossible to disentangle yourself from all that afterwards. It's a poisoned chalice. Bah! Best not to think about it. What difference does that make to how the world works? It will carry on in the same old way whether Bernard Jacquelain is rich or poor, a sucker or a sly devil. What does it matter?'

One evening in June, he invited his mother and Thérèse to his apartment. He felt such joy! It was a ridiculous sort of joy, he told himself, for, in the end, where would it get him? She needed promises, words of love, love itself – why not? She was young. But what she needed most was to own the man she loved, the kind of possession that marriage alone provides. To live with him, sleep beside him, look after his meals, his health, his well-being, to ask every morning: 'What are you going to do today?', and question him every evening: 'Who did you see today? What did you do? Tell me about it.' Someone to give her children. Oh, yes, especially that; when she thought of the children she might have had, something deeply instinctive and gentle, but as yet untouched began to stir within her body and thrill her.

One day, he would come to understand that she could make him happy. But there was not much hope of that while he was living the life he now led.

'What he loves,' she thought, 'is not Renée, it isn't even money . . . It's the luxury. You can fight a rival. But in this day and age, you can't tear a man away from the seductive charms of a car, a bathroom with green floor tiles and a Siamese cat.'

She knew absolutely nothing about his business dealings, but she guessed they had to do with procuring what was superfluous rather than what was actually necessary, deals that fed on bluff, publicity and expenditure until they reached the point where they worked endlessly just to produce enough money to spend, and needed still more to make more. A vicious circle, the illusion of alchemy . . . Bernard said so himself, but it was this alone, this formula alone, that promised a life of luxury.

'My God,' thought Thérèse, 'do you really need all that to be happy?' She had entered the house where Bernard lived, arm in arm with Madame Jacquelain. Everything seemed immense to her, overwhelming. It was a large new building, near the Bois de Boulogne, quite close to where the Détangs lived, a fact Thérèse did not know. A Chinese man in a white jacket opened the door for them and said that his master had not yet returned but that he had ordered dinner to be ready at eight o'clock.

'He'll be here soon,' said Madame Jacquelain. 'Thérèse, my darling, we can take advantage of it by having a look around his bachelor flat. A bachelor flat . . . what would my poor husband have said if he knew that Bernard had a bachelor flat? Do you remember his little metal folding bed in the dining room, behind the wood-burning stove, before he had his own room? This must be a change for him. Still, it's admirable that he has come so far in so short a time. There's the hallway. Here's his little office. Do you want to see his bedroom?'

There was a large mirror in the bedroom in which Thérèse saw her reflection. She was wearing a black dress with a small collar and lawn cuffs. She thought she looked pretty. She had cut out the fabric and made the dress herself. 'It's just as good as the designs from the large fashion houses,' she thought defiantly. 'After all, those dresses aren't made by the gods; they're made by modest working women, humble little women like me.' And every stitch contained so much love, so much desire to look attractive . . .

'He will look at me,' she mused, her heart beating with joy. '"That dress looks good on you, Thérèse," he'll say. I don't have any jewellery, but I have nice arms and a pretty neck. It's true. I have to make sure he notices. The dinner . . . All three of them, relaxed together . . . Madame Jacquelain must be encouraged to have just a drop of champagne, I saw some champagne in the refrigerator (Madame Jacquelain had insisted she see the kitchen and pantry). As soon as she has any champagne, the old dear goes straight to sleep. I remember the day of Bernard's First Communion; his mother fell asleep during the dessert.'

She pictured Madame Jacquelain dozing in her armchair. She and Bernard would hide out in his little office. It was the only room that felt welcoming to her. On the divan, he would offer her a cigarette . . . If she saw he was affectionate and funny as he sometimes was, she would not be able to stand it any more, she would throw her arms around his neck. She would say: 'Be mine forever . . . You need a woman who will pamper you, look after you when you're ill, keep an eye on the cook, because you will dismiss that Chinese servant who looks like a thief . . . Be mine.'

She smiled, looked in the mirror and adjusted the brooch that held her collar in place; it was a little heart made of rubies surrounded by lots of tiny diamonds. A gift from her grandmother . . . 'I was thinking of leaving it to you,' Madame Pain had said – she enjoyed what she called making 'her little plans', her down payments on the future; death seemed to be in her control this way, almost welcomed since it allowed her to offer little pleasures to the living. 'Yes, I was thinking of holding on to it for a little while longer, but I'm giving it to you today so that it brings you good luck . . .' These elderly women – Madame Pain, Madame Jacquelain – they knew everything. Madame Jacquelain would have preferred her son to marry an heiress, 'but that doesn't matter, that doesn't frighten me,' thought Thérèse.

'It's late,' said Madame Jacquelain, also looking in the mirror, with satisfaction at her new dress; she had had it shortened slightly, meekly if belatedly following the indecent fashion of 1921 by allowing her black cotton stockings to show up to mid-calf. 'The table is very tastefully set. This servant, the cook, his valet told me that Bernard invites people for dinner almost every night. The rascal . . . There are flowers strewn on the tablecloth; that's very "high society", don't you think? Now I wonder what we're going to have for dinner.'

'I'm sure it will be excellent,' Thérèse said happily.

'I could give this Chinese servant some recipes, I'm sure,'

Madame Jacquelain continued. 'I wonder if he knows how to make a good mutton stew with apples, or waffles. Those were Bernard's favourite dishes. Let's go back into the sitting room, if that's all right with you, my dear. My son will be back any minute now.'

Thérèse agreed; they waited in silence; after a few moments, they heard footsteps on the carpet outside the door.

'Here he is,' whispered Madame Jacquelain. 'We didn't hear the bell ring, or the key turn in the door, but this apartment is so enormous!'

But it was only the Chinese man who opened the door of a small bar:

'Cocktails?'

'My God, Thérèse, look at how funny that bar is!' cried Madame Jacquelain. She was on the verge of admitting to herself that she and her husband had pointlessly wasted their youth. The world offered more than she had thought, full of mysterious pleasures.

'But tell me now, aren't all those drinks very strong?'

'Some are strong and some are mild,' the Chinese servant replied.

Madame Jacquelain accepted a glass full of an iced liquid the colour of murky, stagnant water; then she was eager to try a concoction made with cinnamon and an egg yolk. 'It must be like eggnog.' It was sweet, with the flavour of fire and ice.

The Chinese man silently left the room. Madame Jacquelain took a few unsteady steps in the middle of the sitting room:

'My little boy . . . Can you picture my little boy serving cocktails to his old mother? I should have had another one, don't you think, Thérèse? We'll drink some more when he gets here . . .'

When he gets here . . . Thérèse looked over at the clock. It was so late . . . She was unconsciously folding and unfolding her little handkerchief.

'I wonder,' said Madame Jacquelain pensively, 'I wonder where my naughty little boy can be. He must have some meeting in very "high society". Some aristocratic lady, perhaps, or a wealthy foreign woman . . .'

'Don't fool yourself,' said Thérèse curtly. 'He's Renée Humbert's lover, the one who used to go for walks with us down the Champs-Élysées on Sundays. The hat maker's daughter . . . Only now that she is very rich and very well dressed, he finds her dazzling, that's all there is to it, he finds her dazzling. Just like all this ostentatious luxury, and that Chinese servant with the long face.'

'I think he's very nice,' said Madame Jacquelain, her face beaming with delight, 'yes, I do.' She was seeing everything through the heady mists of the drinks she'd had. 'And this apartment is very nice too. Isn't that the telephone ringing?'

It was indeed the telephone. They could hear the Chinese man's muffled voice from behind the door replying: 'Yes, Monsieur. Very good, Monsieur. Of course, Monsieur.' He put down the phone, opened the door and appeared for a moment.

'Monsieur has just telephoned. Monsieur sends many apologies. He has been detained. He asks for the ladies to begin dinner without him. He will come back a little later.'

'Well, then,' cried Madame Jacquelain after a moment's silence. 'Let us eat. We mustn't let the soup get cold.'

They sat down opposite each other at the table, secretly glancing now and again at the empty chair that belonged to the man of the house. Thérèse had lost her appetite. 'Eat something,' said Madame Jacquelain, who was gradually falling asleep, 'you haven't touched a thing!'

When the fish was served, a Siamese cat with fur the colour of sable and translucent eyes, jumped on to the table; Madame Jacquelain chased it away with her napkin.

'My dear old Moumoute would never have done such a thing,' she remarked, shocked.

The cat let out a shrill, unpleasant miaow, scratched Thérèse who tried to stroke it and ran off. Thérèse burst into tears. Madame Jacquelain, now sober, watched her cry in dismay:

'Come now, my darling, pull yourself together, think of the servant . . .'

'I don't give a damn about that horrid creature,' Thérèse insisted through her tears. 'Please, Madame Jacquelain, please just let me go home.'

'But Bernard will be home any minute. He'll apologise. It's very rude of him but you are such old friends,' cried Madame Jacquelain.

'I'm not angry, I won't hold it against him, but I just want to go.'

'You're not going to leave me here alone? Wait another quarter of an hour, just another fifteen minutes. Until ten o'clock, all right? At ten o'clock we'll leave.'

They waited until ten o'clock, ten thirty, eleven o'clock. They had finished eating. Every now and again, they heard the sound of the great carriage doors below and the long, muffled rumbling of the lift. 'It's him. He's coming,' the two women thought, their hearts beating faster. But the lift stopped at the floor below or continued rising. The cut flowers sagged on to the tablecloth. Thérèse gathered them up, made them into a bouquet and put them into a glass of water. Poor flowers . . . Where was Bernard? At eleven o'clock, Madame Jacquelain sighed:

'Well, I think that, in fact . . . We'll do it another time, Thérèse . . .'

They took the Étoile–Gare de Lyon metro line and went home.

'I will give him a good telling off,' said Madame Jacquelain, speaking through the noise of the tunnels and trains. 'He is too spoiled. He thinks he can do whatever he likes. He will come and apologise to you, Thérèse. That apartment . . . I'm still under its spell . . . I had never tasted grapefruit before. Did you notice the hand-embroidered tablecloth, Thérèse? He has crepe de Chine sheets. His wife will look after all those beautiful things. He'll settle down one day. He could marry a wealthy woman, but . . . if he found a woman who loved him . . . What do you think, Thérèse my darling?'

But Thérèse refused to say a word.

6

Thérèse got home and went to bed. It was a cloudy February night; a foggy mist slipped in through the half-open window. She did not cry, but her whole body was trembling. Through the partition, Thérèse listened to the sighs and agitated little groans from Madame Pain. The elderly woman slept lightly, restlessly. But at least she slept! How fortunate the elderly were, their dreams and desires gone, they no longer felt regret, no longer felt bitter despair, no longer thought only of love!

'He was so rude! Why would he do that?' Thérèse kept asking herself over and over again. She refused to believe in some accident, that something had prevented him from coming, not even that he had simply forgotten. Especially not that he had forgotten! . . . She would never have forgiven that. She preferred to imagine some well-laid plan made in advance to humiliate her, some evil plan to take his revenge because she had refused to fall into his arms like a whore. 'So what do I have left now? I'll never see him again. I'll never speak to him again. And what about him? Will he pursue me? No, of course not.' He had made himself quite clear. Men don't chase after women who turn them down. There are too many other women, and they are far too easy: 'You don't want to have some fun? Goodnight then.'

'I was too proud,' thought Thérèse. 'When it comes to love, nothing counts, not pride, not virtue. Since he wanted me, all I had to do was give in. After all, men are stronger, more intelligent than we are. If he thinks that this is what love is, nothing more than sleeping around, he must be right. I can't stand up to him, I can't. I'm just an ordinary woman. I couldn't prove to him that he's wrong. I love him, I'm weak. Let him take me, if he wants to. Women like Renée don't pretend to be prudes and they're the ones who are loved, while I . . . If only he had deigned to say some loving words to me, make promises . . . anything . . . even lies . . . But to act so brutally, with such vulgarity . . . And then, because I had refused, to insult me this way! Oh, you're just a little bourgeois woman who needs people to respect her!' she cried out in anger. 'If he wants to humiliate you, why should that matter? Accept it all, since you love him, or else, forget him! And you'll grow old without knowing sensuality, love, pleasure.'

She suddenly thought that she had never spoken those words 'sensuality . . . pleasure', never dreamt, in any case, that they might apply to her. Two words you read in books. But she now realised that other people enjoyed them, savoured them, that other people's lives were, in fact, controlled by those feelings, by sensuality and pleasure. While she . . . !

'But what does the future hold in store for me?' she murmured in despair. 'I'll grow old. I'll help grandmother in the house. I'll make new hats out of a few bits of old ribbon. I'll go to the cinema with grandmother on Saturdays. Then grandmother will die, and I'll be alone. Even if I become Bernard's mistress, I'd still be all alone . . . But at least I will have had a few nights with him, some memories. My God, forgive me! Martial, forgive me! I wanted to remain faithful to you, not simply to your memory but to everything that you loved: a respectable, peaceful, honourable way of life,' she whispered, 'a life where no one does any harm or has anything to hide . . .' and she looked away from the photograph of Martial lit by her bedside lamp. A photograph, a dead man, a ghost. The dead have no power over the heart of a woman of twenty-five.

She slipped out of bed. She looked at the time; her watch had stopped at seven o'clock the night before: she had not wound it up. Yesterday, at seven o'clock, she was getting dressed; she had powdered her bare arms and neck, perfumed her fine hair, that spot at the back of the neck that a man breathes in when he helps a woman on with her coat. She knew all the subtle ways of flirting, the cunning little wiles that are in every woman's blood, yes, even she . . . If she wanted to, she would be able to make herself just as beautiful, just as seductive, just as easy, so she could compete with Renée or any other woman. The watch had stopped; she raised the curtain and looked through the slats of the shutter; it was dead of night. He would be home by now. Asleep. She would go to him, and then . . . anything he wanted. She had taken off her long nightdress; she stood motionless for a moment, naked, looking at her body by the pale light of the lamp; it was a beautiful body, she knew that, a body made for love. She had been wrong, she thought bitterly, wrong to set such a high price on the gift of her body. 'I want him to take me! Even if he casts me away when he no longer wants me!' She opened the drawer of her dresser, her heart pounding, and took out a pair of silk stockings and some pretty underwear. Yes, anything he wants . . . and afterwards, never a word of reproach. After all, she was a woman; she was free. Feeling her way around in the dark room, she got dressed; she put on perfume; she brushed her hair. No one wore a corset then, just a slip and a one-piece dress . . . She understood why now. Everyone around her lived only for those moments of pleasure that they did not even dare call 'love'. She would do as they did. She did not want to put on the ceiling light: a bright light shining through the little squares of glass on her grandmother's door would wake her up. Standing in front of the mirror of her wardrobe, Thérèse held the bedside lamp in one hand and with the other, powdered her wide, terrified eyes, her pale cheeks, her cold, trembling mouth. He would warm that mouth with his kisses. He would say nothing to her, but at least he would kiss her, and, with every kiss, she would imagine what he really meant. One kiss would say 'I won't make you suffer too much' and the next, 'I won't leave you right away . . .' 'If only he could love me the way I love him . . . But no, no, that's impossible! And besides, what's the difference? Does the love you get really matter? The only love worth anything is the love you give.' He would mock her faithful heart. She knew that. She was walking towards love the way you walk towards a fire, in full knowledge that you will only end up seriously injured or even dead, that you will have died for nothing, in obscurity, without honour. She had the sure, blind, rapid movements of a sleepwalker; she picked up the small handbag that had fallen to the floor when she had thrown it on her bed after she got home; she counted her money; she would take a taxi. Some powder, a little handkerchief. The key to come home in the morning. Madame Pain would not be surprised if she wasn't there: she sometimes went out very early to the flower market where they sold such beautiful roses.

She walked quietly through the apartment; her grandmother was still asleep. She opened the door, went down the stairs and on to the street that was shrouded in fog and full of shadows. Was it later than she had thought? Well, that was just too bad. She was determined. She rushed into the first taxi she saw and gave the driver Bernard's address. In his house, everything was still quiet; she didn't take the lift but rushed up the steps, four at a time. When she reached the landing, she had to stop, on the verge of fainting. She rang the doorbell, and it was only when she heard the ring echo through the silent house that a horrible thought crossed her mind: what if he was not alone, what if a woman . . . Oh, how humiliating! She covered her eyes, then her ears, not wanting to see, not wanting to hear a voice, the laughter of a rival . . . She longed to flee but her body refused to obey her; she was in love and her terrified body had drawn her to this very spot. Now her body was in control; she leaned against the door that would not open. Bernard was sleeping; he hadn't heard her. But she had pressed the buzzer very hard. Then she remembered that Madame Jacquelain had put the key back under the mat when they left the night before: her son had asked her to do that if she ever called round when he wasn't there. She bent down and found the key; she silently opened the door and went inside. 'The servant isn't here, if he was, he would have heard the bell ring and come to open the door, and if he does come, that's just too bad! I'll tell him that I must see his master, that it's a matter of life and death. He'll think that Madame Jacquelain is ill and he'll let me in.'

The hallway was empty, as was the large sitting room. The bedroom she walked into was empty. The bed was empty. He had not come home at all. He had spent the night somewhere else. In whose arms? No, he had not intended to take revenge for her coldness; he had quite simply forgotten about her. She fell on to the bed. She would leave. There was nothing more she could do here since he did not even desire her. She stroked the pillow, the bedspread. 'He'll never know that I came looking for him,' she thought, 'but he'll be able to sense a strange warmth, the scent of perfume he doesn't recognise . . .' She closed her eyes for a moment then pressed her lips hard against the delicate linen. 'Enough! Enough! I've had my moment of madness. That's enough. I swear that I will never come near him again.'

She ran out of the apartment.

Outside, the fog had lifted and she saw with some surprise that the clock on the church said seven o'clock. She laughed nervously as tears streamed down her face. 'It's this cold

February morning that's making me cry,' she told herself. 'What a funny time for a tryst! Really, he would have seen at once that I'm not used to such things. You don't go and throw yourself into someone's arms at seven o'clock in the morning. Really, Thérèse, honestly! It's quite obvious that you aren't cut out for amorous adventures. Set the table and see to the meals. Leave it to other people to . . .'

She stopped. No. She would not go home! She would see him. She would know what time he got back, whether he was alone or not, with friends or with a woman. Almost directly opposite his house was a café that was already open, with seats outside on the pavement; it was completely empty in this weather. Too bad! She was dressed in warm clothing. And besides, she would not feel the cold; she was shaking and burning hot. She sat down at a table, ordered a milky coffee and waited. Hours passed by. Every now and again, the fog lifted, allowing a glimmer of wintry, yellowish light to shine through, then fell again to cover the street in mist. Thérèse could smell the sickly odour of rain and swamps; she bought a bouquet of violets from a little girl to block out the unpleasant smell and instinctively breathed in the scent of the flowers. A crowd of people rushed towards the metro. No one even noticed this slim young woman dressed in mourning sitting outside the café. Paris was now awake; you could hear its noises, the shrill bells, the shouts of the newspaper sellers, the taxi horns. The fog had completely gone. From the vast, grey, dreary sky, drops of rain fell every now and then, like tears that are difficult to shed when your heart is too heavy with pain.

It was almost twelve o'clock when Thérèse recognised Bernard's car stopping in front of his house. He got out. She ran across the street and rushed inside the house at the same time as him. They met on the stairs. Terrified, she thought: 'I'll say I lost a piece of jewellery at his place last night, my brooch . . .' But when she was standing facing him, a final surge of pride prevented her from telling any humiliating lie.

'I'll tell him the truth,' she thought. 'I'm not ashamed. I love him.'

In a cool, emotionless voice that sounded strange even to her, she whispered:

'I waited for you last night and you never came. I waited for you all morning and you never came. I wanted to see you, because . . .'

She weakened; he had led her to the lift and they were alone, going up to his floor. They rose slowly together, and Thérèse wished it would never stop, for the lift was dark and she could not see Bernard's face. They went into his apartment; in the light, Thérèse looked at Bernard. He was pale, dishevelled, his eyes were red and stubble showed on his chin, the light, harsh stubble that you find on a corpse. Suddenly, it was she who felt more in control, stronger. She put her arms around him.

'Bernard, my darling! What have they done to you?'

She held him close; she held him as if she were his mother; she understood everything.

'It's Renée, isn't it? She has another lover? You found out last night?'

He nodded. Renée had cheated on him with a man who was old and rich. He was ashamed to be tormented by this. How naïve he still was! He had been suspicious for a long time. The night before, he had been struck by her mother's secretive attitude and followed her to a house that the Détangs had just bought in the woods outside Fontainebleau. There, Madame Humbert had prepared supper and a bedroom for the couple.

'I had no illusions,' said Bernard. In the effort he had to make to speak, to open his trembling mouth, he had bitten his lip; it started to bleed. Thérèse, distressed, watched the blood running down. He was suffering because of another woman, and yet . . .

this other woman was far away. But she, Thérèse, was with him, in his arms. He would feel consoled.

No! He had no illusions. He knew what Renée was like. What insult could possibly upset her? He called her a 'little bitch', a 'slut', and she laughed. Perhaps he should hit her? No, that would make her too happy, he thought bitterly. Forget her? He couldn't. Logic dictated that he simply had to accept her other lover, but he was jealous. It was a feeling that filled him with shame and fury. That woman, that whole world, all those people, that swarm of animals . . . In theory, everything was simple. In reality, he would never forget the lights in those windows, her mother who set flowers on the table and turned down the bed.

'It's over, over,' he cried, 'it's all over! Those people and their vile schemes, their money, their pleasures! I've had enough! I loathe them! I'm done with them! They aren't human beings; they're a herd of wild beasts. You have no idea how much damage they are doing. They don't even realise it themselves. Nothing seems important, they're having fun, joking, making money . . . They make everything they touch dirty, destroy everything. They have lost all sense of integrity and honour. And I don't want to be like them, I don't! Do you understand?' he shouted in a rage. 'I don't want to become a complacent gigolo, then a crook, or a shark, and end up a complete and utter bastard! Help me, Thérèse . . . You're a good woman; you love me . . . Please help me to free myself of them, help me to forget . . . to forget her . . .'

'Her . . . Renée . . . ,' he said sadly, over and over again, 'Renée . . .' and every time he said the name, Thérèse was overwhelmed by jealous despair. Eventually, he calmed down. Silently, hand in hand, they wandered into the large sitting room. These walls, these masks, these paintings, all this strange furniture would all disappear, thought Thérèse. The memory of Renée, that too would fade with time. She thought of those upsetting, guilty dreams that come to trouble the best of souls and then are gone the next morning. In exactly the same way, he would forget Renée and the life he had known, and it would be because of her. He would not miss Renée once he had a faithful wife and a real home. She wrapped her arms around Bernard's neck. She kissed him and he kissed her back. By the time they said goodbye, they were engaged.

7

In the happiest marriages, the husband and wife either know everything about each other or absolutely nothing. Mediocre marriages are based on partial confidences: one of you lets slip a confession, a sigh; a fragment of some dream or desire is shared, but then fear sets in; it is retracted. 'No,' you cry, 'you misunderstood . . . You know you shouldn't take everything I say literally,' you exclaim like a coward. You rush about trying to fix the mask back in place, but it is too late: the *other* has seen your tears, a certain smile, an expression that is hard to forget . . . He pretends not to notice, if he is wise. If not, he becomes fiercely determined, insistent: 'But you just said . . . Listen, I don't understand, you just admitted it yourself . . .' Then you say: 'Swear to me that you don't miss that woman . . . Swear to me that you don't miss that other life . . .'

In the darkness of their marriage bed, Thérèse whispered softly once more:

'Swear to me that you never think about Renée any more . . . Swear that you're happy . . .'

'I am,' he would say. 'Don't upset yourself. Go to sleep.'

Happy? She could not understand. He was bored – and that was an illness impossible to cure. His boredom, a kind of gloomy inertia of the soul, had set in very soon after they were married. They had just settled into a modest, reasonably priced apartment. They had a son, good health, their youth and enough money to live on. Bernard had a job: he worked at a bank, earning two thousand eight hundred francs a month, and could look forward to becoming a senior banking executive when he was forty, and assistant director at sixty. For several months he had tried to broker personal deals with his friends in the United States, but he realised quite quickly that selling American goods in France with government Ministers backing him was easy, but alone, he was destined to fail: Détang did not forgive anyone who dropped him. Bernard reasoned that he had proved his wisdom by abandoning that other life, by seeking a steady, stable position; he had slipped back into the bourgeois existence of his father just as you find yourself sleeping in the bed where your parents died: you shudder a bit; you feel vaguely nostalgic; then you tell yourself: 'This furniture is really old-fashioned.' But it is warm; you snuggle up under the large red quilt; and the old couple had not been unhappy, not really . . . All you have to do is to be like them; you'll get used to it.

Thérèse and Bernard slept in a narrow, warm bedroom; next door, slept their little boy – Yves. In the morning, Bernard went to the office; he came home for lunch; he went back to work; he was not interested in his work; it was simple and soul-destroying. He came home for dinner; he listened to the radio; he read the newspaper; he went to the cinema once a week. He wanted for nothing, really. But he missed everything: he felt that he allowed his professional and home life to touch merely a superficial part of his existence; he went along with everyone; Thérèse understood very well that she did not know the real Bernard, that she caught only brief glimpses of him in sudden, almost terrifying bursts. 'But, really,' she thought, 'what is it that he needs? What does he want?' He misses the money he used to earn so easily, she thought, bitterly. How wrong she was! It wasn't the money he missed, it was a way of life that was fun, exciting, that turned every passing minute into an adventure. For four years now, men had adopted all sorts of new habits: anguish, sadness, despair, crass or heroic attitudes towards death. But they had lost the old, healthy habit of being bored. Many people had spoken of boredom in the trenches, but there it was based on either suffering or hope. 'In fact, perhaps that is what we are really seeking,' thought Bernard, 'to tremble with fear, to feel a thrill, to take chances, to cheat death . . . we should have been offered great new adventures . . . more battles, a new world to build. All we were offered was money and women. One thing still to dream of: a car, a Hispano-Suiza. In the past, when I did dubious deals for Détang or when I was in love with Renée, I had a taste of deep, sharp, almost painful joy, the joy of pride, of vanity, of being alive (vain, false feelings perhaps, but what did that matter!). While now . . . And, of course, there was Renée . . .'

He closed his eyes. He made love to his wife while thinking of another woman. Renée, her whims, her immorality, her mercenary nature, yes, all that was possibly true . . . But her eyes, her soft skin, always cold on her breasts and hips . . . He let out a harsh, deep sigh in the darkness.

'Can't you sleep, my darling?' his wife asked.

No, he couldn't sleep. Shyly, she took his hand. She always was careful with him, behaving fearfully, as if she were standing on a stretch of water covered in thin ice: sometimes it could support your weight, sometimes it would crack and dissolve beneath your feet. Sometimes she believed he was the most dependable of men, honest, lively, energetic . . . her real husband, the one God had given her and who would grow old with her. At those times, she would say something like: 'In ten years we'll buy a little house in the country. In fifteen years . . .' But he would reply: 'Where will we be in ten years?'

Then she would realise he was drifting away from her. He imagined a future that would perhaps be brilliant, wonderful, but instinctively she hated that idea because it did not resemble the present. She only felt comfortable in the present: her bedroom with its pink wallpaper, their large, comfortable bed, the sound of her little boy sleeping in the darkness. She wanted to keep all those things; she wanted nothing more. But he was not content with such simple happiness; he was troubled and anxious; she could not put her finger on what was upsetting him. She did not understand him. Did he regret having married her?

'No, a thousand times no,' he would reply, 'you know that I love you.'

One night, ten years into their marriage, ten years as tepid and constricting as their narrow bedroom (to Bernard it felt as though their existence had taken on the colour of the walls themselves, an old-fashioned pink dotted with pale little flowers), one night he and Thérèse were in bed together. He had turned off the light; he was about to go to sleep when she whispered in his ear:

'We're going to have another child, Bernard.'

She knew he did not want another child. But she was struck by the violence of his response:

'Oh, no!' he shouted. 'That's all we need! What a disaster!'

Tears in her eyes, she tried to laugh.

'Aren't you ashamed?' she protested. 'What about me? I'm so happy . . .'

'My poor Thérèse, think about it . . .'

'We're young. You earn a good living . . . I don't think having two children is so terrible.'

'Terrible? No. But it's one more tie.'

He had whispered those words very quickly and very quietly; they escaped his lips almost unconsciously, betraying him. During the day, when he was in control of himself, he would never have so clearly admitted that he was tired of his wife, of his home, of his son. Never would he have let the truth slip out: that he had seen Renée a few weeks before and she had become his mistress again. But in the darkness, on the verge of falling asleep, sometimes you simply don't have the strength to lie. Well, yes, it was one more shackle that chained him to this mediocre existence. God! Why hadn't he remained free! Renée was just as seductive as ever. He had aged; he was more cynical than before; he would only ask of her what she was capable of giving. He wouldn't dream of leaving Thérèse. Certainly not! But it was horrifying to realise that she held on to him so tightly, that she had forged so many bonds to keep him forever.

They both fell silent, holding their breath. 'He doesn't love me any more,' thought Thérèse. But the idea came and went in a flash: when reality is too bitter, we reject it; the heart protects itself against the truth and tirelessly invents its own dreams:

'It will all pass,' Thérèse told herself. 'We're just going through a bad time. He's tired. He probably has problems I don't understand. Men often don't want children. We already have a son. But he'll grow to love the next one, and . . . he does love me. And I love him so very, very much.'

8

Renée wanted to invest some money abroad. The markets were volatile. Money was flying from country to country the way terrified skylarks, shocked by the sound of gunfire, scatter and then return, only to fly off again immediately in all directions. One of Détang's acquaintances – a Dutch financier – advised Renée to beware of holding too much in francs: disturbing rumours were circulating on the Stock Market. He would gladly have taken responsibility for buying some stocks for her, but Renée had become as wary as a cat: this moneyman was too eager . . . He seemed impressive but did not inspire confidence. His name was Bernheimer.

Nevertheless, any warning from him should not go unheeded. She started to look around for someone discreet who could 'take care of her little savings', as she politely termed it. She did not wish to go to the stockbroker who managed Détang's portfolio: she preferred that her husband remain ignorant of her true wealth – Détang had the annoying habit of merging their two accounts whenever he needed money; ever since the crash of 1929, those times when he needed money were becoming more and more frequent in the couple's life.

Through Madame Humbert, who sometimes saw Bernard's

mother, Renée learned that he was a senior executive in a major foreign bank.

'I wonder if I should go and see him?' Renée thought one morning. She had almost forgotten about everything that had happened between them. One affair among so many others . . . She remembered him because he had been a childhood friend, because his character inspired her with a kind of respect. 'A young man who had such a brilliant future with us and who left it all behind to get married, to take a mediocre job, that's unusual, you don't see that every day.'

'You didn't know how to keep him on,' she had said to her husband in reproach.

'You mean I didn't pay him enough?'

But Détang was brutal in the way he judged people. She thought he had used Bernard as a front, a man of straw, and that he had ended up hurting his pride. It would have perhaps been better to give him the illusion that he was acting freely and responsible for his own decisions. It was a matter of diplomacy, she told herself as she finished powdering her face. In any case, since he had chosen the straight and narrow, she would take advantage of it. 'I'll go to see him,' she thought, 'and consult him about the dollar. I don't understand a thing about it, I really don't. All these important deals on such a large scale frighten me. I'm really still just a little middle-class woman. I want good returns for my money. I don't want to take any risks. "Russian stocks and Government Bonds", as Adolphe Brun used to say. Adolphe Brun . . . how long ago that was . . . And to think that his daughter ended up marrying Bernard . . . How very strange . . .'

Ten years of forgotten memories on one side, ten years of troubling dreams and hidden desire on the other – and this was the result: a meeting with a senior employee at a bank with a client who wanted advice on buying stocks. The interview was brief.

Renée had imagined a completely different Bernard, someone wiser, duller. But he was still young with smooth skin and blond hair. She invited him to come and see her. He refused with an angry gesture.

'No? All right, then. One evening, after work, I'll come and collect you. We'll go for a ride in the car.'

He asked how Raymond was doing.

'Still the same. Still in good form. He misses you. Seriously, you were wrong to drop him. How far have all your scruples got you? What are you earning here? Oh, I see. A pitiful little salary. On the other hand, it's true that Raymond's deals sometimes frighten even me. He's launched himself into important international affairs, you know. It's like walking a tightrope . . .'

'As long as politics help him keep his balance, he has nothing to worry about,' Bernard remarked.

'If you only knew how difficult everything is for me, my dear!' said Renée with a sudden burst of sincerity. 'We almost never see any young men at home any more. I miss the past. Not ours,' she said glancing quickly at him. 'Not the wonderful years after the war, but the old times, the very old memories . . . The walks down the Champs-Élysées on Sundays, the lunches in the Bruns' little apartment . . .'

She let out a little sigh:

'When will we see each other again?'

They agreed to meet the following day after the bank closed. She had her car. They drove to the outskirts of Paris and had something to eat. As they were heading back, she said:

'Let's go to Fontainebleau. We can stop in at my place . . .'

It was a very beautiful house, surrounded by tall trees, set back from the road. Bernard knew it well. In the past, whenever he had come here, all he had noticed was the woman in his arms. Now, he looked at the patio, the walls, the furniture. He remembered what Thérèse had once said to him in a moment of anger:

'Those people dazzle you like the little bourgeois you really are!'

She could be cruel sometimes. Well, yes, he was . . . he had always been attracted by luxury, by these enormous houses, by expensive objects and jewellery. 'Good Lord,' he mused once more, 'what else could I aspire to? As for the war, I joined up in good faith. I realised no one gave a damn about me. When I got back, the only thing everyone shouted was "Enjoy yourself!" ten years have passed. It's getting more and more difficult to enjoy life, but no one has come up with any alternative . . . Sometimes I envy the Germans and the Italians . . .' he thought.

He dropped down on to a large, black divan and closed his eyes.

'This is nice,' he murmured.

'What's nice?'

She laughed; she stood close to him. He stretched out his arms to her as he used to in the past, held her tightly against him and gently caressed her breasts, her arms, her hips.

'Nice, soft, sweet-smelling . . . No worries, no responsibilities . . . I have the perfect wife, and yet . . .'

'What's life like with Thérèse?' she asked. There wasn't the slightest hint of jealousy in her voice, just amused curiosity. 'Do you have any children?'

'A son.'

'Come with me,' she said. 'Come and see my Chinese porcelains. I have a wonderful collection. Look at those pink plates . . . It's very peaceful here, isn't it? You know, this is my house, mine and mine alone. Raymond never comes here. I'll give you a key and when you're tired of the office, of Thérèse, of taking the metro (that's your life, isn't it: Thérèse – the office – the metro? I've guessed right, haven't I? Poor Bernard . . .). Well, you can come here. You'll find cigarettes in this cabinet, this is the bar, there are books, paintings, records, no radio. You'll be able to rest, sleep for a while, and then you'll leave . . .'

'No,' he said. 'I could never leave again.' She laughed and let him kiss her.

9

In 1933, Thérèse gave birth to a daughter – Geneviève – and eighteen months later came a second little girl they named Colette. That same year, the elderly Madame Pain fell ill: she caught a cold and treated it herself with little doses of eggnog that she drank secretly – two egg yolks mixed into some milk laced with rum, half a glass of milk and half a glass of rum. One evening, Thérèse found her looking all red in the face and rather odd, so called for the doctor; he recommended vegetable broth and, after taking Madame Pain's pulse, took the remaining eggnog that was simmering in a saucepan and threw it on to the fire.

'You are over eighty years old, Madame,' he said harshly, 'and such indulgences will be the death of you.'

'It will be a happy death,' whispered Madame Pain defiantly. With feigned humility, she accepted the glass of Vichy water that Thérèse gave her, but as soon as Thérèse was not watching, she got up, opened the window and threw the water into the courtyard. Then she went back to bed. Her temples were throbbing and her legs shaking as she walked. She felt deeply irritated towards a mystical being she could not exactly name so she called him 'someone': this 'someone' sometimes looked like

Bernard, sometimes like the cleaning lady she hated and, tonight, like the doctor. This 'someone' was responsible for everything that went wrong in Madame Pain's life and, recently, nothing was going right. With obstinate perversity, dishes slipped from the old woman's hands, or she would trip on the carpet; everything she ate seemed heavy and tasteless, and whenever she added salt or spices or mustard to her dishes, 'someone' pointed out to her that she was upsetting her stomach. She had gone to live with the Jacquelains, but she missed her old neighbourhood. She liked nothing here; she could no longer hear the sound of the large metal bridge as it vibrated, the plaintive notes that had run through her dreams for so many years. Here, in this new house, the great gates into the courtyard made a harsh, unpleasant noise. The gloss paint in the bathroom smelled foul to her and she couldn't get used to the central heating ('Oh, the gentle humming of the wood-burning stove in the past . . .'). To tell the truth, the entire world was becoming incomprehensible and hostile. In February, there had been fighting in Paris; gunshots had been exchanged at the Place de la Concorde. The event itself did not upset her: she had lived through the siege of Paris, the Commune, the fire at the Bazar de la Charité, the floods of 1910 and the Great War; this was nothing more than another historical event. It was just as she had described the early days of 1914 to Yves, and in a few years' time, she would tell her granddaughters about the 6th February 1934. She had wanted to go out and see what was happening close up: but 'someone' had prevented it. She felt bullied. Growing old was truly irritating. 'Someone' hid everything from her. She had been a mother to Thérèse but now she no longer trusted her. Thérèse thought she was fooling her when she said: 'Of course, Grandmother, everything is fine. Bernard is perfect for me, really he is.' That poor child . . .

'You can't pull the wool over my eyes . . . You can't fool

Rosalie Pain.' (From deep in her past, a very old image suddenly appeared to Rosalie Pain in the little bedroom overlooking a Paris courtyard, and she saw herself as a girl in the Ursuline Convent boarding school, standing in front of the Mother Superior who was shaking her head as she said: 'You're a clever one, my girl . . .')

Over the years, the sick woman's face, once round and rosy, had become like a frozen little apple; the shadow of a sly smile from the past slid across her lips.

'They think I see nothing. They never fight in front of me, but Thérèse . . . Yesterday . . . No, Thursday, the day we had that cutlet for dinner that was overdone (in my day, meat was always served perfectly cooked), well, Thérèse's eyes were all red. I could see right through her. You can't fool me, no, not me. And then . . . the way she behaves with the children. She takes refuge in them; she uses them to build a protective wall around her. In the evening, she sits on a little chair; she puts the cradle in front of her; she takes Geneviève on her lap and it's almost as if she's thinking: "No one can harm me here, no one can hurt me." If a woman is happy with her husband, it's in his arms that she seeks comfort, that she defies the world. She never should have left Martial . . . But no, I'm rambling, it was Martial who left her to go to war. From what I can see, Bernard is cheating on her, there's not a shadow of doubt, and she knows it. Men are all the same. I was cheated on, yes, I was. Cheated on and left penniless,' she continued thinking calmly, for all these things had happened so long ago that she remembered them as if they were sad events that had happened to someone else – a woman with dark eyes that looked even more beautiful when filled with tears.

'I could have had plenty of men to console me . . . and so could Thérèse, if she wanted to,' her grandmother mused. 'But we come from a long line of decent women. As for him . . . I don't know what's got into him. With a gem of a wife like that, how could he not be content . . . ? But that's men for you, that's men . . .'

She pictured these strange creatures for a moment in her mind: all they liked was change; they chased women; they hoped for war. Yes, even though they talked about peace among men, a kind of restless spirit urged them to battle. She shook her old head, then said out loud:

'Still, they won't stop me from eating if I'm hungry.'

She scurried into the kitchen and in the dead of night, made herself a little cream dessert that she spiced up with a few drops of kirsch, then took it back to eat in bed. While she was having her dessert, she was listening; her bedroom was next door to the couple's room. She heard a long sigh; they weren't asleep. Every now and again, Thérèse's voice rose angrily:

'She's your mistress! I know she is . . . I know she's your mistress!'

He replied something that the old lady couldn't hear. Gently, she put her plate down on the bedside table, taking care not to let it clink against the marble top. If Thérèse kept pushing him, he would admit it. Such scenes were dangerous because men always admitted it in the end . . . It was extremely upsetting . . . How could they reconcile afterwards? And you always had to end up doing just that. 'One of these days,' thought Madame Pain, 'I'll take him aside and tell him: "Never admit it." A mistress . . . She listened some more and heard: 'Renée . . . Renée Détang . . .' What? Her again? This was serious. It would have been much better had it been some actress or dancer like the ones Monsieur Pain had in the past . . . But the same woman, ten years later . . . 'She has a hold on him, that's all there is to it . . . Her mother was the same: she had affairs . . . She knew how to hold on to men . . . And besides, they're different from us. They have fun, throw their money around. Thérèse is sweet and cheerful, but she is the wife, the obligation. Men nowadays prefer to run away from obligations (sometimes it is really trying). But duty catches up with us, whether we like it or not. "My dear friend," it tells us, "you wouldn't come with me willingly,"' said Madame Pain with a wry smile, '"so I'll drag you along now. I'll drag you by the hair."' She flinched: 'Oh, she's crying . . . He's making her cry. My poor little girl . . .' She recalled Thérèse as a child: she never cried . . . 'Oh, love . . . how foolish it makes us . . . She won't be able to keep him,' she thought suddenly in a flash of lucidity that was almost painful: 'She should have turned the other way, said nothing, waited . . . She's too young. She doesn't know that time heals all, wipes everything away. She doesn't know that her Bernard will change, that she will change. If they live to be old, they will change body and soul, two or even three times, perhaps more. She can't hold on to the man Bernard is today. She should leave him be, she should forget. Another Bernard will be there tomorrow. I must explain all this to her . . . But I can't . . . It's just too bad, and I'm tired . . . It's such a shame! They should understand. I wonder how she found out he was cheating on her,' she mused again, jumping from one idea to another. 'For me, it was a pair of gloves . . . perfumed gloves that were left in a pocket . . . and another time, two return train tickets to Enghien . . . I cried as well . . . I didn't wait either . . . Well, they've stopped talking now . . . They'll go to sleep. Sleep. My dear little ones, you can tear each other apart tomorrow. It's so quiet! Ah, I don't like it here. I don't like being in this house any more, with my family, not even on this earth. When Martial was a student, I remember he once said that the body is made up of little fragments that hold together for a long time, then, one day, they break apart. When you are ready to die, I imagine that each little fragment quivers and wants to reclaim its freedom, and that is what causes this unbearable sadness . . . Still alive, but you're now in shreds. Am I going to die, then? I've never thought about death before. I'm very old, of course, very old, I'm going to sleep now . . .'

She slid into a brief, light sleep and found herself in a strange place where she could see Thérèse walking towards her. She took her in her arms, stroked her face and said . . . Oh, she spoke such wise words to her! She explained the present to her; she revealed the future. She took her hand and they walked together through wide fields where fires were burning. 'You see,' she said, 'these are the fires of autumn; they purify the land; they prepare it for new growth. You are still young. These great fires have not yet burned in your life. But they will. They will destroy many things. You'll see, you'll see . . .'

She woke up: she could not remember her dream very well, but it left her feeling as if she needed to hurry. 'Yes,' she thought, 'I must tell Thérèse! There's no time to lose. People never talk to their children. I have to hurry . . .'

'Thérèse, Thérèse,' she called out, several times.

Then she fell into a half-sleep and when she woke up, Thérèse was at her bedside putting cold compresses on her head.

'She's had an attack,' she said to someone.

'An attack! How ridiculous,' thought the elderly Madame Pain. 'But of course I've forgotten what I wanted to tell her . . . Yes, the fires . . . Yes, she thinks she has lived, but she's just a child, and he is as well . . .'

She gestured that she wanted to say something; they told her not to speak. But there were so many good pieces of advice she needed to give; she had such a wealth of experience and she wanted to pass it on to her children: that Colette ought to be weaned soon because she was wearing out her mother, that their little Yves was too intelligent, he thought too much, they mustn't say anything in front of him, and that they should really get rid of the cleaning lady – yes, so many things that she could not manage to express, that became transformed into a gentle, childish moan as they passed her lips, or sometimes a mumbled cry:

'Thérèse! Thérèse!'

'Oh, my poor Grandmama, you're in pain, try not to speak,' said Thérèse.

But she was not in pain; she was just very hot. She pitied these poor children standing at her bedside. She stretched out her hand towards them in a gesture that was at once a blessing, a pleading, a caress, an acceptance of her helplessness. She could do nothing for them; all she could do was feel sorry for them.

10

When married couples quarrel, whoever is the first to say the words: 'It would be better if we separated' immediately feels as if he or she has committed murder: love still exists between the couple – love is still alive, but those words kill it. Nothing can ever bring it back to life again; once the lovers have admitted that love could die, the deed is done: nothing remains but its dead body. Once Bernard had said to his wife:

'Listen, all these conversations are getting us nowhere. Since we can't agree, it would be better for you, for me and for the children if we separate . . .'

Once he had said those words, he stopped, turned completely white, paced up and down the room, from one end to the other, then walked over to Thérèse, who had remained totally still, and stroked her hair. There was something fatal in that kind gesture; she could sense it; she stopped fighting; she agreed to the separation.

This scene was the culmination of four years of constant disagreements. 'You are no longer my husband,' Thérèse said over and over again. 'You don't belong to me any more; you aren't mine any more.' She meant that not only did he belong to another woman, but also that he was betraying an entire world of traditions, emotions, joys and pain that they had shared, just the two of them, in the past, everything that had been inalienable, and now, she would have to embody those values alone. For the first three years of his affair with Renée, he had attempted the impossible; he had tried to reconcile two irreconcilable worlds, the world of the Détangs and the world of the Bruns. An ordinary banker, father of a family on the one hand, and on the other, the lover of one of the most elegant women in Paris, a man who was part of Bernheimer's and Raymond Détang's social circle, someone who shared their way of life. And their way of life required money; Renée pressured him to accept Bernheimer's offer of doing business with him, with Bernheimer putting up the capital. Détang would also have an interest in the deal: Détang had an interest in every deal. He was not a Minister; he was not even a Member of Parliament. He was one of the ten or twelve puppet-masters of the time who worked behind the scenes. He knew everything; he was well thought of by all the political parties; everyone treated him with consideration; he got everything he wanted.

'I take my hat off to him,' said Bernard. 'He's made a success of himself. Now, being successful when you are a genius, or are knowledgeable or are exceptionally intelligent, is, in fact, nothing special. What is very tricky is to succeed having none of those gifts; it's like being an academic with no talent, a diplomat who can't find the island of Java on a map; it's knowing how to make a fortune without having done any work, or how to manipulate everyone when you are actually quite mediocre in every way, like Raymond Détang. Now that, *that* is worthy of admiration. There are two or three hundred men like that in France, a hundred and fifty of them in Paris. They are our masters.'

'Those men are evil and dangerous,' Thérèse had said sharply, 'and they will cause our downfall.'

He had listened to her without getting angry; he replied almost with humility:

'It's extremely tempting, Thérèse. You can't understand . . . Everything that is happening now in France is in the hands of these people, for better or for worse. That is why I have to go back to the United States now to place an order for some aeroplane parts for the Air Ministry. It's all been arranged, by Détang, of course . . . He'll take the biggest cut. I hate him but I need to do it: I can't pass this up. Just think what the advantages would be for me: I'll travel, make contacts, and if my transaction is successful, I can hope to start my own business with the backing of a financial magnate like Bernheimer. And then there's the joy of earning a lot of money in one go, the joy of being able to spend it . . . If I listen to you, if I break off relations with them again, we'd be left with an average, dull existence, and this time it would be forever.'

'But that's happiness, that's peace!'

'It's extremely tempting,' he said once more. 'And you, Thérèse, if only you wanted to . . . We could have such a wonderful life!'

'You mean ignore the fact that you're having an affair with Renée? Smile at people I despise? Entertain them here at home? And later on, find one of them who would be a patron for Yves? No, never! Never! Don't ever hope I would do that. I'm just like everyone else, of course: I'd rather be rich than poor, have a car instead of walking, but I won't have anything to do with that world. You already told me about this business about the parts for planes. I asked you then if they didn't manufacture them here in France and you replied: "How naïve you are! If everything were that simple, what would people like Détang and I do?" Well, all that is just . . .'

She tried to express what she felt, a complicated mixture of anger, disgust and fear.

But all she said was:

'All that is bad.'

She might have been able to accept the adultery. So many

women are forced to. You suffer but say nothing, either for the children or because of all the memories from the past. But in this case, it was not simply her husband's heart that was being taken away: he was being entirely changed, and right before her eyes. She barely recognised him. His desires, opinions, dreams, everything seemed foreign to her. My God, she had been so alone ever since Madame Pain had died! A woman cannot love or hate in the abstract: this world that Thérèse detested so very much had taken on the features of a certain face, her rival's face. Every time she hurled abuse at it, she seemed to be cursing Renée. She burst into tears.

'Tell me, really, what has that woman done to have such a hold on you?'

During the first year, he had defended himself; he had sworn that he was not Renée's lover. The second year, he had sighed wearily: 'You're mad, I'm telling you, you're mad,' without admitting anything, but without denying anything. The third year, he could stand it no longer . . . He had become brutal. Yes, all right, he did have a mistress! Yes, it was Renée! He didn't know whether it was love or a sort of sexual passion that would die out one day . . . All he knew was that he wanted her, that he would not give her up, that they were happy together after a fashion.

Finally, he had offered his wife a divorce, or, better still, an amicable separation. That way, the family would save face; the children would know nothing. They would tell them that he was living abroad for business reasons. He would come back to Thérèse's house from time to time, spend a few days at the apartment with her, but they would be living as strangers under the same roof.

'Don't you think that would be best? Simpler?'

'Everything seems simple to you now. You have enough money to support two households. With money, you can do anything, fix anything, isn't that right? Well, what can I do? Leave then, I can't stand it any more. I've done everything I can to keep you these past four years. Go! Yes, it's better if we separate.'

One evening, a few days later, he got up from the table and left to see the Détangs. He looked very handsome and seemed quite young in his evening suit. His wife and child watched him in silence. He was out of place in this little bourgeois dining room, thought Thérèse, and she sadly imagined the dazzling world that was taking him away from her.

'Where are you going tonight, Papa?' asked Yves.

Yves was fifteen. He was a strong boy, stocky, with a neck that was a little too short, a head that was a little too big and wide shoulders; there was something solid about him, something tense and wilful that struck you when you looked at him. He had broad features, but they would become handsome with age. He did not have a child's face; he had the face of a man. The disproportion between his strong, virile face and his clothing, his bearing and his voice, all of which were still childish, made people smile. He had pale skin, three wrinkles across his forehead, a large, nicely shaped straight nose and dark eyes.

'Where are you going, Papa?' he asked.

'To the Opera, to hear the *Magic Flute* by Mozart.'

'You should take Mama with you. Doesn't she like music?'

'No, I don't like music very much,' Thérèse said quietly.

'Your mother doesn't want to go with me,' Bernard replied.

They got up from the table. Yves went over to his father and instinctively stroked the satin lining of his suit. Bernard pulled away.

'Don't touch, my boy. You have ink on your hands.'

'Papa . . . I think that Mama gets bored every night, all alone.'

'Be quiet, Yves,' whispered Thérèse. 'Be quiet. Please.'

'She isn't alone,' said Bernard after a moment of silence, 'because you're here to keep her company.'

Everyone fell silent. The maid brought in the coffee. Bernard drank his quickly. 'It's a strange thing. It's impossible to get that girl to serve the coffee hot.' Then he quickly kissed Thérèse's hair.

'I'll be home late; please don't wait up for me. Yves, you'll be kind enough not to touch my books, won't you?'

He left. The mother and son were left alone. Thérèse walked wearily over to the armchair next to the fireplace. She was nearly forty; her complexion and face still looked very young; it was only the way she walked that at certain moments gave away her age. She sighed and reached for a basket full of clothes that needed mending. Yves made a movement; he was about to say something but thought better of it and turned away without a word.

Thérèse looked at him:

'What is it? What's the matter?' she asked quietly.

'Nothing. It's just that you seem so . . . dejected . . .'

'I have been a little tired recently.'

'I said *dejected*.'

She did not reply; she looked through the basket for her crochet hook and a ball of wool and started working, her fingers moving so quickly that her son was fascinated. When he was a very small boy, he had loved sitting at her feet while she did this kind of work; he never tired of watching the delicate, swift movement of her pale fingers as she unwound the wool. For a long time, he knew his mother's hands better than her features, her face: grown-ups are always half hidden in the shadows to a child; the look in their eyes, their smiles are all too far away, too high above him. But the hands that tuck him into bed, bathe him, stroke him are close by. He had drawn those hands from memory the moment he was old enough to hold a pencil and he had forgotten nothing: not the tiny marks left on her index finger by the sewing needle, not the scar on her fourth finger that she got from burning herself when she pulled his ball out of the fire after it had fallen in, not the little maze of veins on her wrist just below the spot where her long sleeves ended.

'Did you finish your homework?' she asked.

'Yes, Mama.'

'Well then, go and get something to read. But don't touch your father's books.'

He picked up a book and pretended to read. His eyes constantly wandered from the page as he studied one object after the other in the room, as if he were comparing them to some internal image.

'Mama,' he finally said, 'we have a nice house, don't we?'

'I think so . . . Yes . . . Why are you asking me that?'

And immediately, she regretted her words. She knew very well that he would not reply. A child – and he was still only a child – never explains himself. Especially not this child . . . And besides, she knew what he meant: 'Since it's so comfortable here, since our apartment is so pretty, so clean, so nicely furnished, why does Papa always rush away?'

On the mantelpiece, between a lamp and a small silver vase full of holly branches, sat some photographs that Yves had seen there for as long as he could remember: Madame Pain as a young girl, slim and smiling with her fine hair, one of Yves when he was three years old, one of his two little sisters and one of Martial Brun. Yves had always looked at this one with strange curiosity. 'He was one of your mother's cousins,' he'd been told, 'and he was killed in the war. He was a doctor.'

This evening, as he often did, Yves walked over to the mantelpiece and picked up the photograph. This thin, bearded man with deep-set eyes, his uniform and military decorations seemed to belong to a different age. He studied it attentively and with fascination. He had died six years before his own birth, in a great war. That fact linked him in a way to a mythical, even legendary, historical past, and at the same time, brought him closer to Yves himself: for Yves, like all the young boys of his generation, believed he was destined to go to war. In five, ten, twenty years, war would break out. Everyone seemed to hate war, and yet everyone expected it, just as one fears and expects death, or rather, the way a bird fascinated by a snake trembles and lowers its head without thinking of fleeing. War . . . He held the framed photograph in his hands and sat down next to Thérèse.

'Was he killed at the beginning or the end of the war?'

'Who?'

'Your cousin.'

'After a few months.'

'How was he killed?'

'Didn't I ever tell you? He died under fire,' said Thérèse, 'when he went to save a wounded man who had been abandoned.'

Yves closed his eyes to better imagine the scene that he pictured so clearly; it seemed so vivid that it was almost painful. Those great fields of mud during the war, so often destroyed, a dying soldier caught in barbed wire, another who crawls towards him in the glare of the rockets, finally takes hold of him, lifts him up, carries him away. Then both of them are hit by a hail of machine-gun fire. They both fall to the ground. And before their bones are crushed and scattered, death unites them so that these soldiers are no longer alone but together, brothers in arms, along with the other bodies already fallen. Thérèse told him the story of how Martial died:

'The man he saved is still alive. He's a farmer from Burgundy. After the war, he wrote to me and told me what Martial had done for him. "Your husband was truly brave, Madame. He gave his life for me. He was a good man."'

'Your husband?' asked Yves.

'Yes,' said Thérèse, blushing as he looked at her. 'I had married my cousin Martial in 1914. We were only married for a few months.'

'Why didn't you ever tell me that, Mama?'

'I don't know. I didn't think you would find it interesting.'

'But I . . .'

He stopped.

'You?'

'I'm . . . I'm not his son, am I?'

'Martial's son! Think about it, my darling: he died six years before you were born.'

'Yes, that's true . . . It's a shame . . .'

'What are you saying?' cried Thérèse. 'Have you gone mad?'

'I would have liked to be his son. He has an honest face, and also, what he did was good, it was brave.'

'But, Yves, your father was also brave. He was barely older than you, he was eighteen when war broke out. He enlisted, he fought in the Aisne, in Champagne, everywhere. He was wounded, decorated. He's a brave man. You can be proud of him.'

'I think,' said Yves, 'that I would have got along better with Martial . . .'

'You shouldn't say that, my darling.'

'Mama, did you and your first husband ever have a son?'

'No.'

'Well, do you find it fair that he died without leaving anyone behind to . . . well, to miss him?'

'But I missed him . . . I cried over him . . .'

'No one to admire him either? Yes, I know. You're going to tell me that you admired him. But it's not the same. If I had been his son . . .'

'In a certain way, you are his son, just as you are the son of all the men who died in the war for you,' said Thérèse.

He looked at her, bit his lip and finally whispered:

'But Papa didn't die . . .'

'Are you saying that you don't love your father?' asked Thérèse, taking his hands in hers and looking deep into his eyes.

'He's the one who doesn't love us any more. Don't tell me any silly stories, Mama. I'm fifteen years old, I know certain things. I know that you want to separate.'

Thérèse hesitated for a moment, then decided to tell him the truth. It was true that they were not getting along together any more; they would separate, but he, of course, was always to love and respect his father.

'You know that you mustn't judge your parents, don't you, Yves?'

'I know. I'm not judging him. He's free to do what he likes . . . I just don't understand him.'

'Alas, no one ever understands their parents.'

'But I understand *you*,' said the young man, hugging his mother.

He rested his head on Thérèse's shoulder for a moment, then pointed at the photograph of Martial that had slid down on to the carpet:

'And I understand *him*.'

Part Three

1936–1941

1

The negotiations for the aeroplane parts that had begun in 1936 were only concluded two years later: the engineers had stated that the American parts were not suitable for French planes. The question was discussed in Parliament. 'I'll deal with Parliament,' Raymond Détang had said. 'We'll sort it out one morning when the benches are empty. We won't allow those troublemakers to prevent us from making a pretty packet. Why should I worry about the engineers? They're specialists, and specialists only ever see *their* side of a problem. This is much greater, on a much bigger scale than they could imagine. The aeronautics industry must take inspiration from the current minor difficulties in order to overcome them through a brilliant approach, an approach that is . . . French, I could not put the matter better, Gentlemen' (he was speaking to a panel of experts). 'Do you understand what I mean by that? A bold, aggressive plan that transforms the drawbacks of this business into an advantage. I can just picture our workers, our engineers, our scientists toiling relentlessly to solve the problem, becoming passionate about it, finding a solution, for it is impossible not to find one. Nothing is impossible given French ingenuity, Gentlemen, is it? I have never seen, nor will I ever see, anything but the greatness of France and the power of her Air Force, for, Gentlemen, we must not forget the times we are living in. A storm is brewing in the East. What will you say to your fellow Frenchmen, what will you say to your sons, sons who are perhaps destined to fly these planes in order to defend the Maginot Line, when they reproach you for not having done everything in your power to strengthen our Air Force? You had all the resources of American industry in your hands, they will cry, and yet you did not take advantage of that? Why did you hesitate, pull away? Because of some insignificant details? Did you not have faith in the engineers of your own country? Ah, Gentlemen, allow us to act. Let us put our faith in the clear, luminous spirit of France that relishes overcoming difficulties . . . what am I saying? . . . that rises high above problems when confronted by them, like a bird on a mountain top who seems to gather strength from the very air that the weak find impossible to breathe!'

The Gentlemen on the Expert Panel finally agreed and the order was passed through Bernard Jacquelain who, a few months earlier, had been made director of a private company that was financed by Bernheimer and secretly by Détang.

Neither Bernard nor Détang knew exactly what to think about the business of the aeroplane parts: the experts were equally divided and never managed to agree. The issue, however, soon was being discussed beyond the field of pure technology. It became embroiled with ideological and political considerations.

'To tell the truth,' Détang said to Bernard, 'no one understands a thing about it. I have six reports on my desk that all contradict each other. Why should I believe the ones who sit on their high horse and shout "Beware!", and stop me doing great business, when very highly esteemed men assure me I can go ahead? Everyone says: "This is a very serious matter." There are no very serious matters in the times we are living, my boy, because if people truly wanted to consider how complex and serious everything was, they would have no choice but to shoot themselves in the head. And if you want to do that, there's always time . . . What can I say? All we can do is to trust our common sense, and mine is telling me that it would be a shame to miss out on this deal because three fools out of six want to be paid to change their minds. And I certainly am not going to do that! I don't buy men. Everything is above board.'

Bernard wanted to study the matter but found himself overwhelmed by contradictory reports and technical details.

Until 1937, every aeroplane part was manufactured separately, by skilled workers who knew their craft. Now, however, the aeronautical construction companies had machinery that could mass-produce planes on an assembly line. This was a very hard blow to Détang. But for certain types of plane, the old methods were still used. 'The French Air Force will be the better for this,' said Détang. 'We'll have to use the American parts for some of the planes and others will be manufactured under the new system. We'll end up better equipped than we could have hoped. When I say that in France, victory emerges from the jaws of defeat, I'm telling you the truth!'

'As far as I'm concerned,' thought Bernard, 'it's nothing to do with me. I really hope he won't find anyone who will consciously sabotage our country's Air Force. They must examine the matter from a technical and practical point of view and take responsibility for it. As for me, I'm just the broker.'

Nevertheless, Bernard spent the entire year of 1938 as if he were being swept along by a violent storm. He slept four hours a day. Bernheimer made him responsible for multiple deals. They juggled the figures. Millions flowed through his hands, or rather, the symbols, the signs of those millions. He handled the paperwork that represented them, but he was so short of money that several times he was unable to pay Thérèse her maintenance (they had agreed a certain sum that he would send her).

'But I'll make up for it next month,' he wrote to her. 'My dream is to put money aside for Yves, just for him, to have when he's twenty. I remember how furious I was at having no money when I was young. I don't want my son to feel the same way. Yves has a wise, confident nature. Money won't be his master, but it will be a good servant.'

Thérèse and Bernard hardly saw each other any more. According to the agreed plan, he came back to live with his wife when he returned from his business trips. 'No, this is horrible,' Thérèse had told him on the third day, 'I would prefer a proper separation. The girls have forgotten you; they'll just get attached to you again and will suffer when you leave us.'

'I won't leave Yves . . .'

'I know. Yves is seventeen. There's no point in hiding the truth from him. He can go and visit you at your place as often as you like. But I'm begging you, don't come back here.'

'Not ever, Thérèse?'

They were alone in the small, very peaceful sitting room. He would have preferred to keep his wife. He was not without affection for her or the children. It was even strange how much they meant to him, he thought. He would have liked to make them happy. But there was too much excitement, too many pleasures, too much to worry about on this earth to allow him to be faithful to her loyal heart. 'Good, brave Thérèse . . . When all is said and done, she is the only one . . .' He thought that, one day, much later, when he had enjoyed everything, experienced everything, exhausted everything, when he was tired of parties at Vaucresson around Bernheimer's swimming pool, and the wild nights at Juan-les-Pins, and the hours spent with Renée Détang at Fontainebleau, when he was bored with the pleasure and the pain caused by money (but pleasure and pain were inseparable . . . it was a double-edged sword that whips, excites and wounds the human beast), yes, when all those things finally meant nothing to him, he would come back to Thérèse. He made a point of asking her if she would take him back one day, if she could truly forgive him one day. For several nights afterwards, he dreamt of the look in her eyes: she had said yes; she had looked up at him, she had even smiled at him with difficulty: 'Yes, of course, I'll take care of your arthritis when you're old.' They had spoken completely freely, even with more trust than they had ever shown one another in the past.

'You're not a bad person, my darling, why are you making me suffer?'

'You're suffering because you want to. You have to compromise, come to terms with life, with love, with everything. You remained the wife of that admirable but stupid Martial who used to say: "You don't make compromises with your conscience or anything of that type." My poor Thérèse, you are destined to be a victim, yes, you are, along with all the others who think like you. This affair with . . . you know who I mean . . . you think she is a monster. And yet, it's no longer a question of passion, it is more self-interest, habit . . . Even she tells me to go back to you. I could promise you that I would only be a friend to her in future. But you have to understand, I can't give up that world. It's my life, my career.'

'Be quiet, you're horrifying me!'

'Thérèse, the world is despicable. Men are stupid, cowardly, vain, ignorant. No one would appreciate us being scrupulous and altruistic. Believe me. I learned lessons during the war that I will never forget . . . Out of humility, out of a kind of respect for decency, I'm letting you raise your son with the ideals of the Brun family. I'm wrong though. I should open his eyes to the truth.'

'You've already done that, you know . . .' murmured Thérèse.

After this meeting, the married couple separated. Bernard had not rented an apartment; he lived at Claridge's Hotel on the Champs-Élysées. Two or three times a year he went away on brief car trips with Yves. In his father's mind, that was meant to bring them closer, allow them to have long conversations, to share secrets, but they seemed to feel embarrassed and ashamed when they were together. Even conversations that began on quite a friendly note often turned into arguments.

During the winter of 1938–1939, Bernard and his son went away together to Megève. The young man expressed naïve joy at the prospect of seeing snow for the first time and of learning to ski.

'I won't tell anyone where I am,' Bernard thought. 'I'll do nothing but look after my boy. A week to make peace with my son, because I can tell he really holds a grudge against me. I must learn how to get to know him and make him love me. He'll see that I'm not a pedantic, unpleasant companion. When I was his age, I would have been happy to have a father like me.'

And so, one January evening, they set off together by train. When they pulled back the blind that covered the carriage window, they could see the dark countryside beneath a clear, icy sky.

'Let's hope it snows,' said Bernard.

He had been counting a great deal on this first evening on the train to get closer to his son. He asked him about his studies, his plans for the future. He talked to him about politics, about women, about everything an adolescent might find interesting. 'I should have done this sooner,' he thought. 'He's not fifteen, any more; he's eighteen. At his age, I was about to enlist.'

And the memory of his youth made him silent and shy, because between a child and his parents, the obstacle is never the man someone has become, but the man he used to be. The young man of twenty he once had been, but was no more, sealed his mouth closed, now that he was a father.

They simply exchanged the most banal words, then Yves went to sleep. Bernard remained awake in the passageway until very late that night. He smoked and watched the little blue lamp flickering on the ceiling.

He had not given anyone his address in Megève but the hotel was full of his friends. The very next day, he and Yves were invited to lunch by the wife of a well-known Member of Parliament. The men were wearing ski clothes, their fat potbellies stretching out the colourful sweaters, their cheeks red, not because of the pure air they had not yet breathed in, but because of the wine and aperitifs they had drunk at the bar. The women were thin and heavily made-up. The older men talked about Russia, Danzig, Germany, the imminent war. They ate smoked salmon marinated in dill while describing the scramble of enemy planes massing towards French cities: 'And there's nothing we can do, nothing. After the first night, boom, and everything will be flattened.' While tucking into their kidneys flambé in Madeira sauce, they all spoke as one: 'Thank goodness this is the land of miracles! As soon as we think we've had it, wham! We pull ourselves up and the world is amazed!' Over dessert, ice cream swathed in hot melted chocolate, they confided to their neighbours the gist of what was contained in reports received by the Foreign Ministry: 'All this, of course, is just between us.' One man, with a dark beard and moustache and a Toulouse accent, pointed out that the Germans did not have enough food and so could not go to war. Everyone was in agreement about the deplorable state of chaos that France found herself in: 'What we need is someone with a firm hand, a real leader,' they said. Through the hubbub of voices, the clinking of glasses, the laughter, you could hear a shrill sound, like a fife: it was a woman asking a former President of the Council, 'But why don't you take power, Monsieur? You should, Monsieur', as if she were offering him a slice of foie gras. The former President, who was short and well-fed, with very fine white hair, shook his head without replying, a cautious, greedy look in his eye, as if to say: 'Well, well, why not? Take power . . . Hell! . . . I must think about it.'

Yves felt a sense of nightmarish unreality. As a child, after reading adventure stories, he had sometimes dreamt that he was in a cave full of jabbering beasts. And now he was re-experiencing the very same painful, grotesque feeling. During dessert, they lit cigars, and the smoke made him feel even more uncomfortable. He glanced longingly through the windows at the grounds covered in snow. Finally, he could stand it no longer. Let them talk if they want, let them argue endlessly, sort out Europe as they see fit, destroy Germany (verbally), make quick deals in armaments or trade stock portfolios! As for him, he no longer wished to be with them. He took advantage of a moment when his father wasn't paying attention to slip out of the room. He gave a message to the porter: 'Please tell Monsieur Jacquelain not to worry; I'll be back this evening.' 'Do be careful, Monsieur, the weather is going to change.' He fled in the direction of the mountains.

2

Yves would never forget that day he spent alone in the Savoy mountains. The weather did change, in fact. Snow began to fall, covering the trails. Some young people climbed up in front of him, skis over their shoulders. He regretted not having all the equipment like them, but what he most wanted was to be alone, to breathe the pure air and put his thoughts in order. Up until now, his inner life had been that of an adolescent: no logic, bursts of admiration or rebellion; no reflection, just blind desires. He had to learn how to think like a man. To know exactly what he wanted and to act according to his own will. First of all, he had to recognise the true characters of his mother and father, for he sensed deep down that there he would find the crux of the matter: he had to follow one or the other of them. 'To judge your parents is bad, of course,' he thought. 'But they are primarily responsible for that. They are the ones forcing me to make this choice.' He had always been, as he naïvely put it, 'on his mother's side', but his reasons for leaning towards her were emotional, and that was not enough. He did not wish to be unfair. He wanted to try to understand his father. He was not an evil man. He was not a dishonest man. He had a quick, brilliant mind. He had fought bravely in 1914. Grandmother Jacquelain had made him read the letters his father wrote from the front, when he was eighteen, nineteen, twenty, amid all kinds of danger and hardships. They were moving, delightful letters, funny and full of daring. In one of them, he talked about the son he would have one day: 'I'll have so much fun with him! If he moans about going to school when it's raining in the morning, I'll enjoy telling him: "What would you have said if you had to spend the night in the woods like your father did in 1915, soaked to the waist and your boots full of water?" He'd go to school, sheepishly, while I, I'd stretch out in bed until noon. Ah, those will be happy times . . .' 'Not everything is ugly in war,' he continued. 'A bomb explodes and the shrapnel forms a plume of pinkish white smoke that looks like the froth on top of a sorbet . . .'

Reading those lines, Yves had wanted to cry over his father as if he had died. And yet, he had not died. His father had come back and had begun to live his life with such cynicism, such bitterness!

'All in all,' Yves thought, 'if anyone asked me what I think of him, I would have to say: "He is part of an evil set that out of spinelessness, blindness or deliberate treason is causing the downfall of France." And since he belongs to those people, since he deals with them, shares their profits and their pleasures, does that make him . . . a dishonest man? Oh, no, that's terrible, I couldn't say that! And yet . . . That Détang, that Bernheimer . . . those women . . . And the worst part of all this is that other people are almost ashamed to judge them from a moral point of view, because they have transformed morality into something grotesque, childish, which only deserves to be ridiculed. If I said to my father: "It's wrong to profit from a man like Détang! It's wrong to increase unemployment in our country by buying things from abroad that we could manufacture here! It's wrong to speculate on the devaluation of the franc, like Bernheimer is doing. It's wrong to avoid paying taxes by sending your money outside France as you've bragged about doing in front of me . . ." What would he say then? He'd just shrug his shoulders. What a terrible generation they are! Why are they afraid? It's clear they are afraid, and of everything. They spend the whole time fearing: fearing for their lives, and for their money. Why should those men, who at the age of twenty willingly risked their lives for nothing, now sell their souls for banknotes?'

He walked through the snow in no particular direction, lost in thought. A bitter wind had risen up that whipped the back of his neck and behind his ears. It felt good, that sharp wind biting at his skin. He was content far away from everyone else. He had always been rather anti-social. As a child, he had dreamt of being like the sailing explorer Alain Gerbault, dreamt of escaping Europe (what appealed to him was not the peace of a desert island, but steering a boat on the high seas, the storms and the danger). Yes, he was happy when he was alone. Everything was calm. He had a perspective on people and things that was clear, tranquil, objective and implacable. His father . . . he had wanted to stay alive. He would never allow himself to give up his one chance at life. He had never given himself entirely to anything; he had held back a part of himself, remaining defiant, reticent, egotistical – in war, in peace, in love.

'I won't be like him,' thought Yves, 'not me. Anyone who wants to save his own life ends up losing it. I will offer up my life. I will disregard it completely. I will know how to sacrifice myself if need be, yes, I will.'

A strange, prophetic sadness took hold of him.

'They are the ones who are offering us up to be sacrificed,' he thought. 'They say there will be a war, that it is inevitable and imminent. They are the ones who have laid the ground for it. They claim they fear it. I don't know, perhaps that's true, but, at certain times, they seem to welcome it. Or maybe they are fascinated by it? Perhaps they have now gone too far to step back and they feel we're on the brink of an abyss? But what is certain is that it will be the young men who are first to fall into that abyss.'

He climbed the mountain faster and faster. He stopped, out of breath. He had been walking for a long time. The short winter's day was ending. The setting sun was red.

'That's a sign there'll be a wind coming up,' said a farmer who was passing.

There was an inn nearby where Yves ordered some milk and toast. The room was empty but for a dog and her six little puppies asleep on a bundle of hay. When Yves went to stroke them, she bared her teeth at first, then, after studying him, she left Yves with her little ones. He picked up one of the puppies, slipped it under his jacket and went outside. It was nearly dark. In certain places, the snow glistened. Yves leant over and tried to see Megève, but a thick fog hid the town. He could not even make out the waterfalls that fell down the mountain, cracking the ice; he could tell they were there only by the smell of cold underground places and their deep, solemn sound. Yves stood motionless for a very long time, stroking the warm fur of the little dog that sighed and whimpered softly. Yves was thinking of many things, some clear and sharp, others as confusing as in a dream. In the life of every man worthy of the name, there is a moment when he takes sides, when he decides once and for all whether he is for or against a certain way of life.

'What I need is solitude,' thought Yves, 'and for things to be clean and clear . . . Something that resembles this mountain, something austere, harsh and strong. I want to live far away from cities, far away from people. If I were a believer, I'd become a priest.'

He walked a few steps in the snow and breathed in the pure, sweet-smelling mountain air.

'I'll become a pilot,' he thought. 'I know very well what my father would say . . . that I'm naïve, that there are as many shady deals and schemes in that profession as in any other. I know that . . . But the effort and danger it demands redeems everything. And at least being a pilot is work that requires you to offer yourself up entirely. What will Mama say?' he continued thinking. 'Well, little dog,' he whispered, putting him down on the ground; the puppy immediately rushed away, tail in the wind. 'What will she say? And what would he have said . . . the man who so wished to be my father, I'm sure of that, the man who died, hoping, perhaps, that he had left behind a son? Yes, what would Martial Brun have said? And what will my real father say, and not the father of my dreams?'

He could hear him now:

'But think about it, my boy. It's all very well and good, but . . . there's not much in it for you, you know? It's true that you get women.'

Women! Making money and making love! A good steak and someone's bed . . . He shook his head angrily and went back to the inn. He had a bit of cash with him; he would spend the night in a sparse, bright little room. He sent a young lad to Megève with a letter for his father:

'Please forgive me,' he wrote, 'for not coming back tonight, but I can't stand the people we met and you're part of their world. Forgive me. I don't wish to be harsh or insolent. But I know you won't be angry, you'll simply make fun of me. I have my return ticket with me. I'm going back to Paris alone tomorrow. Once again, forgive me, Papa.

'With love,

'Yves'

3

Bernard learned of Bernheimer's death over the phone. It was a stifling hot night in August. He had spent the night at the Détangs' place, in their house at Fontainebleau. That summer of 1939, no one left Paris. The Détangs gave a large dinner party. As soon as soup was served, the word 'war' was uttered by one of the guests.

'No! That's enough!' cried Renée Détang. 'You don't know what you're talking about! It's not true; don't you know that another war is impossible? My husband has seen the President of the Scandinavian Bank. It seems that war isn't possible, because the Germans don't have enough railway trucks. Didn't you know that? It's the latest news, you see. And I beg of you, please let's talk of other things!'

The dinner party had been very lively. Détang was in particularly good form; the passing years did not seem to affect him. He was fatter and had a healthier complexion than ever. Bernard had known him for so long that he really no longer saw him. But that evening, he was struck by one of his features that he had either never noticed or had forgotten: Détang's eyes. They were shining and completely blank. They reminded him of the sparkling surface of a mirror; they reflected the outside world, they were happy when everything around him was joyful, full of melancholy when others were sad, but on their own, they expressed nothing. He walked over to Bernard and put his hand on his shoulder.

'Tell me, are you coming away with us? We're going to Cannes a week from Monday. From there, we'll take a little trip to London.'

Then he lowered his voice to make a remark about a woman who was walking past. Whenever he talked about women, the blood flowed up his neck and behind his ears in a slow wave of deep crimson.

'To tell the truth, women are the only thing I really like, and I like it more and more,' he said in a different voice, a low, hoarse voice. He quickly walked away from Bernard.

The same man, two hours later, woke Bernard to tell him that Bernheimer had died. The Dutch financier had gambled on a drop in the value of the florin and had lost. The florin had not been devalued. Bernheimer lost everything and had just died. In his own debacle, he had dragged down many business deals that had seemed to be solid and profitable, including one that involved Bernard Jacquelain who, a week earlier, had loaned him every penny he had. As for Détang, he had blindly bet everything on Bernheimer:

'I'm done for,' he said to Bernard. 'That will teach me put all my eggs in one basket. Someone offered me the chance to bet on the Dutch florin increasing in value. I refused. I trusted that foreign bastard. Trusting people will be the death of me. I should have had him deported. Are you listening to me, Bernard?'

'I'm listening,' Bernard replied after a moment's silence.

'Have you been hit hard, too? You as well?'

'I'm going to lose everything.'

'Ah, my dear boy, my first thought was to blow my brains out. Then I told myself that there would be plenty of time for that later.'

'Have you known for a long time?' asked Bernard.

'Since five o'clock this afternoon.'

He hung up. Bernard let out a deep sigh and got out of bed. He felt the peculiar sensation of disbelief that follows the announcement of a disaster. 'Come on now! Could something like this really happen to me? To *me*? It simply isn't possible!'

Mankind can only easily get used to happiness and success. When it comes to failure, human nature puts up insurmountable barriers of hope. The sense of despair has to remove those barriers one by one, and only then does despair penetrate to the heart of man who gradually recognises the enemy, calls it by name, and is horrified.

'I just have to start all over again,' Bernard had thought. 'These things happen. I'll get a loan.'

Calmly, thinking clearly, at first, then more feverishly, then with desperate rage, he had tried to imagine anyone he knew who could help him. The bank in London, the Americans, that important French company. Come on, come on! He wasn't just anybody! He was Bernard Jacquelain! But . . . in truth . . . Who was Bernard Jacquelain? Had he brought anything new, anything of value to the world? Something of genius? A considerable body of work, a new invention of any kind? No. When he thought about it carefully, he had built his fortune with telephone calls, conversations, lunches, a kind of savoir-faire, by knowing how to deal with people, the ability to talk about anything, to have the latest facts about everything, an ability that was to real work what smoke was to a flame. Ninety-nine per cent of the careers in Paris that had been established in the past twenty-five years were just like his. Bernard let out a low groan. Suddenly, the realisation of the disaster rushed through him in a wave, carrying in its wake all his fragile hopes. He was finished. The bank in London, the one in New York, the French company whose President he knew so very well, all of them would drop him, because it was in no one's interest to save him. Quite the contrary. There had been too many financial scandals in France in the past ten years; everyone would be afraid, fearing to become compromised by helping one of Bernheimer's old friends . . . He was abandoned, ruined. He would fight. He would try to get extensions for his debts, loans. In vain! What was more, he had been happy. And that was unforgivable. Now they would make him pay for his good luck. There would not be enough mud in all of France to throw at him, to prevent him from getting back on his feet again. Who was on his side? Not his family, not a powerful collective. Connections. That wasn't very much. Connections were all powerful in times of success, but weakest when it came to failure. There were simply a flimsy kind of support that crumbles as soon as you put out a hand to grab on to it, he knew that. A crash, a collapse. No way out. Détang, without a doubt, was dying of fear that thanks to the scandal, everyone would uncover his shady deals from the past, like the aeroplane parts, for example (how had that actually panned out? He knew he had earned his commission, but for the rest . . . Détang had mentioned in passing that in the end he had 'made the Air Minister responsible for it all, but not without a great deal of difficulty, and he had had to spend more than twenty per cent in backhanders'). If that old deal ever surfaced, people would take advantage of it to bring him down – Bernard, who had played only a minor role.

For the first time, a deep sense of terror rushed through him. Perhaps what he had done, which was so commonplace in certain circles, actually deserved the punishment that was raining down on him? But he immediately banished that thought. What a joke . . . He had not conned anyone. He had not betrayed anyone or stolen anything. From a legal point of view, no one could be blamed for the crash itself. He had been thrown by chance among a group of men who meted out honours and wealth to each other. Almost in spite of himself, he had been pushed to the forefront. He would have been mad not to behave like the others. Why should he have refused? Why? In the name of what? Everyone was involved in some shady business, everyone lied, everyone schemed. The only difference was that some of them were hypocrites and others were not. He had been smug and open about the scandals; he had enjoyed them; he had wallowed in the mud with joyful, cynical delight. The next generation would make him pay dearly (he was thinking of Yves) not for the sin itself but for the brazenness of the sin. Perhaps . . . he didn't know . . . He felt very weary. He opened the window and took several deep breaths of warm air that seemed to stick to the back of his throat like tar. He thought about death. He was desperate. Renée? She had stopped caring about him a long time ago. And what about him? He had no illusions. It was so strange; he had always believed he was the only man in the entire world who had no illusions. He now realised that, on the contrary, no one had ever so carefully constructed such a wall of smoke and mirrors and lies around himself. He had believed that he was rich, powerful, loved. He discovered he was poor, weak and alone. Renée, like Détang, would drop him. He could sense it; he was sure of it. One day, Détang had told him: 'In life, like in a shipwreck, you have to cut off the hands of anyone who wants to hold on to your raft. Alone, you can float. If you waste time trying to save others, you're finished!'

He waited impatiently until daytime to go to the Détangs' house. They did not let him in. He was told that Détang had gone out. Renée, too, was nowhere in sight. He rushed around until nightfall. He warned all his friends. He telephoned London and New York. He desperately tried to save himself; he could, perhaps, have got some support from Détang by threatening him with exposure, with gossip, frightening him, but he could not bring himself to do that. It was too low, too cowardly. A surge of morality put an end to that temptation: 'Ah, no, not that, not that! That would be the final blow! I couldn't look Yves in the eye after doing something like that.' Yves . . . 'And what about Thérèse . . . ?' he said very softly. He found himself out in the street. He fell down on a bench, looking so pale that a passer-by walked over to him and asked if he were ill. He said no, thanked him, stood up and continued walking. He kept going, blindly roaming the streets of Paris. He found himself in his old neighbourhood. He only became aware of it when he was on the street where he used to live, that dingy street with its lace curtains at the windows, cats wailing in the gutters, the sound of the bells of Saint-Sulpice and the fountains in front of the church.

Like a sleepwalker, he crossed the road. From his key ring, he found the smallest one, it was flat and worn, the key he had not used for three years. He called out a name to the concierge, climbed up the three flights of stairs and opened a door. He was home.

4

Father and son left together the day war was declared, Bernard for the Lorraine region, Yves for an Air Force camp in Beauce. Just as you go into a house where you used to live, feel your way past the familiar furniture, so the women of France, without feeling shock or making any apparent effort, fell back into the way they behaved during that other war. They recalled, for example, that you must not go with your husband to the station when he is about to leave, that the final kiss must be given at home, far from the crowds, in a dimly lit room; they remembered that the soldier would walk away without looking back and that they must not shed any tears, as if they knew, instinctively, that they needed to save their tears for the future.

In the hall, Thérèse and Madame Jacquelain (very old now, her face pale and wrinkled, still very petite with innocent, misty blue eyes) kissed the men who were about to leave. Thérèse's two daughters, aged six and four and a half, hopped about, understanding nothing, and wanted to laugh, though they did not know why. At first, Geneviève, the elder girl, had seemed surprised and saddened by their departure. She had blond hair and grey eyes and looked like Bernard, while the younger one had her mother's smooth, soft skin and dark eyes. Geneviève had asked in a quiet, worried voice when Papa and Yves would be coming home. 'Soon,' they said. That completely reassured her and she began to laugh with her sister. Of the two men, it was Bernard who was leaving for the front, Bernard who would be in real danger, but 'there's the Maginot Line', thought Thérèse. Yves would be safe for three months. After that . . . the danger of flying, battles in the air, bombs . . . God! What a nightmare! Everything felt like a sinister, hazy dream: her husband had come back to her two weeks ago. By what miracle? In response to her fervent prayers? Only God knew why. He had come home – the moment she had been waiting for, for three years, the moment she had lived for, the moment she had imagined more than a thousand times: the sound of the key in the lock, a hesitant voice: 'Thérèse, are you there? . . .', that tall masculine figure in the entrance hall and suddenly, he was by her side, his face changed through suffering . . . Yes, she had pictured all of that in her dreams before living it . . . And the night that had followed . . . in her arms, her husband, shaking with sobs, cruel, furious, sharp sobs, in which wounded pride and remorse were mixed with love, then his falling asleep, relaxed and trusting, and her own feeling of divine peace! How sad, how very sad – only two weeks and then the war! She had lost Bernard twice. As for Madame Jacquelain, what was horrible, inhuman about this war, she thought to herself, was that the past was returning in a way that only happens in dreams, or, perhaps, in the afterlife, the way you imagine hell. Every now and again, she got a bit confused; she turned towards her grandson and called him 'Bernard' in a loving voice.

Even Thérèse felt a strange, foreboding sense of reliving the past. She was herself and someone else as well, the Thérèse of the past who was still alone, married for one night and soon to be a widow. Martial . . . The stifling hot little entrance hall seemed full of ghosts. The dead, normally so quiet and unobtrusive, suddenly seemed alive, reclaimed the place, the importance they had when they were still living. Everyone thought about them, missed them, whispered: 'If only they could see this . . .' or: 'Thank goodness they aren't here to see this.' Everyone talked about their virtues; they would prove themselves worthy of the dead. Bernard felt a deep, inexplicable sense of shame. He preferred the way he'd left in the past, that was for sure. 'I was innocent then,' he thought bitterly. 'I waltzed into that butchery as if I were going to a ball. Now, I know . . .' He thought back to a time when he had faith in everything: in the great wisdom of the government, the alliance with Great Britain, the superiority of bayonets over shells. He wondered if Yves had the same illusions. He did not understand Yves. Yves hated war. It was as if he were giving his life to something higher than war, something that might not even have anything to do with war. He was simply offering up his life.

Meanwhile, they continued to exchange banalities:

'You'll be so hot in the train!'

'Thérèse, you won't forget to post the letters I left on my desk, will you?'

'No, don't worry . . .'

Letters! Business! The crash! Money! The only good thing about the war was that it interrupted all the legal proceedings. But Thérèse would have very little money on which to live.

He walked over to his wife and kissed her on the forehead and cheek without saying a word. He left first, with Yves following behind; the door closed; Thérèse fell into a chair, her teeth clenched but without shedding a tear.

'It's too much. Twice in one lifetime, it's just too much!' said the elderly Madame Jacquelain, sounding passionately resentful, as if Thérèse were to blame for the war.

The children had said nothing for a while but now had recovered and were jumping around Thérèse, trying to take hold of her hands. She gently pushed them away and felt her heart breaking.

'Come on, Mama, come with us,' they said over and over again, trying to pull her up. She resisted, because her legs were shaking and because she was afraid to go back into the dining room they had just left, where she would see the ashtrays full of cigarette ends, the chairs pushed back from the table, the place settings of the two men, the men the war was taking away from her. She still had the memory of agony like this from before . . . The clothes that have to be put away, the books with a few ashes from a pipe between their pages, the scent of lavender and cigars that gradually fades away, the cold, empty bed.

The children looked up, and seeing their mother so still, were worried. And yet, she seemed composed and calm. Age and sorrow had caused a kind of light in her to die out, or rather, to shine only rarely, a dim light where, in the past, a bright flame had burned. She finally stood up with a sigh.

'Come along, my darlings, let's tidy up.'

Fortunately women still had that left. Fortunately their empty hands could be kept busy with folding, with caressing the clothes and the linen. Fortunately their tears could finally fall this evening, one by one, on to the mending. Fortunately there was the shopping to do, children to care for, dinner to make . . . Fortunately . . . how very fortunate the fate of women!

5

Two months after being mobilised, Bernard found himself in a small cold, grey town in Lorraine. War had not yet begun for him; he knew only one enemy – solitude, the worst of all, the enemy that comes from deep within your heart and overwhelms you, even in the middle of a crowd. Suddenly, the world had disappeared from view, just as the curtain in a theatre closes and instantly hides everything on the brilliantly lit stage; you are alone; you have to leave the theatre that was so warm and pleasant and where you could forget about life, whether you want to or not. You find yourself back on the dark streets, in a cold wind. For twenty years he had believed himself to be showered with good luck; he had had friends and money, experienced passion and pleasure. But now, there was nothing. Everything was gone. Everything that had been enchanting, superficial, light-hearted had disappeared, abandoning him. He did not have a penny. No power, no contacts, no mistress. He was alone, in a sad little town. The street was sinister, with dim lights, a bluish cast to the windows, a dull, relentless blue that caused a kind of despair and depression in your heart. Every now and then, the sound of the air raid sirens and nearby explosions announced the approach of an enemy plane. Bernard could go to the barracks, a hotel room or the dining room of the Grand Café. Normally, that was where he took shelter. He spoke to no one. He leafed through the newspapers from Paris; he listened to the gramophone.

It was there, one evening, that he learned of the death of his son.

He was alone; he had ordered a black coffee that he did not drink. Outside, it was raining. He was handed a damp telegram. The son of the hotel proprietor, a boy of ten, to whom he sometimes gave sweets, had not seen him come in since that morning. Knowing that Bernard often spent the evening at the Grand Café, it occurred to the boy he might find him there. He handed Bernard the telegram, smiled and looked at him shyly, inquisitively. Bernard, surprised, opened the envelope and read:

YVES PLANE CRASHED THIS MORNING AND CAUGHT FIRE BOURGES AIRFIELD STOP OUR SON KILLED STOP COME HOME STOP DO THE IMPOSSIBLE STOP THERESE

He looked up, noticed the boy who had not moved; he looked very frightened.

'What is this lad doing here?' he thought.

'Is something wrong, Monsieur?' the child asked; he liked Bernard and saw he had gone pale; the officer's face was slowly turning ash grey. Bernard did not reply; he took a few pennies out of his pocket and mechanically pushed them into the boy's hand. The boy ran off. Bernard picked up the telegram again. Once more his sorrow caused deep incredulity to rush through him, then, little by little, passionate denial. No! His son could not be dead. No! Not that. Not his son. Dead without honour, in a stupid accident! Why, an accident? Why the plane? Oh, he never should have allowed . . . He knew better than anyone why some aircraft were lost in accidents that seemed inexplicable, why there weren't enough tanks or armoured vehicles, why they didn't have enough weapons, the reason there was chaos everywhere, why, why . . . He knew. He looked around him, horrified. He felt as if everyone had guessed, everyone was thinking: 'He killed his own son.' He sat there motionless, eyes staring out blankly, very pale, too weak to stand up or leave this noisy place. Now he felt despair run through him, an emotion that was barely human, something primal, savage, that roared through him in a wave. 'My son, my little boy, my child, my only son . . . It isn't possible! It can't be you . . . God would not allow such a thing! Is there a God? There must be, because He is punishing me. Let Him punish me, chastise me, kill me, but not you! He must let you live! No, no, it's too late. I can't hope for a miracle. He is dead. I'm going mad . . . It's not my fault. That business with the planes has nothing to do with this . . . Accidents happen every day and I never ever thought . . . But now that idea is haunting me, killing me . . .'

He threw back his head violently and noticed that the barmaid was looking at him with curiosity. She knew him well; she thought he was a handsome, likeable man.

'Not bad news, I hope?' she asked.

He said nothing for a moment, looking lost.

'I'm afraid so,' he finally replied. 'Do you think I could telephone Paris? Can you get me a line to Paris.'

He gave her the telephone number of his apartment and waited.

An hour passed. Some officers nearby were playing dominos; others were reading; some were in the midst of noisy discussions. You could hear the knocking of billiard balls, doors banging closed in the kitchen. Someone had put on the gramophone that played an old tune, an insistent, vulgar song, with words that kept repeating:

Don't you worry, Bouboule!

His neighbours automatically started singing along:

Don't you worry, Bouboule,
Don't make your life a hell
And everything'll turn out well

Bernard was called to the phone. Inside the glass booth, with graffiti on the sides, scribbles such as 'Titine and Suzette' and 'I love Lili', with those obscene drawings and the noise from the café all around him, he heard Thérèse's soft trembling voice; she confirmed the fatal accident (up until now he had kept hold of a frantic hope that it was all a mistake, that the cross he had to bear might be far off in the future).

'What about his body?' he heard himself ask. 'Have they recovered his body?'

Yes, his remains had been saved and pulled out of the burning plane. Both his legs were broken but his face was intact and two small photographs he kept close to his heart had even survived.

'Ah, really? Really?' Bernard whispered eagerly, finding a kind of mad consolation in the thought that his son loved him, that his son kept photos of his parents with him, for they could not be any other photos.

'One of you and one of me, Thérèse? Our child had our photos with him?'

'Mine, yes,' said Thérèse very quietly, with difficulty and with infinite pity. 'The other one . . .'

She hesitated.

'The other one was of Martial.'

'Ah?' said Bernard.

She could hear the husky little sob that made his voice shake.

'I'll see you tomorrow. I'll ask for leave,' he said very quickly. 'When will we . . . ?'

He could not say the words: 'When will we bury him?'

She understood.

'Thursday,' she said. 'Eleven o'clock.'

They said goodbye. He slowly opened the door. He heard two officers nearby speaking to the barmaid:

'One of my friends who's studied the question tells me there's a group of old crates that have a fatal tendency to crash to the ground the first time they try to take off. Apparently some of the parts were bought from America and didn't fit our planes.'

'That poor young man,' the other one said.

They both suddenly fell silent when they saw Bernard. He realised that the barmaid could not have resisted the temptation to read the telegram he had left on the table and had told the officers the news. They both stood up respectfully when Bernard passed by them. He saluted them and left. Outside, the street was quiet, cold, grey; the fog that drifted over the river spread a sickly sweet, damp odour over the marshland. Shadows covered the town. In the sky, tiny stars, so far away . . . Behind him, the shrill, tinny sound of the record that was almost finished playing:

Don't you worry, Bouboule,
You're the kind who knows what's what
Just stay cool and you won't get shot
They'll get your mates, but what the hell
. . . .
Don't you worry! . . . and everything'll turn out well

'Yes, every time a man said: "As for me, I actually don't give a damn . . .", every time a man thought: "If I don't take advantage someone else will", every time a woman whispered: "You are completely ridiculous . . . Look around you . . .", every time, every time . . . and without realising it, every one of them helped to cut short an innocent life. When I blindly signed the contract that Détang drew up, when I cynically thought: "I don't want to know the ins and outs of this deal. I'm just an honest go-between . . .", every time I pocketed some money, you could say that I was sabotaging with my own hands the plane that killed my son. But what if his accident only happened by chance? What if my conscience is making me feel guilty for a crime I did not commit? But then, there will be other planes that crashed because of me, other children who died because of me, Bernard Jacquelain, a man who was no worse and no more dishonest than anyone else, but who loved pleasure and money. Just like everyone else, my God, just like everyone else! Not wanting to be taken for a ride, refusing to make a drama out of our dirty deals, our little schemes, not accepting the worst and believing:

Don't you worry, Bouboule,
. . . And everything'll turn out well!'

6

The army was beaten in Flanders, beaten at Dunkirk, beaten on the banks of the Aisne. There were no supplies left. It was only the civilians who clung to insurmountable hope in their hearts; in the cafés in the Lot-et-Garonne, they even tried to establish an imaginary line of defence south of the Loire, but the soldiers no longer had any illusions. The soldiers knew that the army had lost; they could even see the day approaching when there would be no more army, when amid the mass of an entire population in flight, soldiers would disappear, just as the debris of a ship sinks to the bottom of the sea during a storm. Regiments had lost their leaders; groups of soldiers wandered about, adrift among the people who were fleeing. Ten men who had miraculously escaped the enemy walked behind an exhausted officer; his bearded face was thin, his eyes burned with fever. The officer was Bernard Jacquelain.

After the battle of Dunkirk, in which he had fought with a kind of savage despair, he took the path along the sand dunes, followed by these ten men. The rest of the regiment had been taken prisoner. For four days they had lived in the dunes, without food, but suffering especially from a lack of water; never, thought Bernard, never would he forget that hideous thirst, intensified by the sight of the sea. Just as the Germans were about to reach them, they had thrown themselves into the water, swimming along the coastline, beneath the bombs, in the unimaginable chaos of the sea: floating all around them were barrels of supplies from the British Army, wreckage from the battered boats, the living and the dead. Finally, Bernard and his ten companions had made it back to the lines still held by the French. But that very night they were attacked by enemy tanks and forced to flee, and, since then, their retreat had continued among the Belgian, Dutch and French vehicles that were beating a path towards the south, along with lost children, women forced to give birth in ditches, common criminals running free on the roads, ministerial cars carrying archives, government trucks packed so full of official files that some of the documents flew out of the windows. Cannon, carts, baby carriages, tandems, wheelbarrows, herds of cows, machine guns covered in foliage, exhausted horses, men . . .

Sometimes the civilians hurled insults at them; in a house where they asked for something to eat, the refugees who were camping out in the kitchen shouted that it was shameful, that the soldiers had only got what they deserved and that they hadn't even tried to fight back. But most often, people simply watched them pass by with gloomy indifference.

In one village, right in front of an inn, a little boy who was playing in the dust got up, went over to Bernard, blushed and asked him if he would like a glass of beer.

'My mama's the owner of the café. She told me to offer you something to drink, because you're a soldier, like Papa . . . 'Cause we don't know what's happened to him,' the child said sadly.

For a long time, Bernard stared at the handsome little boy with dark eyes who looked like Yves. Or perhaps he was just seeing him that way? Everything reminded him of his son.

'Would you like a beer?' the boy asked again, surprised by Bernard's silence.

'Yes, thank you very much,' Bernard finally said, 'I'm very thirsty.'

The child disappeared into the house and came back a moment later carrying a small bottle of beer and a heavy glass. Bernard drank some, then took a few small coins out of his pocket, but the boy refused to take them.

'Mama said that she wants you to have it for free.'

Bernard sat on a bench alone, in the sunshine. It was a stormy day; in the distance, thunder continuously rumbled, and anyone who thought they were hearing cannon fire was afraid.

The soldiers had found something to eat and wanted to share a melon and a hunk of bread with Bernard. But he couldn't swallow a thing. He chewed on a piece of the bread then left it on the bench beside him. Then he covered his face with both hands and pretended to be asleep. His fellow soldiers studied him for a moment. A big lad who looked like a farmer cut his bread in slices before putting them into his mouth from the end of a knife; he stopped and looked at Jacquelain:

'Poor guy!'

They realised that Jacquelain was crying; a tear ran down through his locked fingers. The men tactfully turned away and pretended to be telling jokes, laughing among themselves to give their lieutenant time to pull himself together.

After a few moments, Bernard seemed calmer; he lit his pipe and fell into a deep, bitter trance. An endless wave of cars streamed past along the road. He could see pale, exhausted faces covered in dust. Children were asleep, curled up in a ball on top of suitcases. A horse-drawn wagon passed by in which some old people (evacuees from an old folks' home) were dozing on the benches, their heads resting on bundles of sheets. Then there was an ambulance, going at the same speed as the other vehicles. A small Citroën went by, full of crying children: the lad driving looked about fifteen; there was no adult with them. Then it was time to set off again. The

Germans were getting closer. They were marching towards Paris and the French Army was fleeing ahead of them. The little group formed by Bernard and his ten men also took the road to Paris. Some people were saying there would be a battle at the Seine.

'What battle?' thought Bernard. 'The battle has already been fought and lost. And it didn't happen yesterday, nor, as everyone believed, on the day the Germans entered Belgium. The Battle of France was lost twenty years ago.'

They kept on walking. Night was falling. The air was an unbreathable mixture of dust and the stench of petrol. Bernard walked on:

'Lost . . . lost . . .' he said over and over again, quietly. 'We've lost . . .'

The earth was growing darker, but the June sky above was lit by a dim glow, and in the tender dusk, enemy planes flew overhead, soaring unchallenged, masters of the heavens.

7

At ten o'clock, after receiving an order – no one knew where from – the long column of refugees was forced to leave the main road that led directly to Paris. One group turned back the way they had come, another was sent on a detour towards Melun. Bernard thought he would rejoin the French troops in the forest of Fontainebleau, but he very quickly realised he was wrong: the forest was full of refugees and the main body of the army was retreating south. The forest looked like an enormous gypsy encampment. People were sleeping, eating, dying on the mossy grass (the forest had been bombed).

Apart from the melon and stale bread they had eaten at midday, Bernard and his soldiers had been unable to find any more food. Bernard did not feel hungry; he was no longer in pain. He had only one desire: to sleep. But behind him, the soldiers were whispering:

'My God! Some soup! A glass of wine!'

One of them, the farmer, shouted:

'This forest is so big!'

Bernard sighed. He had crossed this forest of Fontainebleau in his car so quickly and so often, in the past. It had been a forest full of lilies of the valley, couples in love, people taking leisurely strolls, but now it had become a place to take shelter (and how precarious it was!) for so many desperate people. The night was full of voices calling out, vain cries:

'Mama, I'm scared!' 'Jacques, Jacques! Has anyone seen my little boy Jacques? I lost him when the bombs started to fall.' 'Can anyone give me a litre of petrol?' 'Can you spare a bottle of milk for a child?' 'Can you lend me a blanket for my sick father?' 'Monsieur, Monsieur, my husband was wounded in the bombing. He can't hear me; he isn't replying. Where can we get help? He's going to die.'

Bernard walked quickly away, taking such great strides that his exhausted men could no longer keep up with him.

'Will we ever get out of this damned forest?' they asked.

'I think we're going around in circles, Lieutenant,' said one of the soldiers.

'No. Follow me. I know a house where we can spend the night. It isn't far from here.'

They found themselves in the middle of a clearing shaped like a star. He hesitated, got his bearings, then took the path to the left.

'Follow me! Be brave!'

They were headed towards the Détangs' house. It was close by, down the road, an opulent house full of soft beds, wide divans, cupboards stuffed full of food, wine cellars with champagne. Where were the owners? They had fled, no doubt, as soon as they caught a whiff of disaster. They must have crossed the Loire without any problem. Behind them, the bridges had blown up, throwing fiery stones, twisted metal and, sometimes, human remains upwards, into the sky. But the Détangs would be safe. No doubt they were crossing the border at this very moment, with their money, their jewellery, their trunks, leaving everyone else to manage as best they could, the others who lacked their cunning, who had not known how to invest their fortune so it was safely abroad while there was still time, the people who had not understood, not taken precautions, who had kept faith.

Perhaps Bernard was wrong? Détang could very well waver over what he should do: flee, since his political position was compromised, in danger, or take the attitude that he was someone who 'does his duty right to the end', counting on a future of profitable changes in alliances? Bernard could just hear him:

'First of all, do not be a fool! Coldly weigh up the pros and cons. Think of me. *My* situation . . . *My* way of life. *My* power. *My* house. *My* wife.'

But most importantly, there was Renée's money, money she had placed abroad a long time ago. Nothing could prevail over that. Influence, contacts, reputation, all took second place to money. Had Bernard forgotten that? He should have remembered.

He took a few more steps.

'We're here,' he said to his men.

It was a very beautiful house, all white, surrounded by a large estate. Bernard pushed open the gate. It was not locked. The front door wouldn't open.

'It doesn't matter,' said Bernard. 'There's a shutter that doesn't close properly on the ground floor. Here it is. Let's go in. The sitting room is this way.'

'Is this your house, Lieutenant?' asked one of the men.

'My house? No. It belongs to one of my friends. There should be plenty of food. You can eat all of it, if the refugees haven't got here before us.'

They walked into the sitting room, in single file, their heavy army boots creaking on the beautiful parquet floor. The windows were carefully blacked out by long, dark velvet curtains that were drawn across the casements. They could safely put the lights on. The chandeliers shone softly, lighting up the enormous rooms that were in the most terrible disorder. The Détangs had certainly gone away. Everything shouted it out. Bits of string, wrapping paper thrown on the floor. Raymond's desk empty, its drawers wide open. How many letters and compromising documents had been pulled out of this desk and hastily thrown into a suitcase, or torn up and burned. Bernard raised the shutter on the fireplace, saw the remains of a recent fire and smiled.

Here was Renée's little sitting room, and her jewellery box, too heavy to carry, which had been emptied; open boxes were strewn all over the floor. Bernard imagined the jewellery sewn up in a soft leather bag and hidden between Renée's breasts, her soft, cold breasts. Oh, God, to detest her, despise her, and still love her! She had been his downfall.

'Thérèse . . .' he whispered, as if to exorcise Renée's memory.

He continued leading the men towards the dining room. All the silver was gone, the dressers empty. The Détangs had forgotten nothing. Their car must have been full to bursting. If a lot of people had run away with so many belongings, it was hardly surprising that the journey was very slow and difficult . . .

'Well,' thought Bernard, 'they spread the evil ways that, in the past, were the exclusive privilege of a small, select circle, who by that very fact could not do too much harm. They democratised vice and standardised corruption. Everyone has become a schemer, a gambler, a profiteer. And hence . . . a traffic jam in which the guilty had to suffer along with everyone else. There is a kind of ironic, bitter justice in all these events. Ironic and terrible,' he thought.

The soldiers, dumbstruck at first, had also begun to feel the instinct to pillage rise up in them.

'I'm telling you, it's contagious,' murmured Bernard.

They had found the kitchen and broken open the cupboards; they came back into the dining room carrying tins of foie gras, preserves, sugar, coffee, chocolate; two of them went down to find the wine cellar.

'It's further down, to the left,' shouted Bernard. 'Push the door hard!'

And when they returned, carrying a lot of bottles, he quietly said:

'Eat. Drink, my poor lads. All this is for you.'

Suddenly, even he was hungry. He cut a slice of pâté, drank a glass of champagne and, leaving his men at the table, left the room and walked through the empty house for a long time.

He went into Renée's bedroom; he walked over to the large bed. Everywhere there was chaos, visible signs of panic. The sheets had been dragged on to the floor; he could picture her semi-naked body leaping out from under the covers when Détang had come to wake her up. She must have run, still undressed, to where she hid her jewellery, taken it out of the box, hidden it between her breasts. She had not been concerned about a single living soul; she had felt sorry for no one. Not a child, not a dog, not an old servant . . . All she loved was her jewellery, as cold and dazzling as she was.

'Did I really love her?' Bernard wondered out loud.

He seemed to be waking from a dream. Her body . . . yes. Her shoulders, her hips, yes . . . But then there was her mother with the eyes of a Madam in a brothel, her bastard of a husband . . . He pictured her lying in his arms and remembered the way she made love, had love made to her; there was something brutal about it, something cynical, greedy and harsh within her . . .

He walked through the next room; it contained the wardrobes where she kept her dresses. A few of them had been thrown to the floor; he kicked them away, thought she must have taken the most beautiful ones with her. Tomorrow, or next month, in some nightclub in Lisbon, or Rio, or New York, she would be dancing, graceful, indifferent; men would court her; she would talk about the awful times she had been through during the fall of France; she would make everyone feel sorry for her: 'We left everything behind, lost it all . . . We feared for our lives . . .' Their lives, their precious lives . . . Why had he ever met this woman? Why had he listened to her? And yet, he still had feelings for her. She had penetrated his being like poisonous venom.

'I'm having an attack of moral virtue because I'm tired and miserable,' he thought sadly. 'But if things had worked out . . . The war will end. Everything will settle down. People like Raymond Détang will always find a way to swim to safety.

'And I . . .' No! There was the death of his son. Directly or indirectly, he was responsible.

When he went back into the dining room, his men were asleep. Some were stretched out on the floor, others had not even left the table and were snoring, their heads resting on their hands. None of them had even had the strength to look for a bed. He did the same; he threw some cushions down on the rug near the window and lay down, his face hidden in the crook of his arm. But he couldn't sleep. He kept thinking about his son. How much time he had lost, how many years when he could have loved him . . . He had always been too busy with his love affairs and dreams of wealth. His child had been growing up at his side; he had barely noticed him. He had sometimes looked down at him and thought vaguely: 'When he's fifteen, I'll take an interest in him . . .' Then: 'When he's eighteen, I'll teach him about life. I'll make a man of him.'

He fell asleep and dreamt of his son. The boy looked at him but did not recognise him; he let Bernard walk over to him, then leapt back and ran away into the distance. He ran so fast when he was twelve . . . his black hair falling down over his eyes. He also dreamt of Martial Brun. He often thought about him now, ever since he learned that a small photograph of Martial had been found on his son's body. Why? What did Martial symbolise to Yves? In his dream, he found himself murmuring: 'You know, he wasn't so great. There were thousands like him. He fought well in the war, but I . . .' He chased after Yves' shadow, Yves' ghost, but Yves could not hear him. In one leap, he jumped over a metal gate that jangled softly. As he fell to the ground on the other side, he landed on the gravel that crunched loudly beneath his feet, crunched . . .

Bernard suddenly woke up, rubbed his eyes and heard the sound of boots on the sand in the garden. In the clear June night, he could see two, three, five, ten men coming towards the house. Soldiers? He leaned forward. There was something odd about their uniforms, something he did not recognise at first but which, suddenly, stopped him from shouting out. Green uniforms, long boots . . . it was the Germans, the Germans, so soon.

He bent down, shook the man next to him by the shoulder, putting his hand over his mouth at the same time to stifle his cry of surprise. The man woke up, took a moment to understand, then whispered:

'Right.'

'Wake the others,' said Bernard very quietly.

The Germans were already in the entrance hall. The Frenchmen waited, helpless and anxious.

'Let them take us and get it over with,' one of them finally said. 'The war is over.'

But his comrades did not want to surrender:

'*I* have a wife and kids!'

'Who's going to take care of my old parents?'

They surrounded Bernard, expecting him to save them. They were trapped like rats. He was the one who knew the house. Was there another way out?

Yes, the servants' entrance.

'Follow me.'

But when they got to the kitchen door, they could hear someone speaking German. They went back up into the dining room. Bernard thought for a moment, then said:

'We'll barricade ourselves in here with the furniture, then I'll open fire. When I start, you can get out through the window. Wait for the right moment and get away as fast as you can. I'll keep on firing. They won't all chase after you because they'll think there are several men defending the house. You might get caught, but that's the way it is! There's nothing else we can do.'

'You'll be killed, Lieutenant.'

'It doesn't matter,' said Bernard. He walked over to the window, counted quietly: 'One, two, three.' At the same time, he fired towards the enemy and his ten men jumped out of the house on to the lawn. The Germans returned fire. One of the men was hit and fell to the ground. The others made it to the woods. Bernard continued firing. As he had predicted, the main body of the troop remained where they were. Two or three soldiers rushed off after the men who had escaped. A hail of bullets broke through the glass panes but, miraculously, Bernard was not hit. He continued firing. His mind was a blank. He finally felt a sense of peace.

The battle lasted for quite some time. When it stopped, when the Germans had broken down the doors, they found Bernard, leaning against the wall, arms crossed over his chest, his useless weapon thrown to the floor at his feet. He was not wounded. He surrendered with no further resistance. That same night, he was sent to join a group of prisoners of war in the forest of Fontainebleau and left for Germany.

8

Unhappy? No. He was not unhappy. His fellow prisoners, like himself, were still not used to thinking of their lives as real. They were living a nightmare that would end, suddenly, in a flash, just as it had begun. Someone would unlock the doors; the barbed wire fences would be taken down. They would be told: 'You are free.' Every evening, they thought: 'That's one day less . . .' Another day that had ended; a day that brought them closer to freedom. The most difficult moment was when they woke up. In their dreams, they were reunited with their families, on a French beach at the seaside; they could see their wives smiling, hear their children's voices. Then they would open their eyes and see their sleeping quarters with the rough, wooden walls. Every morning at dawn, they would hear the murmurings of the priests who were prisoners as they said Mass in front of a small portable altar at the foot of their beds. It was like being back in the monastery, or the barracks, or the worst years of boarding school . . . At forty years old . . . 'It's hard at our age,' said the man next to Bernard, a man with white hair and a weary, worn face. There was talk of freeing the soldiers who had already fought in 1914, but there was talk of so many things. The atmosphere in the camp made it easy to believe in dreams, in illusions, in lies; they whispered the strangest stories to each other: 'You're going home, you're lucky,' the young men told Bernard, the ones who had left school and knew nothing of life but the hell of Dunkirk or the vain rush to escape along the roads of France and who now celebrated their twentieth birthday in these fields of snow. Going home? Home to what? How would they, these beaten soldiers, be greeted back in France? They had no idea; they could not imagine it. Each envisaged his return according to his own desires and his own anger. Neither love nor hate had died down within them. Quite the opposite, those feelings grew more and more heated, poisoning them with violent intensity. Sometimes, in the silence of the night, they could hear a prisoner sigh, sob, curse some unknown person, or call out the name of an invisible woman in despair.

The camp was located in a snowfield. It was the first winter the prisoners spent in Germany. It felt as if winter and the war would never end. Sometimes flakes of snow would fall softly and swiftly; sometimes it blew through their shelter as hard and round as grains of sand; but there was always snow, with its silence and a melancholy, blinding whiteness that stretched to the horizon; they had not seen the earth underneath since September. There were no forests, no towns, no mountains in sight. Barely a few undulations, shallow hollows, folds in the white shroud that in summer must surely be meadows, fields, plains? The prisoners did not know; they had arrived at the camp last autumn. Far in the distance, a sparkling path looked like a railway track or a stream covered in ice. They studied it for a long time. It was a road, a way out towards the world of the living. They were not alive. Not entirely. They automatically carried out their daily tasks. They worked, read, went for walks, ate, organised games and performances, but only a part of them was really involved; the other part slept, but it was a troubled sleep from which they would only awaken on that blessed day (when would it come? when?), the day they would be told: 'Well, it's all over. You can go home.'

'When? My God, when? When will this trial be over?' Sometimes Bernard thought that if it were possible to cut open the hearts of his companions, you would find those words engraved on their bleeding flesh. But they rarely spoke them out loud. They were ashamed. Life in the camp had reduced them to a strange kind of uniformity: they all looked the same. They only became themselves, only regained their unique personalities when carrying out tasks from their former professions, when the shoemaker put new soles on a pair of boots, when a priest said Mass, when a teacher prepared a talk for the student prisoners who wanted to continue their studies, or when letters and packages arrived from France.

Then, the jealous men, whose faces were normally grey and gloomy, allowed their torment to show; the ones in love would stare out into space for a long time, their eyes shining, lips slightly parted; the ambitious men who felt that others, in Paris, were usurping their positions, bit their clenched fists in silent rage, and the simple men, nodding their heads, would quietly say:

'Seems like my wife is having a hard time getting by, all alone . . .'

Or:

'It's cold back home too, they say.'

Or even:

'The cows are all dying . . . Everything is in chaos . . . The baby's nearly ten months old. And to think I've never seen him . . .'

Someone would then reply:

'Don't think about it, come on, my boy. That'll get you nowhere . . .'

Each of them would then retreat into his own dream. That did not prevent them from having lively discussions, laughing, playing cards or chess, or, among the intellectuals, passionate arguments over what they had read in the past, plays they had seen ('Do you remember Dullin in *Richard III*? One night, in 1930, Ludmilla Pitoëff . . .'), but the deepest part of each prisoner's heart, the part of the soul that is immutable, impossible to share with others, that part still slept, taking refuge in the kind of sleep that was their salvation, as well as in dreams, or in those desperate little words, the question that obsessed them, repeated almost mechanically and to which there was no reply (at least, not yet . . .): 'When? My God, when?'

The long evening passed. The snow fell. Every few minutes, a beam would light up the sky and then the barbed wire fences with all their sharp little spikes would sparkle, like a forest of cactuses.

They could hear the crunching of boots on the frozen ground, the sound of rifle butts striking the hollow earth, brief orders shouted out, a drum roll in the distance. Outside, everything was dark. It was the time of day when the prisoners who had lived in the cities thought about the towns they had left behind, the clusters of lights along the Paris boulevards, the tall white billboards outside the theatres, the gleaming train stations, the reddish haze in the Paris sky . . . A bad moment, another bad moment to get through. It was the time when they began to confide in one another, shyly, revealing half-secrets. No one spoke about himself, nor of his family, but in the abstract, deliberately coldly, impersonally, starting a conversation that always revolved around the same theme: 'When will we finally go home? When will the war end?' Each of them endlessly sought some meaning in such a cruel ordeal. The priests (there were many of them in the camp) were the only ones who felt peace, certainty: suffering was a gift from God. 'Rejoice, ye who suffer,' they would say. But the men whom the century held in its snare did not understand; they were indignant, they revolted and continued to seek the meaning of their pain with difficulty, in vain. They beat their fists, so to speak, against a silent wall; their blows returned no sound.

Sometimes, Bernard would grow pale and cover his eyes with his hand.

'What's the matter? Have you seen a ghost?' one of his fellow prisoners would ask, looking at him.

Yes, a ghost . . . This was the time when ghosts appeared. The ghosts of the dead and the missing invisibly filled the camp. He felt like crying and begging forgiveness.

9

When Thérèse got out of bed, the city was still plunged in darkness. It was the second winter of the war, cold and full of endless snow. No one swept it away any more, and since there were very few cars, the snow did not get crushed beneath their wheels, as it had done in the past; it formed a kind of blackish mire that seeped through worn shoes and froze the feet of the passers-by. There was much poverty in Paris; the city still hid it, though. It was not visible in the streets which, in spite of the war and defeat, retained a look of carefree opulence. Poverty was hidden, out of shame, inside all the houses that had no fires lit; it took a seat around dining tables with little food on them. The manual workers and farmers were less affected than the middle classes, the skilled workers, those with small private means who, like Madame Jacquelain, had first watched their income disappear, then their capital; now, she had only what Thérèse could give her to live on, and that was not much. Thérèse was receiving the allowance she was entitled to as the wife of a prisoner of war and she had a few thousand francs that Monsieur Brun had put away in a savings bank in his daughter's name.

Living off this minuscule income would take a miracle, but Thérèse performed that miracle day after day; her daughters had more or less enough to eat; they were warmly dressed – so many sweaters had been unravelled, washed, re-knitted, so many dresses patiently mended and underclothes patched up in the silence of the night! The only thing she could not manage to get was coal, and on the harshest winter days, the children and the aged Madame Jacquelain stayed in bed in their freezing cold little apartment. Madame Jacquelain complained. 'I would happily change places with you,' thought Thérèse. Her legs ached after standing for so long on those dark mornings; she waited in front of shops that were half empty, ran her errands, stood in the metro and every day climbed up the five flights of stairs to their apartment. In the evening, after the dishes were done and the children asleep, she would allow herself a moment's rest, a respite; she would sit down at the empty dining room table; she would hide her head in her hands and imagine the moment he would come home, the moment she would hear Bernard's footsteps behind the door, his voice, his soft little cough. She loved him so much! Neither separation, nor time, nor age – her greying hair – nor Bernard's infidelity, nor everything she had guessed about his life, none of it was stronger than her love. She sometimes reproached herself for thinking more about her husband, who was alive, than her son, who was dead. But her poor little Yves no longer needed anything except her tears and her prayers, while Bernard perhaps depended more on her than her son ever had. What was most important was for him to remain alive, to make sure he had parcels, tobacco, sweet treats if ever it was possible, warm clothes for winter. He needed newspapers and books and, most especially, even so far away, he needed to feel her love, the devotion she had sworn to him. She thought back to her rival who had gone away. 'Has he forgotten her? Does he still think about her?' She had always been jealous: her heart was filled with jealousy and loyal tenderness. Alone in the small dining room with its dark corners, she imagined the letters she would write to him, letters full of passion, reproaches and cries of love. But then her gaze would wander to the mirror above the mantelpiece, and she would see her face, her dull skin, her hair that was starting to look like silvery foam (the same hair Madame Pain used to have) and her wide, anxious eyes, burning and red from her tears. 'It's too late . . . It's ridiculous, I'm an old woman. I didn't manage to keep him when I was twenty.' It was that feeling of embarrassment and regret that forced her to hold back when she wrote to him. Her letters were brief, in spite of herself. 'If he's changed, if this ordeal has made him mature, he'll understand, but if he's stayed the same, what's the point?' she thought. She would never tell him how difficult everything was, never. She did everything in her power to reassure him: 'I'm getting by. We want for nothing. Your mother and the girls are as happy as they can be during this sad time. As for me . . .'

She stopped. What could she tell him? She was a woman with no hope and no future. She was no longer young or beautiful. 'I gave up everything for you, to help you,' she sometimes thought sadly, but without bitterness. There was not a drop of hostility in her heart. But she had no illusions: she was old. If war had not broken out, if death and mourning, suffering and work had not destroyed her strength and her health, she might have had a few more good years after Bernard came back to her . . . The memory of that made her come alive again: 'He came back once. I thought I had lost him but by some miracle, we were together again, I got him back. And just when I feel the most despair, he'll be given back to me again!' She stood tall; she carried on with her daily chores, endlessly interrupted, endlessly repeated; she took up her darning (but where would she find any wool tomorrow?), she carried on mending (but this was her last spool of thread), she calculated how many ration tickets were left for meat until the end of the month; she patched up the worn-out slippers. Every now and again, she got up and went to throw a shawl, an overcoat, on to one of the beds, for it was horribly cold. Every so often, when her eyes were too sore and swollen, she would stand up, switch off the light, pull back the dark curtain and watch the sleeping city, the inexpressibly dark, silent city. It was winter, wartime; neither would ever end, or so it seemed. There would never be another spring, or peace. The street lamps along the empty avenues would never be lit again. The deserted buildings would never come to life again. Never. And yet, in the centre of Paris and for the privileged few, life went on, more or less the same as before the war. There were still expensive restaurants, women who wore perfume, brilliant theatrical performances, well-fed men. But in these houses, beneath every roof, sitting beside every lamp, there were so many people in mourning, so many tears shed, so many bitter memories!

Lost in thought, Thérèse tapped her thimble against the frozen window pane. It was still snowing. The snow fell on to the prisoner of war camps, on to the barbed wire fences, on to the deep forests she imagined in the heart of Germany. What was happening to him, her prisoner of war? Would she ever see him again? And when, my God, when? When would this war ever end?

The clock ticked in the silence. Thérèse sighed and went back to her sewing.

They were short of money. The two women pooled their resources; everything that could be sold was carefully examined and weighed up (in Paris, there was a market for silver, gold, precious gems). A few small pieces of jewellery, some silver spoons, the gold necklaces that belonged to the little girls, Bernard's cuff links and his watch, all these things disappeared one by one. They hid from the children whenever they needed to take something out of the cases where they had been locked away at the beginning of the war. 'The girls are starting to understand; we mustn't upset them,' their grandmother said. But she soon realised that nothing amused Geneviève and Colette more than these secret meetings, the whispering of the grown-ups who rifled through chests of drawers and held lockets, rings, silverware in their trembling hands. Geneviève, who was blonde, cheerful and cheeky, jumped with joy as she said over and over again:

'This is such fun, my God, it's such fun!'

All these treasures were sorted through with great care; they saved faded ribbons and Thérèse entrusted her daughters with the task of carefully folding them up: everything was useful, the smallest bit of thread, a needle, a metal button. Everything was in short supply. For certain middle-class French families, life was becoming like surviving a shipwreck. They had to ration coffee, chocolate, cheese; a pin discovered in the hem of a skirt was a lucky find; they saved old rags; they hoarded old newspapers. For the children, it was an amusing, endless new game. Thérèse sold everything that had any value at all. She returned that evening with a bit of money in her handbag: the next day was safe; the children would have enough to eat. She looked for work, but since she couldn't leave Madame Jacquelain, who was almost always ill, or the little girls, who were still too young, she could not get a job. One day she remembered that in the past, she had been unrivalled at making flowers out of felt and velvet. She spent her very last ration tickets to buy some thread and used some old gloves to make a little bonnet that the hat maker on the corner bought from her. Thank God! Women still liked to dress well. People still found the means to buy accessories. And so Thérèse managed to earn a bit of money.

10

Winter ended. At first, no one believed they would ever have enough sun and light to make them forget the harshness of the past season, but summer brought Thérèse other problems: both of the children had caught whooping cough and since they were also anaemic, they were taking a long time to recover. It was stifling hot in the small apartment.

In August, Thérèse saw that the children were getting worse, so she sold her winter coat. It was twelve years old and made of grey squirrel, one of the rare gifts Bernard had given her. Next winter, she would have to see. Perhaps it would not be so cold? She must not think of the future, just deal with what was most urgent. Furs were selling well; she got enough money for her coat to rent a small country cottage, about two hundred kilometres from Paris. She settled in there with the two children and Madame Jacquelain. It was so peaceful! There was a small garden, a bench on the lawn, a little stream that flowed through a meadow. For the first time since the start of the war, since Bernard had left and her son had died, she felt almost happy. Her happiness was tinged with sadness, but she was calm and confident. She had worked so hard; she had given so much of herself that she had atoned, or so she felt, for all of Bernard's sins. Her love was not blind:

emotions felt with eyes wide open are the most deep-rooted and the most painful. She had not forgotten her suffering, how he had abandoned her, but she forgave him, and with all her heart. He too had suffered. She imagined his nights in the stalag, and his thoughts. He would come home. But what would be in his heart?

'It's just that we don't have enough time to start our life together all over again,' she thought. 'If I were twenty years younger . . . But at our age, the furrow has already been marked out; we have to follow it to the end, whatever the cost, and too bad if the earth has been poorly prepared and is full of pebbles. Too bad; it's too late. The bread we eat will be hard and bitter. Too bad for us. We did not sow our fields well.'

She knew, though, that she had nothing for which she could reproach herself, but she accepted the mysterious fact that in marriage, the innocent person must often pay as dearly as the guilty one. But she also had faith; her own efforts, her tears, the death of Yves would not be in vain; they would bear fruit. Perhaps in the near future? Perhaps only for their children, when she and Bernard were gone? She did not know. Such thoughts ran endlessly through her mind. She was a woman whose face was tired, whose hair was turning grey, but she was always calm and smiling; no one could have guessed that she still had so much passion within her. One day, she found a photograph from the past among some old letters. It was a group photo of Martial, Bernard as a teenager, Renée and herself; it must have been taken around 1911 or 1912. Her entire past, all her old memories swept through her at once. She called her daughters to show them the picture: 'Come here, come quickly and see your Papa when he was young!' Her eyes were shining, her lips trembled, but she smiled.

'You were so pretty, Mama,' said the little Geneviève, 'and you're still pretty.'

Thérèse glanced at the mirror and thought that, in fact, she was still quite attractive. Then she smiled sadly. Alas, that was not enough . . . For she could not imagine that Bernard had aged, that Bernard had changed as she had. But whatever he looked like, she loved him.

It was autumn. The house was rented until the 1st November. Thérèse sometimes wondered if she would not be wiser to stay in the countryside all winter. She would be able to get food and keep warm more easily than in Paris, but what would Bernard say if he came home?

The children were now well again; they ran through the fields, played on the road and went to fetch eggs from the henhouse. The nights were starting to get cold. In the morning, they picked icy peaches; the juice flowed into their mouths as cold and sweet as sorbet. Little Colette picked up a dead bee she found in the centre of a dahlia. People were starting to light the first fires: in the little tiled rooms in their houses, the kind of fires that give off the smell of smoke and roasted almonds, a sweet perfume that lingers in the air; and fires, in the fields, that burn the weeds and prepare the ground for the next harvest. All around Thérèse, in the town, on the roads, in every house, a woman was waiting for her prisoner of war to come home. There were so many of them, and Thérèse had listened to their hopes and disappointments (more often than in Paris where she never saw anyone and where everyone talked only about food and how expensive life was), so often that she almost lost the confidence and faith she had felt at first. So many wishes, so much love, so much work . . . all in vain . . . Here, a child is born who does not know his father. There, an ill, old woman realises she is going to die without ever seeing her sons again, prisoners of war. And elsewhere, people have worn themselves out trying to keep a little farm going; the women's health is suffering; their youth is fading because of having to take on work that is too hard for them. It was announced that soldiers who fought in the last war would be shown clemency; some men had already come home, but so many others were still missing, far away. People talked about them, kept their memory alive, but in spite of everything, little by little, their features became blurred in the mind, like the faces of the dead. Every now and again, the ones back at home got used to being alone. From time to time, even Thérèse imagined something she would never have believed possible a few months before: another winter without him, another summer, perhaps . . . She had to live. She had survived after Yves had died. She would perhaps end her days far away from the only man she had ever loved. She was approaching the hardest moment to be faced when separated from the one you love, the moment when you finally get used to your pain, and then, you are only half alive, because that pain meant you were still fully alive. It was a bleeding, gasping kind of life, but now even that pain had disappeared, leaving nothing but a sense of mournful resignation.

It was a day like any other. It had rained a bit in the morning. The children had gone into the woods to gather chestnuts. They wore clogs and the prickly green shells cracked beneath their feet, making the smooth, shiny chestnuts spring out, as if from tiny catapults. They found foxglove in the forest as well, on long stems, and the last ceps of summer and clusters of greyish mushrooms that looked suspicious but which tempted Geneviève.

'Are you sure they're poisonous, Mama?'

'Quite sure, darling.'

Colette secretly took off her shoes; she left her socks on and put her little feet down on the soft, spongy moss. The two little girls shook the branches of the trees and a light crackling shower of rain and golden leaves fell down on to them.

At midday, because they were far from the house, Thérèse suggested that for lunch they make do with the snack she had brought just in case, some bread and butter and goat's cheese. Then, for dessert, and the best treat of all, they would roast some chestnuts. She soon managed to light a fire between two flat stones.

The children watched the fire for a long time, fascinated by the beautiful colour of the flames in daylight, a coppery pinkish colour.

'This is nice, Mama,' said little Geneviève. She let out a contented sigh and curled up against her mother's threadbare skirt like a cat. They ate the chestnuts, then explored the forest to its edges, right up to the place where the fields began, the wide, dark purple fields, all furrowed and undulating. They fascinated Thérèse. She could not say why. Soaked with rain and sweat, this fertile land reminded her of her own life.

They spent the whole day in the warm woods where there was still a gentle torpid heat; it felt as if the branches, the grass, the dead leaves had soaked up and kept bits of sun and light, while the October wind blew through the rest of the vast countryside.

The smell of smoke reached Thérèse. There were fires everywhere, those purifying pyres of autumn. When Thérèse and her children finally headed home, the sun was already setting; the clear, reddish sky was a sign that the next day would be cold. The crows were cawing. The road seemed long to their tired little feet; Thérèse had to carry her youngest daughter in her arms. Pools of mud shimmered, all pink. Colette soon fell asleep, her head on her mother's shoulder. She was a sweet burden . . . but a burden nonetheless. 'To tell the truth,' Thérèse thought sadly, 'I've always had to carry them alone.' It was dusk; it was cold. She felt tired and weak. She listened vaguely to the children's babbling; she replied to them without thinking. She continued with her thoughts; a kind of internal pulse beat within her; one question, always the same, obsessed her:

'When will he come home?'

Perhaps it was because of the physical fatigue, or hunger (for she had eaten almost nothing so the children could have most of the lunch), but she suddenly gave in to a feeling worse than despondency: for the first time in her life, perhaps, she was overwhelmed by black despair. Yes, for the first time . . .

Yves . . . She had found consolation in the nobility of his death, by her faith in eternal life and by her conviction that so many young lives could not be sacrificed in vain. But she had never before experienced a despair so deep, so darkly seductive. 'It's all over,' she thought. She would never see her husband again. And besides, what was the point? She had always been a fool. She had been betrayed and abandoned. Her son had died for nothing because France had been beaten. Even if he came home, Bernard would not look twice at this woman with her grey hair, a woman he had not loved even when she was young. As soon as he was back on his feet, he would start seeking out life's pleasures. My God, could he actually be right . . . ? What was the point of so many scruples, so much suffering? No one would thank her for it. She felt abandoned both by God and man. So many prayers, so many tears . . . All in vain . . . The war had been going on for ages, and was still going on. Her husband would not be returned to her.

She raised her eyes towards the heavens in an instinctive gesture of supplication.

'If you have not abandoned me, Jesus,' she whispered, 'give me a sign, just one sign! Do not test me any more.'

But the reddish sky continued to sparkle, pure, icy, brilliant. The wind was growing piercing and cruel. Perhaps, after all, this silence and this indifference were the signs she had asked for?

She put Colette down on the ground:

'Come on now, walk for a while. There's the house. I can't any more.'

Surprised by her mother's tone of voice, normally so gentle, Colette looked up at her, said nothing and trotted along behind her, head lowered. Geneviève, who was always full of energy, ran on ahead. They pushed open the little grey gate; its bell made a soft tinkling sound. They went into the house. Thérèse saw her mother-in-law sitting at the table, her head in her hands.

'She's sleeping,' said the little girls.

Thérèse walked over to her; the old woman was not asleep. She turned her trembling face towards Thérèse; she was crying.

'My God, what's wrong?'

'Bernard . . . Bernard . . .' stammered Madame Jacquelain, 'he's coming back . . . He'll be home tonight . . . He's been released . . . The telegram . . . it's been waiting here for you since eleven o'clock, my poor child!'

The hours that followed were like a dream. Everyone was excited, rushed around, got dressed, tried to organise a car (the station was a few kilometres away). It was already dark when the two women and the children stood on the open platform in the wild, blustery wind. The stars shone and shimmered; the railway tracks gave off a pale light. Their four faces looked out into the distance with the same expression of joy, disbelief and anguish, for, to those who have suffered, happiness seems so inconceivable, at least at first.

The little girls, who had forgotten their father, wondered if he was kind, not too strict, if he would play with them, buy them presents. Madame Jacquelain felt as if she had travelled back twenty-five years and would see a young man appear suddenly, stepping briskly off the train, a young man with a bold look in his eyes, the Bernard of the past. And Thérèse . . . Thérèse alone thought nothing, remembered nothing. Her entire being was filled with expectation and love.

They heard the sound of the train, like whispering carried on the wind; then harsh, metallic noises, the wheels of the train hammering the bridge. Finally came the roar and the smoke of the engine. People stepped off . . . women carrying wicker baskets . . . children . . . 'My God, where is he? Where is Bernard? I must have been dreaming . . .'

Then a voice spoke, very close to her:

'Don't you recognise me, my dear Thérèse?'

She looked up. No, she did not recognise this pale man with very deep-set eyes, walking so slowly, who came towards her and kissed her.

'Bernard,' she whispered, and it was only when she felt her husband's lips against her cheek that she understood it was really him, and she burst into tears. She also understood (one glance was all it took, a sigh, one brief sob that Bernard tried to stifle as he kissed her), she understood that he had changed, he had come back more mature, a better man and, at last, he was hers, and hers alone.

ALSO BY IRÈNE NÉMIROVSKY

SUITE FRANÇAISE

Suite Française begins in Paris on the eve of the Nazi occupation in 1940. As Parisians flee the city, human folly surfaces in every imaginable way: a wealthy mother searches for sweets in a town without food; a couple is terrified at the thought of losing their jobs. When Némirovsky began writing *Suite Française*, she was a highly successful writer in Paris. But she was also a Jew, and in 1942 she was deported to Auschwitz, where she died. For sixty-four years, this novel remained hidden and unknown.

Fiction/Literature

ALL OUR WORLDLY GOODS

Set in France between 1910 and 1940, *All Our Worldly Goods* is a gripping story of war, family life, and star-crossed lovers. Pierre and Agnès marry for love against the wishes of his grandfather, the tyrannical family patriarch. And their marriage provokes a feud that cascades down the generations.

Fiction/Literature

DIMANCHE AND OTHER STORIES

Written between 1934 and 1942, these ten stories mine the details of social class; the tensions between mothers and daughters, husbands and wives; the manners and mannerisms of the French bourgeoisie; religion and personal identity. Moving from the drawing rooms of pre-war Paris to the lives of men and women in wartime France, here we find the beautiful work of a writer at the height of her career.

Fiction/Literature

ALSO AVAILABLE

Fire in the Blood

Jezebel

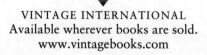

The Wine of Solitude